The Tribe
Beraud Rock 2025

This **Second Edition (Revised and Expanded, 2025)** includes restored and newly integrated chapters, expanded continuity with *The Alloy*, and minor stylistic and structural revisions. No part of this publication may be reproduced, stored, or transmitted in any form without prior written permission from the author.

First Edition published 2025.
Second Edition published 2025.

ISBN: 978-1-7643565-4-1

Evolution decides which gods will rust.

Author website:
https://www.peterbarrett-author.com/peterbarrett

Acknowledgments

Thanks to my partner Donna, Graphic Designer and Book Design editor. Cover image art work by Peter Barrett. Cover art designed by Donna Crotty.

About the Author

Peter Barrett - Pen name: Beraud Rock, was born and grew up on Christmas Island in the Indian Ocean. He has spent a lifetime reading Evolutionary Science, Science Fiction, History, and comics as a child. He was not exposed to television until age eleven.

Peter has a fascination and passion for the natural world and our place in the Universe. Peter's world changed the day he examined tiny insects through his photographic lens and discovered their beauty and makeup. He is equally fascinated by the human animal, their degrees of humanity, the complexities of society and the future of the human race. Themes in his writing include Artificial Intelligence, sentience, problem-solving, disaster, and the evolutionary timeline and makeup of life on Earth.

He holds two University degrees, neither of which is related to his previous careers as a Cook, Photographic Technician, and Ophthalmic Technician. When not writing, he spends time with his partner, his chickens (Chooks, as Australians say), wildlife, and grows his own food.

Prologue

Deep within the magma and enormous heat the bedrock began to crack and shatter. Volcanic vents at the seabed erupted and giga-tons of gases started to spew forth bubbling, hissing, shaking its way to the surface spreading out and up into the atmosphere with ever increasing quantities. The amount of Methane that was being emitted in the Atmosphere equaled a millennial's worth in an afternoon, oxidising quickly into CO_2. Huge geysers plumed through the ocean upwards from great to low pressure breaking the surface of an ocean unobserved, a quiet sea beyond human eye. Giant turgid areas as if formed by an enormous propeller wash. The atmosphere began to convect in enormous plumes, clouds increasing the temperature rising in an evolutionary lament more cryptic than the world could ever grasp.

The Physical Earth, an analogy of a panicked terrified sweat and grime covered distorted face of uncontrollable fear as one would see in a doomed person peering over a parapet to a distant place that contains their end. A judgement as sure as energy cannot be destroyed. The ultimate sacrifice had come too soon, the certain end of the Earth, the Doomsday clock clicked the last stroke. A die cast, a stone dropped to the depths, innocence lost.

As the Earth heated up the population panicked. The founded fear of tsunami from earthquake activity led people to seek high ground and swept the people of the great cities into the mountains. The freeways, a frustrated humanity, a crawl. Tent cities grew up along the highways. Family disintegration, separation, dislocation. Comfort to death, abandoned ship, evacuation, terror, confusion, lament, loss. Violence, theft and chameleon behaviour, men become boys, boys, men, girls women, women, boys. Loss of nutrition, bad advice, middle management insanity, poor leadership, tribalism, and false gods on altars held aloft like broken kites.

.

Diesel stench and petrol fume residue, sludge pyres of burning oil and gas explosions, partially submerged cars, and children's floating toys, dead pets and human heads. Floating aircraft, partially floated submerged apartment blocks and beached ships, helicopters in trees, old wood enclosed television sets adrift to the wafting stench wind. Birds whirled in the sky, flocks aloft lining out to the horizon to perceived safety like the Cretaceous flight for survival. Mass land invertebrate exodus followed the human wave, snakes and unseen spiders, deer, ants and packs of lost dogs. Farm animal flocks of chickens and pigs, horses abandoned cats, roamed aimlessly, free, instinctively aware yet not knowing. No Ark, no religion, no gods but free range.

As the weather warmed dramatically the sky grew dark. Then came the storms, seething masses of cumulus fury sweeping the sea and dwindling areas of solid ground. The sheer amount of rotting vegetation clogged to a standstill. The clouds of sulphur and carbon dioxide gas choked the atmospheric meridian to a grey apocalypse. Day never came again, a millenia night, temperature dropping, hope receded. Plants dead, photosynthesis a past evolutionary tenet, marine Carbon Dioxide lethal, water-cycle admonished and pardoned, silence then a roar as the next wind storm battered as the trees vanished with their break. The ash fell as heavy rain, hot and wet, then dry and constant, matting the surface with toxic sludge, no growing, no food, exhaustion, pain, terminal tiredness, and finally, sleep.

"Cyclops, I think we need to get the hell out of here," Ye-Min said, starting to feel nervous about their time in a place where three piles of broken and discarded androids reached high in the sky. "This is all too potentially dangerous," she said to the mono, the Artificial Intelligence Sentient Monoglass (AISM) cylinder attached to 990's shoulder, like a metal parrot on the white android. Both of them were facing in the direction of the strange fence and past the discarded Android piles beyond. 990 was crouched like a depressed spring and seemed ready for something. Cyclops piped as if in reply to the non-verbal stance of the Droid;

"I think that option has expired. Flight in this situation would be certain death, I have sent a link for you to your tablet then you will understand," the Mono piped deadpan through her headset. In her crouched position a chill came over her, she rummaged for her tablet in her pack, looking through the gaps in the grass mounds behind expecting something bad to come though suddenly and accessed Cyclops's feed.

The tablet's feed showed Cyclops's eye view, the crystal clear AISM's vision past the discarded Android pile and the fenceline, a distance she was unable to see well but a good distance for the Military recce eye-glass, in its element here. She guessed several hundred figures were milling past the fence on a flat plain and then discerned they were running fast in their direction. They seemed to know they were there, she looked to see if it was something else but her heart sank with dark realisation, and the red eyes of the oncoming hoard told her otherwise. She estimated they were still perhaps a few kilometres away. The figures came into sharp clarity as Cyclops zoomed to full distance with his super clear vision, only then did she understand the mono's visual ability and also what they were facing.

The closest figure came into view, a tortured machine, an Android like 990, two metal arms two metal legs but with threatening appendages protruding from its exo-skin, some seemed organic and some machine, blades, saws, spears, knives, rotating blades, a mace-like swinging tool. All the figures that came into view carried malevolent weapons, pikes, rotating chainsaws, spinning wheel devices like hole-saws, drills, flame torches, one had what she seemed to be a rocket launcher on its shoulder, another a pack that looked like a flame thrower, the machine grasping a pole with a lead attached. She saw others that had more than two legs, a three legged machine Android scuttling like a crab.

She had seen enough and rose to flee, Cyclops's voice piped urgently through her headset. *"Min, retreat to the furthest mound back, but stay in sight and lie down prone, don your exo-suit helmet and gloves. The threat is only to the front, they are not flanking us, if they come upon us 990 will fight for your protection, until then I have made my decision."* "Fuck, Cyclops, what decision?," she uttered in sheer terror, the mobs ground-swell now audible and she could hear what sounded like war screeching cries and a metallic jabbering. "*Air strike,*" Cyclops, piped deadpan. *"Go!, now!,"* Cyclops yelled, the first time she had heard the mono raise its voice. She fled back to the furthest mound, her pack in one hand like a fleeing schoolgirl and grabbed at her knife in a pitiful attempt at some comfort, the terror invading her ability to think clearly.

The next moments went like a slow motion, she laid prone and in sight of 990 as Cyclops told her, she was shaking but alert. Her vision seemed to improve, 990 becoming clearer about ten metres in front of her, gazing above the mound then back to her position. She looked at her tablet, the feed still active with Cyclops's sight, and reached for her exo-suit helmet, still attached to the back of her pack. The images on the tablet showed the mob were now about two kilometres away from their position.

The sky was suddenly interrupted by a high pitched sound, as a monumental explosion detonated on the plain, her helmet went flying away, the force of the impact so great, her whole body left the ground momentarily as if on a trampoline. The blast wave swelled over them with great speed, her ears popped and a mass of grass and dust horizontally seared over her position, like a storm tempest, the afterclaps thundered as the terrain seemed to crack with the blastwave, a massive uprising of dust and black smoke rose above the mound and into her view.

She raised her head and saw the Tablets view, grabbing the device with squinting terror. The mob had been dissected and pulverised, some survivors struggled on, pieces of metal dragging and falling off, the plain ahead a mass of metal shards and broken Android torsos, metal heads rolled with the throng, a smoke haze and raised dust obscured the rest of the survivors. She saw the smoke billow, the blast radius looked kilometres long, a vast line of destruction rose upward. She strained to see what had been left and noticed some of the Androids had been miraculously untouched and still advanced, passing the smoke boundary of the explosion and cantering as if nothing had occurred.

Suddenly, she whirled around and sat up, a sound behind her rasped and an Android came into view, 990 was already advancing upon her, the Android cantering to her position. The warlike machine that had surprised her had two enormous meat cleavers, one in each hand, she raised to a standing position and for a reason she didn't understand discarded her small camping knife, the Android now five metres from her.

The expectation was terror and death but she stood firm and calm. As the Android spun to strike like a blender, both blades turning in both hands, she ducked, and shifted down on her feet, crouching smoothly behind the machine, in one timed motion, the blades missing, the Androids arms flailing in front of it with speed as it failed to connect. She grabbed the head of the Android from behind and spun the machine's skull, the head cracking and lifting from the socket of the torso with a crunch and electronic hiss, the head falling onto the ground, the torso remained standing for a moment then fell like a ruined statue, then falling heavily onto the grass, the head socket emitting a sharp burning smell of electrical rubber and seared metal. She felt shocked, the action was partly subconscious, she had known what to do and was in control as she surveyed the rear for more threats.

990, had reached her position, and had hesitated as it saw her despatch the Android. Cyclops, she noticed, had been left on the farthest mound and was attached to a metal pole that looked like it may have been from the fence line, looking out towards the advancing army. 990 grabbed her and shoved her to the ground expertly, she, for an instant thought 990 was attacking her, but then she was released and 990 crouched beside her, then stood back up again in an instant and surveyed behind them just as she heard another massive strike on the plain.

The blast seared past again, a white blast wave, like a super fast water vapour. 990 held firm, its feet ground into the grass with the force, as the thunderous explosion shuddered her this time, the sound, a terrain-busting *Hammer of Thor* krumping resonance. A mighty crack sounding on the billard-ball plain.

She covered her head instinctively with her arms and hugged the grass, the sound seemed to linger, a whining crack, then another concussing thump like the bass sound of all bass sounds, which made her stomach feel like she was on a roller coaster coming back down from a ridiculous height. Pieces of dirt fell from the sky like mud rain, bits of wire and small electronic parts shattered and rolled down from the sky in an electronic rain and bounced on the grass mattress that was the mound area she noticed peering from under her arm

4

protection. A large piece of light debris hit 990 and bounced away on the grass partly aflame.

She sat up instinctively and saw that two more Androids had appeared in concert with the mighty explosion, walking slowly through the descending smoke haze, behind their position. Her ears rang like an intruder alarm inside, the sound a bleating sine wave from the blast. The nearest Android was about ten metres away, it had a flamethrower and the hiss of the pilot flame was audible as it advanced through the descending haze of the dust from the missile strike. The other machine carried a pole that had a selection of saw blades arrayed at the front spinning with intent about another two metres behind. Both were like 990, but with red eyes and scarred with black streaks, probably she thought from the strike on the plain. She still felt calm as they approached and didn't know why. She stood up again and her stance was automatic, facing the threat but slightly turned and still, waiting. She glanced down at the cleavers, but left them in the grass, knowing they were useless in this situation but not knowing why.

990 sprinted past her at speed at the nearest Android, tackling the machine into the ground with a pounding thump, the Androids strike like a *Minosaurous* in the deep, a lightning bound. The two machines ground into the dirt, as 990 ripped the flame thrower pole from the tank, and in one motion flung away, rolling while throwing the still lighted pole at the machine. The Android floundered on the ground from 990's force, the fuel shooting from the tank under pressure like a severed artery, the spray rising then falling in a heavy mist down on the machine and around on the grass. She saw the Android momentarily try to rise again as she dived behind the nearest mound.

As the Android rose to a sitting position like a drunk awakening on someone's lawn, it ignited, and a plume of napalm soared like a blow-torch upwards in a mini spearhead shaped explosion with a mighty soaring flame cloud. The

5

surrounding grass caught fire and hissed out quickly, then the shell of the fuel tank landed, a half mould, the side of one internal tank sheared away, having been cast into the sky with the explosion. The tank landed with a thud, and bounced with a quivering of metal over the machine's flaming torso and rolled flaming to a halt.

The next threatening machine advanced unconcerned. 990 was standing between the Android and her waiting for the response, 990 having risen and regained position in an instant, her seven foot mechanical companion standing in front of her. There was a short standoff, the machine turned to look at its smouldering companion as it passed the wreckage, now two metres from 990, the fiery Android on the ground with one dead arm extended; locked towards the sky like a burning candle on a napalm cake.

The approaching machine charged 990, the saw-blades rotating a whirring rasping sound. 990 stepped to the side and took hold of the pole, stepped inside the machine's gait and tripped it, using one of its own legs, sending the weight thundering onto the grass in a heap. 990 raised the pole in one movement and speared the Android through the front torso, the saws cutting through the mid section of the prone figure and spinning out a mass of electronic goo that splayed in a wet arc, some hitting her in the face. As she stood again, ready for the next attack, she wiped away the hot burning material in a fast reflex seeing 990 scan around again behind them. *"Air strike successful, the mob has been neutralised,"* Cyclops piped suddenly from the forward mound.

"Min, are you ok?"the mono piped again. She looked at 990, *"No more flanking Androids, clear at the rear,"* 990 piped, looking at her. She looked at 990, then back at Cyclops, realising she was breathing hard, her cheek hurt, and she turned to look at the far plain from where the army had advanced, a billowing dust volcanic-like cloud, pieces of wire and parts still falling as if an airliner had disintegrated above.

6

She wiped her eyes and sat down reaching for the first aid kit in her pack, still scanning the smoke haze for any more marauders. 990 helped her with the wound, the Android quickly administered some solution and a cream and covered the burn like a veteran trauma doctor early in a shift. *"Hold it for me while I tape it,"* 990 asked, the Android kneeling on the grass beside her. She looked down at her legs and saw another wound, a piece of metal had penetrated her exo-suit leg, 990 had already seen the wound and was cutting the pants away a little to access the site.

The Android looked back momentarily as if to confirm there was no danger, then continued the triage, scissoring the pants open and removing the silver piece of jagged metal from the gash, her blood flowing freely down her leg. 990 quickly administered some spray and stapled the wound closed with the stapler from the kit, tapering her leg like a sewing machine. *"Ahh, fuck,"* she called out in pain, looking at the sky, 990 ignoring her and wrapping the wound with terrain bandage; treatment at a blistering pace. "It's ok Min, you are ok, 990 said, looking at her, finishing the treatment and placing a heavy metal hand on her leg in *machine comfort*, which surprised her; the android having a bedside manner.

She watched and noticed the Android had large gouged scars down its face when some blast material had struck the exo-skin. *"Those injuries would have severed my head off,"* she thought, looking at 990. With the wound bandaged she saw it was a large gash but not life threatening, 990 applied some antibiotic with a syringe in her arm finding a vein instantly and withdrawing the needle.

She glanced again at the rear, the twin suns almost set casting a redder light than usual due to the dust from the missiles, the mounds losing definition in the failing light. Despite her injuries she thought a better version of her was now lying here wounded on an alien plain. Her education flashed through her

7

mind, the years of rigour. *And here I am. Fighting robots with cleavers.*

Squinting, still lying on the grass on one elbow and looking back at Cyclops, she strained and looked above the far mound, the smoke still rising, where Cyclops was, still attached to the pole. "Cyclops, explain to me how you can organise an air strike? I am already super-curious, ..but thank you as well. I have to say it's been quite the day," she said dryly as she softly spoke into her headset, the AI still directed out towards the open billowing fired plain.

2

Memories of the corrupted, broken farce of the mission flooded Ye-Min's consciousness. Everything she had strived for—the dream of a new home for humans—was gone. Her mission had become something else entirely. **Something dangerous.**

Darkness enveloped them as they moved across the billiard-ball ground. Away from the protective mounds, 990 and Cyclops guided her under the green-lit moons, leading her toward a safer stretch beyond the burnt plain. Her neck ached with cold. Her wounded leg throbbed. But she kept pace with the machine.

I don't feel the same way anymore, she realised. *Fear here isn't the old fear—panic, retreat. It's survival. It's a fight.*

Poor Tom.
Had they really tied him to a bloodied totem pole?
Had she?

The childish worship of a space-helmet effigy... the crude stick-face grinning inside the exosuit visor... the stone altar smeared with sacrifice... These fragments pressed in on her.

Nothing in her astronomer-trained mind could reconcile her transition from scientist to warrior—from orbital calculations to drawing a bowstring as though she'd been doing it all her life. She had been awakened to consider a deal, shaped into a pawn for reasons she still barely understood.

Maybe I still am.

Ahead of her, 990 stopped. The android surveyed the ground sloping toward the distant river—a silver-green snake sliding through the night desert. Ye-Min crouched instinctively, letting the mounds and shadows hide her.

A new memory surfaced: Ecologist Jessica Neuer being hauled aboard the lander, wild-eyed, begging to return to orbit. A rare field day turned terrifying. Why did this come back now? What had Jessica *seen, even felt* that none of them had understood? *And what is she like now, alone in this wilderness? Neuer, not like the others, different.*

The darkness thickened.
990 turned, his tiny orb-eyes dimmed for security.

"We camp here."

3

Ye-Min unfolded her small photograph, then gazed out at the twin-suns in the vacuum, *Gemmi7a* showing the dark side of the planet, their speed 7.8km/sec which meant that they orbited Gemmi7a twenty two times a day. She could see the weather satellite streaking in the far horizon of the planet, a small white dot lit by the suns, in Geo-stationary orbit, moving with the planet's spin, mapping the terrain and providing data about the weather. The planet's green tinge lit the boundary between dark and light where the sun's glare hit the far side of the orb's day, contrasting the dark-side facing the ship, a grey, dark conglomeration of patterns. A continent was still visible, swirling masses of low altitude cloud and delineations of high terrain. Mountain ranges and rivers flowed to the ocean like veins slit, the fluid weeping into another liquid mass, consumed and recycled, back to storm laden skies visible with the flashing of strobe at portions of the equatorial band.

She sat quietly at her observatory console, the *Ate Successions* Astro-physics lab, the *Flexible Atom Acrylic Glass* window allowing a one hundred and eighty degree view of the planet and distant constellations, several screens reflecting her facial features. *As if in assessment, concentration, commitment and focus,* she thought, seeing her faint face in the terminal's reflections. She liked to think about the Universe to relax, after a few hours of analysis, to think about what she knew, what was real, and then what might become of them, the planet. *Have I done it right? The calculation of the elliptical revolution?. Was the temperature going to drop below about minus eighty degrees centigrade, a chilly -112°F? during the night time? Yes, it was going to get cold as the planet tracked to the outer orbit away from the twin suns, very cold,* she thought.

She had also established that they were almost as close to the Twin-stars as they would travel in the calculated revolution, therefore they were in Summer, the seasons determined by the distance from the stars, unlike Earth, the planet's tilt determining the season. *In our favour,* she thought. The planet had a slow rotation, warming the surface of the planet on the day side longer, as a function of the three moon tidal pull on the planet, effectively slowing its spin. Longer days and longer nights, an increasingly warming day over a longer duration, then an increasingly colder night over a longer duration. That explained their long days and nights being twenty hour days and twenty hour nights. She also thought about the frequency of severe storms on the planet's surface as Dong-hyun Han, their Meteorologist had discovered via the orbiting weather satellite, a slower spin meant a less variable climate, but more upper convection from the planet's surface to the Stratosphere and increased cloud cover, with additional atmospheric moisture. "I must talk to Akseli, he might have some theories on the effect of the continents on the tides which is a factor here," she said to herself. "Mmmm, yeah, slow rotation, long revolution around the the two stars," she pondered, "Only effect I don't know yet is the revolutions of the stars in respect to one another, this could be interesting"

She bent down from the chair and released her buckle and stretched her legs, floating straight up, never taking for granted gravity which was still a Science-Fiction dream if generated on an orbiting ship. The only reliable form of generated gravity, the Linear Acceleration of the ship when travelling close to the speed of light. She pushed softly from her chair to get to the Flexible-Atom-Acrylic-Glass, a straight timed float, breaking her glide with a light touch, looking out at the planet, her fingers touching the amazing *Flexible-Atom-Acrylic-Glass.*

Now, that is Science Fiction in reality, she thought, running her fingers across the surface, the friction creating a slight contact impression with light colours radiating outwards. *Not glass,* rather an impermeable liquid, sentient-molybdenum alloy, flexible armour, unique in its toughness but also flexible to heat and cold with large tolerances, to withstand temperature range within deep space environments., super tough, even with micro-meteorite resistance.

She also thought, while inspecting the planet's day-side now radiating a magnificent green-blue glare, *Why did I get my Mothers side of looks and not my Dad's?,* her stunning complexion and attractive good looks complicating her world in many ways, making it easier in many others, lots of sexual attention but not much substance, at times feeling like a female pigeon wanting to flee the same old tail-feathers, momentarily remembering her last potential relationship that almost went somewhere, *well, it might have got started,*she dryly mused. She could see a storm on the planet's surface, a dark mass of convection cloud on a distant continent that had a distinct wide sea channel running through the upper portion, where the top of the massive land mass had seemingly split like a crust off a slice of bread. There seemed to be a desert there, the ochre pastel exhibited no green, reflecting yellow into the exosphere.

She thought about her work which typically involved judgement and error, mass calculation and fine adjustment. The spectacular star driven void of the Universe was an ancient constant, immune from human nonsense and speculation, banter, introspection, self-absorption, cruelty, destruction, and pointless conflict. *"We are all like that.*

Recognising humans evolved from under the feet of roaming instinctual Dinosaurs and needed a defence to survive, something more than fleeting ability and cunning route to buried den. Consciousness was the weapon, the ability to know that you existed and think about it, unfortunately a precursor to eventual morning television, she thought smiling, thinking of her Mama's television set, something never turned off, just emitting. *The human mind, a rotating drum of rehashed boredom busting action and ninety percent nonsense."*

The unfolded photographic print remained quite still in front of her weightless face, a small four by four inch white bordered memento she looked at occasionally, when she felt lonely while gazing at the twin stars, stars that seemed to laugh at her existence, knowing they would be burning for another four billion years, about four billion years after her demise, her chemistry broken down into Carbon and Hydrogen again, and if she died in space, she would return eventually to the galaxy that made her, interstellar gas and atomised elements before the Universe contracted and got cold, the stars extinguishing, one by trillion one, then a dark void ready for the next cataclysmic eruption to create another Universe.

This was the bit that she disagreed with. *The cataclysmic explosion part.* Her Astro-Physics colleagues presenting the evidence, she still thinking that there was another scientific explanation, although she was at sea on a doubtful raft trying to explain why, but it gnawed at her occasionally, her great question and unknown hypothesis. *"I think something else, an unknown element or a bending of time might do this, "* she thought speculatively. "

She gazed at the photograph of her family, her Dad and Mama, a fine crease through the print intersecting his smiling face, her Mama looking deadpan, a trait of hers in any known photograph no matter what the scenario or mood. She looked at her Father, long gone now, who had died of a stroke on a factory floor in Shanghai three days from retirement. Her Mother in the stark light of reality, simply a selfish cow, still not knowing, or really caring what she did, more concerned with the neighbour next door who had several ailments, seeing the need to lecture her when she visited on each one, about someone she didn't know.

"Gee, Mama, aren't you a bit interested in what I do?" She remembered thinking, sitting in her mothers complex mortise

and tenon joinery three seater, her mother entrenched in her nightie rambling like a wind-up malfunctioning toy, the television blaring diatribe and morning nonsense about how cold it was and what you can and can't eat, continuing to listen to the monologue with increased grenade-like smouldering depression, *"Ah, yes she was in hospital again, poor dear, rotator cuff you know..."* , how many times did she have to hear that one. She sat there, the inane presenters striking a pose, interviewing good looking people who were having a great day, with the constant digital clock showing in the right hand bottom corner, a bubbly reporter explaining how windy it was in some highway cul-de-sac.

Her Dad she missed, he was actually interested in her life, he used to ask things called "questions" about her life, the Physics, being a Taikonaut her preferred Chinese term for Astronaut. Now he was gone, "back to the stars," leaving her walking a Ningbo street, feeling like an abandoned child, a vacant and guilty feeling, like she should try harder but knowing it wouldn't matter, her Mother had crossed the line into self-absorption, routine flummery, and *"indoctrinated television brain-rot"* as her Father liked to term morning television.

The last time she left so frustrated she remembered walking down the cold apartment block street, snow lightly falling and staining the white pavement, tears in her eyes, the further she got from her Mama's apartment, the better she eventually felt, the feeling subsiding in her subconscious filling in the uncomfortable gaps with explainable kind alternatives to quell her guilt, stopping on a bridge to watch the frozen river beneath the ice, then looking up and seeing two geese looking straight at her standing on a distant rock as though they understood.

The comm's traffic awakened her from her family pondering. Something on the surface was going on. Turning up the volume, she could hear Tom, Tanya and Jason talking in urgent tones. *Sounds like the Lander.* Jessica Neuer sounded frantic, troubled, like she was being helped, shuffled somewhere on board.

4

Jessica Neuer placed the soil sample into the bio-container and sealed the crew top lid. "That's the four samples from the river edge" she thought, "Quadrant 12" she reminded herself, careful to make a mental note of her sample area. She scanned the swift current, "No fish in there I suspect" she thought, considering the observed obvious lack of larger animals on the planet"s surface to date. She adjusted her beanie, laughing to herself, "beanies and off-world Ecology, we imagine space-suits and lakes of methane, not here my friends, not here" She breathed deeply, "The air" she praised in scientific wonder, "So fresh, so clear of particle dust here," she took a long breath through her nose, remembering her city home among the worn tire highway and the belching fossil-fuel traffic, the odd electric vehicle, in the maze of queued petrol-diesel humming metal, smug and silent, deadly to a pedestrian used to hearing for danger on the road, the electric heavy weight searching for somewhere to charge the potential fire-storm and future landfill batteries.

After some collating of tins and recording her finds paired to the sample quadrant, she started back up the river bank, a small rise of broken twig and dotted mineral pebbles, she noticed masses of tiny black ants, scurrying across cleared grain paths in winding intent to subterranean homes among the sedge. Stopping and finding unoccupied footholds so as not to disturb the frantic creatures she took her bag off her shoulder and rummaged through the contents grabbing her camera. "I love the macro lens on this" she thought, bringing the camera to bear and adjusting the focal-length to a 1:1 ratio, so detailed an area of where the ants were running, the edges blurred, the focal area tiny and sharp. Briefly a single ant stopped within the focal area in contrast to its colleagues, de-accelerating fast to a body-motionless statue, its feelers grabbing a stone momentarily and turning it in examination like a beach-ball being grappled by an array of beach-goers

17

arms some competitive game. "Wow, five segmented parts", she said out loud, softly. "And look at that!, hah, hah, ten legs." laughing to herself. *Ye Min was right.* Their breakfast meeting had taken her slightly aback, Ye Min was very perceptive as a Scientist, able to deduce very well from Astronomy to Ecology. *Ten legs for increased stability on terrain. But stability from what?*

She gave herself a lecture on insect locomotion, uttering in a Professor-like upper-class English accent, "Look at you guys, hah!, ten legs, one, two, three,... my goodness, ...so these ants have greater stability to compensate for their rigid exoskeleton, a fast stride and tripod gait to compensate and therefore balance, their nervous systems are not fast enough to compensate for their fast movement, Dr Neuer", She continued her thought out loud, "So ten legs, not six, a different stage of evolution?, a more rigid exo-skeleton? A harsher environmental adaptation? Wind speed? Perhaps, another unknown factor that adaptation has compensated for? That is amazing to this emotional Earth bipedal human, girls", taking several fast shuttered photos to try and catch the movement still.

The wide river coarse was in front of her, moving swiftly in a great mass, a blue and grey turgid wash breaking to a shallow stony section away from the banks in the centre of the water runway, swirling around and buffeting against some large unmovable boulders, the foaming augment of water, small detritus, ripped grass, a larger log twirling like a water wheel, pushing around the bases of the monoliths with floating debris like a crowd surging in a tear shape flow around a lost traveller at a busy subway station. Away from the river bank small strange shrubs like Acacia with protruding stems and Pineapple-like fruit atop dotted the rising vegetation beyond, a wiry grass cover, sections of dirt patches and broken stone, weathered, ancient, placed like monuments in small depressions and rivulets where the water was tempted after rain to flow in slight downward courses to the river main, untouched sentinels, the rivulet coarse with filtered sand and small pebbles, different colours and shapes.

Winding far in the distance beyond a curved tree-line the river introduced a far mountain chain glistening in the morning twin-sun haze, a slight mist above the water moving slightly with the flow and up in small eddies. Behind her the tall forest trees stretched far into the Southern horizon within a rugged valley, tortured stone plug pillars of long extinct volcanoes weathered to wrinkling infants poking like accusing fingers from the Forest anarchy canopy. The night brought heavy rain, the encampment in a small grass clearing protected by the tree line from a constant buffeting wind. "Water, she thought, lots of water, two Hydrogen, one oxygen downpour of monumental proportions" driving them to break camp due to the water pooling and move the terrestrial based energy tents from a forming lake to higher ground, sputtering, cold, wet steaming, a broken deep sleep from uterus to external world. She remembered someone calling out "Akseli, pick up the pace you old Nordic lug", Akseli Koskinen, the missions Geologist uttered an unintelligible response she couldn"t hear but brought laughter to others, eventually the new encampment set, dying of murmuring re-organisation, then silence again, the rain halting shortly after.

Her companions had spread out in a ten kilometre radius, the AI drone patrolling the perimeter checking, photographing, mapping the quadrants, assisting the Scientists "with thoughtful AI manners", she mused. A speck away to the valley moving without variation in height confirmed her thoughts, the drone skirting the tree-tops. Akseli the Finn was in the forest examining the ancient volcanic plugs of mineral makeup. She put away her lunch-box in the canvas bag, stood to ride down her trousers and sat again, "A little more time left to just sit here for a moment", she thought. The storm had moved a little closer, flashing bolts down to the terrain in strobe-like angular whiskers. "About five kilometers away" she thought, "better watch its track"

Akseli, she recalled, was selected for the mission based on his research on Plate Tectonics and Volcanism in small planetary bodies but also for his mechanical Engineering ability, the duality of positions vital, much like an Antarctic expedition. She recalled the selection process, "pretty unique actually and very smart" she thought, "Based on Ernest Shackleton"s way of loosely selecting his expedition personnel"s makeup, the Antarctic Explorer, selecting Scientists mainly for show to secure funding but also solely people of loyal, hardened character gained from life experience, not necessarily having both skills but equally sought. "After all," she thought, we are here to colonise, not explore per se, do I have both? she asked herself,a little maybe, most of my work life has been in the elements, nothing like Tom Auer though, wasn"t he picked off a Salzburg street?", she pondered. "Yes, that"s right, she remembered a Cargo ship crew member, retired, interviewed, selected. Tom was in charge of logistics and safety, "a highly trained jack of all trades" she thought. She remembered meeting him just before Cryo-sleep, assured, funny, polite. "Can"t question his skill-set" she thought. "Who else", she thought. "Ahhh, yes, Tanya Gery, the super-fit athlete, tri-athlete, explorer, mountaineer, electrical engineer, and all round nice girl, yeah, Tanya", she thought, again I only met her briefly, really nice, she would be Tom"s partner in a way, assisting with logistics, passengers when they joined us, it was very rushed in the end, surprised we didn't have an accident before take-off", she thought grimly.

She thought of her other colleagues, Dong-hyun Han, the Korean Meteorologist, was releasing the weather drone today, a small AI capable type that could send detailed information flying through the Troposphere. Ye Min, the Chinese Astronomer was on board *Ate* ,examining the twin-sun orientation and seasonal variation and the tidal interactions of the three moons, of which the gravity pull was considerable with four tides a day.

20

A morning storm broke the concentration with a mighty crack, startling her concentration, "Ohh", she uttered breathing out with a moment of surprise raising her head to gaze out towards the direction of the sound of thunder shaking the air waves which grumpily flashed and cracked like a fighter jet far beyond the mountain range in some dark valley to her East contrasted with rays of twin-sun shards in pillars striking the ground, the falling rain, curving to the mottled puzzle-lighted below in a vignette of grey striated pattern like a fine piece of fabric over a white background.

As if in a climatic conversation with the land below, a shift in the wind swirled confusion then settled in a sweeping gust, shifting the grass sedges creating a whispering din, hissing away across the tops of the tufts surrounding her like a green foaming sea as she stared back across the plain, like an imaginary hand was caressing the area in enquiry and search. The fresh smell of musty oxygen and damp wood, a little methane-like tang accosted the wind in ballet unison, tingling her nostrils momentarily sending a small shiver within her, "Still cold," she thought," creating fists with her hands to access a little extra warmth, turning to pick up her canvas ally full of planetary samples.

She reminded herself of the initial aerial survey by the teams drone of the area, which had reported increasingly predictable plant habitat but little of animal habitat beyond insect-like life, small wasps with twin-dual purple wings that made nests in rock crevasses, butterflies, delicate golden wings, a fine fibrous membrane with arterial veins striating outward to the oblong wing structure, more elongated than Earth species, "adapted to gliding?" she thought, "rather than fluttering" in the planet"s abundant katabatic wind descending down the mountain range slopes to the forest valley below. In fact all the insects seemed to be adapted to gliding adaptations with flapping ability, even the small bees that had oddly larger wings, when in a swarm, the tone between buzzing flight and gliding flight, a rising and dipping resonance like a straining air-conditioner inverter, part mechanical but naturally lamenting.

After examining the ants, she sat briefly on the river bank, drinking from her water bottle and eating several prepared snacks of dried type crackers, mixed nuts and raisins, keeping a lid from her container under the meal while eating making sure no food fell off, bio-security was paramount here, nothing alien, "apart from the most invasive of all she thought,....us". She stared at the vast plain where the sedge-like wiry grasses dominated, growing from damp soil and the minute weathered grains of desiccated pebble that had eroded over vast amounts of estimated time and washed like an inland king tide beyond the forest territory. "So amazingly beautiful" she thought. "Even this sparsely grown grass environment" The bed below of pebble-miniature around the sedge cover of grass contained the array of gravel, pebble, silt, coarse sand, clay, conglomerate mineral and silica dust, slivers of blackened quartz, amber pieces discarded from presumably the forest and particles of yellow algae and purple fungus on rotten sticks accompanied by the wash. She scanned the grass tundra wondering, examining, predicting this planet's course through time, its future in Geology and evolutionary course, "so, are we at a crossroads with this world? Has oxygen just reached the level to promote larger species, although they will take thousands of years to emerge?" She mused, placing the container in her sample bag, still the canvas carry she always had, which was comfortable, an object teasingly ridiculed by others like she was still a first year student.

Another thunderous crack shook the plain, "Crap", she said, looking up at the darker sky, the storm was going to hit for sure, lower now, rolling in like an explosive mass, swirling cloud, gusting force wind across ground after a direct hit. She grabbed her bag and made for a collection of large boulders back from the river, making strides through the sedge, still careful to avoid the ants.

The sound of the small pebbles crunching under foot, an increase in wind, and the sound of swaying grass tussocks singing. The boulders sat irregular but smooth eroded and with a convenient overhang she had explored before, just in case shelter was needed. The lightning flashed again, sending the landscape a lighter colour for half a second, shadows from the sedge like a puppet show lighting, spots of rain, then a little small hail, "Double crap" she blurted, reaching the boulder formation at pace,, tiny bits of ice twinging like a kids bullets across the stone like a Western movie. She huddled under the rock overhang, moved to the back of the about three meter triangle shaped enclosure. Her radio blared and scared the hell out of her, "I"ll never get used to this thing" she said out loud, sitting down with her canvas bag, the samples clanging roughly.

The radio scratched, rasping their perimeter frequency, *"You ok Jessica?, storm approaching from South West if you didn"t already know, but I know you, you may be spaced out with a strange plant or something"* "She replied smiling, yep, ok, under a rock at the moment, thanks for asking, what are you up to, blowing something up?" There was a pause as Tom seemed to be laughing and was confirming something to someone in the background, *"Hah, Hah, no need for me to create a scene yet Doc, good, good, just checking in on everyone so, you say, under a rock meaning you are trapped and cutting your arm off?* She dipped her head and laughed at the quick one-liner, "No, Tom, under a rock overhang, sheltering" *"Very good, glad to hear that,* he replied with intentional dryness, *"You are still in quadrant twelve, yes?"*

"Yep, correct, thanks Tom" *"So back at base camp at five-thirty Jessica, that"s 3 km SW from your position at the moment, and two hours casual walk away, it being at the moment 15:30, do you want the drone to assist?* "Copy, thanks, ah no, I can find my way back, I"ll be there" *"Good one Doc, see you then, ...otherwise I will have to blow*

23

something up..only joking" Tom"s receding laughter was cut short by the end of the transmission as she placed the radio back on the clip just near her left shoulder.

She watched the rain seeth down, heavy angular with the wind in long driving bursts, hitting the small stones and sending them flying among the sedge. She noted the water pooled and ran away from her hiding place in the direction of the river now unseen, the darkness and tempest was flashed at times lighting the scene like a floodlit stage of grass and stone, a medieval set for a Shakespearean play, an expected hooded character at any moment walking in the gloom. *"The ants"*, she wondered, probably why they were massed before, preparing dams around the nests, *"Same instinct, same low pressure sense in the atmosphere?, maybe"*

It was then as the rain tempest scoured the grass and the wind blew in clouded haze that she thought she could hear voices. Thinking that it was just the wind, echoes on rock or sound of falling water, but then realising it was none of those. Slowly, a primal dread came over her, where she was, things talking to her, inanimate things.

Her breathing paced like a metronome, and a vague feeling of a blood pressure drop within her system, making her shake a little. The darkness of the storm amplified her terror and she crouched in the gloom like a scurrying insect fleeing danger. As the next lightning strike lit up the surroundings she grabbed her bag and fled into the howling buffeting rain driven mist and sprinting towards the forest and where the trail was back to the scientists camp like a hiker being chased by a predator.

5

The Altar Priest watched as the soft light fell upon the helmet, highlighting the face within, the sun's rays sparkling the mineralised grain eyes and setting it blue and green, striking, and resembling a stare of solidified cruelty. The eyes were encased in a false cover but smiling a haphazard wrinkle, the mouth resembling a nervous murderer's grin. Silent and waiting, it seemed to suggest movement, but the only shift was the sun's light and slow cloud shadow on the slightly crafted nose, patchy and mottled with red ochre and brown smudge.

The head seemed content and judgemental at the same time, waiting in its protected hemisphere for the unsheath of steel or pouring of oil, lighted wood, wisp of chain or strike of rope. Around the waiting crafted Templar, the cleared rough dirt oval was encased by a crude fence of rough tree-branch stick stakes, strewn haphazard pebble and angular moved stone, placed with intent and seemingly magical reasoning as if to some parchment directive, now hidden with its cloaked makers.

A makeshift tilted gate at the end knocked on wood slightly with the breeze, blood patches mottled the ground, the fallen tree totem pole in the centre waiting with attached ethernet cable restraints seemingly moving but optically alluding to the clouds shifting above, leaning slightly right, the base reinforced with a crude earth covered, protruding rocks wedged around the circular exit from the earth.

Donghyun Han sat cross legged on the rough dirt floor near the makeshift stone altar, the one they used for placing the spacesuit helmet, in times of judgement. The Altar was a waist-size pillar of mottled grey lichen covered stone that the unbeliever had dragged from the river. "Ha," he uttered softly. "The rope had rubbed his hands raw and bleeding, this had taught him discipline and the way, the path was long, but those unfeathered in the eyes of the Altars knowledge would learn, community is everything, those who progress and temper like a well kept lawn will find the truth of the tribal cauldron, it boils but does not spill," he lamented to himself as he heard a sharp crack, then muffled squeal, and some soft laughter, shifting with the breeze.

The space suit helmet had been fashioned to his *Altar Priest* direction. He and the Mistress had established earlier that this was the *twin-sun tempest leader*, it had been found written on the rock painting Akseli had discovered, and he had a memory of the effigy, the tempest leader, *Hexibarber*, this also was written. He suspected, they would receive more instruction from the Mistress and her voice from the Forest in contented time, there would be, sometime in the near future, a celebration and ritual grooming of the unbeliever. The *Flexible-Atom-Acrylic-Glass* visor had been removed. *Whatever that is, probably some unbeliever cunning, a veil of some sort.*

He could see the ancient unbeliever writing on Hexarber's head that had been cleansed according to the way. A pair of marble size mineral eyes had been secured inside within a stick fastened frame, resembling a fashioned wooden human-like skull, a paper-mache type skin had been applied, dyed in the blood and rubbed in the dirt, this had been the Temple Mistresses task, she, working on the effigy long into the night under the sourmoon configuration, the unbeliever had assisted, she had said, complaining of his wound.

Akseli has been instrumental in the application of the mineral way, he thought. They had collected a variety of minerals from the alluvial plain, some translucent, some amber and large clumps of *quartz,* a *talc slab, gypsum conglomerate,* and *orthoclase rudiments.* He didn't know what the names meant but the *Mineral Master* did and that was just and allowed. He reminded himself of the correct passage, *which now needed to be assessed,* he thought, according to the appropriate healing

26

quality, and placed on the *Geological table* their wonderful unbeliever-carved half log from the forest raised on our two supporting altar-approved stones. From the ends, hanging and weighted, the elementary tassels hung, crafted beautifully from the correctly inert coloured unbeliever string cable in a platted array that suited the Mistress. *This is very important, the minerals must be collated and kept for future healing dances, the Mistress will dance naked with the stones around the pole and we will watch and be cleansed and engorged and will be safe from the weather and storms and any unforeseen planetary portent,* he mused with delight.

The encampment was struck suddenly by the twin-sunlight breaking through the orange clouds, a mist down low on the plain, the three moons still high, two in inverted half moon, the other a small sliver as if looking forward to the new moon dawn away from its sisters. Some late stars were in the blue bracken sky, still white and glistening sharply with the new day haze and atmospheric dust, some grazing the distant blue darkened plateau, the broken and burned *Unbeliever* monster atop like an ancient artefact upon a portent laden temple.

Akseli, the Mineral Master entered from the far gate, a swishing of the stick frame, he looked up, Akseli was grinning as he made his way across the circular area past the totem. "Altar Priest," Akseli said in greeting as he sat down next to him in the dirt, Donghyun, smiling. *Our friendship is stronger than ever,* Donghyun thought. "Greetings Mineral Master, how is our lost spaceman, that poor excuse for a Sailor?" *I wonder what a Sailor is,* he mused.

"He is starting to see the way I think, the carving has made him submissive and more willing, on paper of course. We shall see what motivation he has when the festival starts," Akseli said looking up at the moons as if he had been hard done by, then back to Donghyun, who smiled and looked at the totem in the distance, its shadow impinging long and black on the fence, misshapen with the undulating slats.

"Indeed, are you looking forward to the dancing of the Mistress?" "Ahh, yes my friend, she strikes a masters chord below, ..I" Donghyun interrupted placing his hand on Akseli's shoulder, "Patience my friend the festival may secure the Mistress and the wife Templar for enjoyment, *Although,* he thought to himself, *I have no sexual desire, nor can I raise the member from its stupor.* "The moons have predicted such, I..." There was an interrupting shuffle. Katie Arnold appeared in a crudely fashioned dress, sewn with unbeliever fabric and lengths of unbeliever string of different colours, almost touching the earth, her hair tied back with the cloth that was smooth on one side and stayed on things on the other side.

She was wearing shoes fashioned from some unbeliever substance, a spongy rock material and a grass headband aloft like a Queen's crown. *Queens crown, I don't know what that is but it has to do with an important head,* he thought. She shuffled towards them, smiling as if approaching old friends after a long absence. "Ahh, we were just talking about you my temptress, Akseli was just commenting on your grace and poise. "Thankyou Mineral Master," she said smiling looking at Akseli, he beaming and grinning at her in anticipation afar. "Where is Ye our majestic huntress?" Donghyun said, Katie sitting down on the earth facing him, the dirt totem shadow receding in the morning progression.

"She comes, anytime soon, I would think, she has been busy skirting the far valley, the Findus fool is still at bay" "Oh yes, the bastard of the Unbeliever monster, he indeed is my favourite" Donghyun, thought briefly about why Findus and the Sailor were aggressive towards their party. *They just don't want to be a part of the group"* he mused. *And where is that adventuring whore, the stupid Geary?, she would feel his weight against her naked skin when she was found, no one, and I mean no one eludes the Altar Priest,* he thought angrily.

Ye-Min entered the makeshift gate, smiling. He looked at her tight brown tattered trousers, a roughly made top of unbeliever fabric from the strange things that when discovered flew up into the sky like heads on a string. Her black waist height hair was falling across her tall strong frame, bow secured at her back with the forest crafted arrow shafts in her silver quiver, a cylindrical bottle given to her by the Mineral Master, secured round her waist with a long unbeliever cable that had a strange end which in his dreams the unbelievers placed in the sun-rock. "Ahhh, here she is, my amazon queen, come and sit *Delilah,* discuss the current unbeliever status," *Amazon Queen and Delilah, now where did I get those names from?,* he thought.

Ye-Min stood beside them smiling in greeting the others returning the nonverbal transaction while releasing her quiver and un-shouldering the bow, Katie, looking at the ground then at Ye-Min in a mixed expression of friendliness and envy, Akseli looking at her bow, now on the ground with interest. Ye-Min then gathered her gear and placed it nearby, then sat next to him. While the others talked to Ye-Min inquiring of her adventure, he thought to himself, *Is it because they were resentful that his leadership would threaten them, or perhaps their group's high standing among the ways of the plain, a conundrum, and yet who would question such a strong following? If we think so, then it must be always the case, the Tribe ticks every box of agreement without too much thinking that can confuse the way.*

After all, we have a bold set out plan for enlightenment, provided for with shrub pineapples daily. They have the Altar, the primary hearing judgement, a place where the great Hexibarber, the suit-head, could adjudicate a just sentence. Ye-Min reached out and took his hand, "You look deep in thought Altar Priest," she smiled sensing his quandary. "Ahhh, the burden of Priesthood weighs heavily ," he replied.

Ye-Min smiled in reply, turning around, her hand still in his to the sound of Anders Pedersen coming through the gate, naked waist down his member dangling, adorned with a tight fitting long sleeve vest, his grass wreath tightly fitting around his head, an Altar-like adornment. He wore a belt made from the unbeliever cloth, a camping knife attached, sheathed but menacing in length, a small cape of fabric stained with dirt and green grass marks was attached to his neck, fluttering as he approached. He smiled at the others.

"Ahh, we're all here, no, wait, …where is the Mistress?" Kylie Albott's voice barked out suddenly as she too came through the sacred sweeping sound gate after Anders, "Here my chickadee, did you not notice my grace in the distance coming to the altar?" "Oh, apologies, Mistress," Anders said, looking at her in mock embarrassment. Kylie smiled, looking down at his appendage then back to Donghyun, glancing at him with recognition. He smiled in satisfaction, turning to the others, "Ahh, my children, we are all here, Hexibarber is not impatient but willing and masterful," the tone of the group grew more serious all sitting up straight within the circle.

Donghyun raised himself to his feet and approached the space-head, soothing the top of the helmet with his hand as if turning a mounted world map globe, looking over to the Totem with a raised eyebrow, then back to the others. "Shall we bring the unbeliever within the contextual judgement?" *"Bring him in,"* they all said in unison. Akseli stood and walked toward the gate, opened it then left it open disappearing for a moment then slowly coming back through with

Tom Auer on a length of tower cable, attached to a metal collar around his neck, limping heavily, his injured arm dangling, smeared with blood and dirt, naked and forlorn, half asleep or dead, he wasn't sure. "Mmm, no matter" Donghyun said to himself, "The ceremony will be no less impressive" "Come Thomas, my Sailor friend, Hexibarber awaits your call of absolution and piety, will you join us?, I wonder, a pineapple treat awaits, and maybe, just maybe a little extra treat," as he looked at Kylie with a naughty glance. "Go fuck yourself Donghyun," Tom unexpectantly replied.

Donghyun lowered his gaze, the others silent. He motioned to Akseli to tie him to the totem, turning and addressing the others still seated in the circle.

"What is it my friends that these two, Findus, the deluded Geary and the unfortunate Sailor seem to think is not right?" The others looked at him with smug smiles and pursed lips, as he walked towards Tom now secured to the pole, who was looking at him with a certain intent, a dried blood trail extending from his forehead to his chin that had winded its way around his nose. "Do I not satisfy the group's needs?," he asked the others, turning with inquiry, the others replying in unison, *"The needs are met, the needs are met."*

He turned to Tom, he could see he was clearly in pain and struggling with his standing position against the pole. "My needs are not met," Tom added, still looking at him, shuffling his feet to carry his weight with the pain. "Indeed, Thomas, I dare say, not yet, may I and Hexibarber enquire about your current needs?" "To shove that space helmet up your arse," Tom replied, looking at him, then away to the fenceline in apparent disgust. "Well, that's uncalled for unbeliever," Donghyun turned and faced the others, smiling and feeling slightly embarrassed as the others watched him. "There is certainly not a lot of belief here," Donghyun laughed, the others following suit. "Hexibarber is most displeased," Donghyun said, pressing his chin against his chest while looking at his captive.

31

6

The crew of ten, and cryogenic passengers of eighty six, aboard the Ate Succession entered orbit around 'Gemmi7a' in 4038, two months shy of the original arrival estimate. The planet, one and a half times larger than Earth had been briefly probed and water had been found in a large sea with four large continents and it seemed that Plate Tectonics was present, a water cycle existed, gas exchange and plants were observed. Organic life, with a degree of slow rotational variation, and small day-night transition near the latitude at the meridian.

The exosphere admitted a ray of orange, reflected off the Nimbus-Cirrus tails of windswept clouds in the outer atmosphere, the vehicle descending, metal-petal wings astride, twisting to the rock plateau, the sound echoing across the grass plain and through the ancient forest.

The Captain, James Aegean Williamson looked at his First Officer Kate Arnold as the craft wound down the drives after a successful landing on the planet's surface, with an ironic smile and certain relief. "Piece of cake ... .woooooah," She called, the entire deck confirming with laughter, some groaning and comments too quiet to make out.

"We are down and safe, my friends, welcome to *Ate Succession's* arrival at the end of the Universe.." "The cabin was unanimous in its celebration, with much astonishment, relief and reserved professional caution, the ship's Systems Engineer and Second Officer Kylie Albott embracing the third Officer Anders Pedersen, a small boned blonde embracing a Nordic giant.

James Williamson released his helmet and set it aside noticing his reflection in the windscreen, revealing a man of forty odd, chiselled face, a nose longer than he would have made for himself avoiding the twenty years of military ribbing and predictable friendly joking. His thoughts turned to assessment given the successful landing, they had all only been awake from cryo-sleep for twenty four hours, the Starship in orbit around Gemmi 7a, the chosen Exoplanet, the last bastion of human collective technological endurance, ability, politics, money failure, redesign and eventual rushed preparation and launch.

Awakened campers, he thought, after a night of anticipation, professionals descending into childish themes after too many drinks, a rare treat of alcohol before the big day. Before going into sleep he remembered the strain with some relationships after a year of pre-deep space flight preparation. Not unexpected but still solid professional ability, experience and career calibre. *No walks by the sea out here. No getting out, to clear the head,* he mused. *In the end people were complex walking unique basket cases, clever, skilled, qualified or not. He continued* to think, seeing his reflection in the Flexible-Atom-Acrylic-Glass window momentarily.

A greying short crew cut hair on his sweaty head showed the strain of the flight physically, contrasting with the contented expression of success and relief. He reached over to Kate Arnold and embraced her, she still holding her helmet in one hand, "Well done, Bill," she said with sincere respect, using his nickname. "Great job Katie,"he replied, momentarily grabbing her with both arms to her shoulders after embracing, emphasising his respect for her ability mixed with elation and relief of the landing"s success. Smiling they both clicked back to flight mode both commencing after flight checks, there was whirring, clicking, whistling and several audible thumps as the landing gear adjusted and secured the craft that had landed on high stone strewn plain, with rocks no larger than tennis balls and the odd basketball.

The exploration craft on the plain was high above the distant fields below that streaked green and brown partially obscured by the massive overhang of rock on which they sat but also low lying cloud. The stone plateau swept down on one side, at suitable walking degrees of elevation to several other graduating plateaus that tilted down to the flat land below. In the distance a storm was sweeping the distant mountain range and forest below, harsh driving rain and flashes of light, casting eerie vignettes of patchy light on the ship's hull and surrounding stone as if the rocks were an audience to some portent. Far down below barely visible was a wide river that looked grey and oil-like, slimming its way to a blue black sea only discernible by the vast white- cap scape, windswept and marine raw.

Spots of precipitation blotted the glass, visible from inside the cabin, running in forms of string down the surface, condensating inside the craft like a warm greenhouse of human odour and strain. "Jason, are we anywhere near our Landing Zone?" "Right upon it Captain Kate," Jason Findus the Navigator said dryly with a smile, turning to her revealing his youthfulness of twenty five, school boy good looks and an air of high intelligence.

His still attached helmet hid his red movie-star like hair and broken stubble, tattoos of success and scars of a fire he had managed to survive in a training accident. Kate Arnold rose from her seat, a thirty year old Navy pilot, bottom of her elite class but far more suited to flying Starships, short crew-cut brown hair, right weight for her height of five feet eleven, green eyes with natural leadership gait, much like an old respected General before a major campaign. "Batteries are hot" someone lamented, the cabin now a flurry of hands pushing buttons like the end of an Earthlike long haul flight with the sounds of rustling, crew standing, stretching out long seated limbs and sore sides, quiet chat and stale air, and comments to confirm or deny, waiting for orders.

"Thankyou Jason" Kate said humorously. Standing to adjust an upper console and peer outside the Glass front portal and back again scanning her crew for signs of discomfort and flight discipline procedure. She saw Anders Pedersen intently staring at his console, manipulating the touch screen with typical Third Officer Dexterity, his huge frame belying his manners and light touch. Anders Nordic blonde hair, tied back to disguise a Viking but unable to hide a tattoo of a ship poking above his collar above the suit. "Ander"s are we good at the moment?, are we secure on the platform?" "Yes Katie, he said looking up, I was just having a look at the atmosphere composition, it is quite still amazing we have this oxygen-Nitrogen mix almost identical to Earth, ..but er, yes we are secure landing gear locked seals ok, ... wait, yes I can confirm, stable on the platform, no signs of damage with the descent." "Thanks Anders, well done," she smiled at him, turning to address the cabin.

"Ok, listen up everyone, fantastic effort, we are here, after many years flight time and an immense amount of toil from the mission planners," she glanced a *"are we ok"* look at her Captain, who nodded and listened intently leaning forward both hands on a seat in front waiting his inevitable turn to address the crew and be recorded for the moment to be sent back to Earth which would take a little shy of three years.

"It's scary, exciting, monumental to be exact." She started laughing and began to get teary, looking down at the floor composing herself, the crew shuffling quietly but smiling and showing their solidarity with her feelings. An incessant alarm was still bleating in the background, she paused which was enough for her silent command to be attended to by Kylie silencing the alarm. "Thanks Kylie, is that anything serious?," she smiled, Kylie smiling back shaking her head,

"We, ah, all of us here have been working our butts off, to put it mildly and we have accomplished arguably the most dangerous part of this mission, we have eighty-six passengers in the freezers who will I hope also be happy. We are.".., she looked up and composed her tone, assuming her General-like self again,

"Still a happy, professional bunch, this is a great day, remember this day," she said slowly nodding looking around at her colleagues, "Remember this day, as we are all that remains, and now our chances got a little better" She made a stoic face to the crew who replied with clapping and praised comments. "And without further pomp, I give you our Captain for further torture.." Anders beamed at her his respect, Jason smiling started to chant a friendly "Captain, Captain, Captain..." James started to shake his head, looking at him with pretend annoyance and impending consequence, she saw Kylie Abbot at the back small in the cabin, looking large in her ability even in shadow, her suit shining from the cabin light, contrasting her librarian teenager-like looks.

"Yep, we are here, that's all," ...in a pretend exit he started for the door, the crew in unison called a "aaaahhhh" "Only joking," He twisted around, returned smiling and stood scanning his team. There was paused silence, seemingly a moment of communal sighing and serious tiredness, waiting for his speech.

Katie stood arms folded like a child awaiting a lolly smiling at her Captain, Jason had his hands on his head, Anders was seated still touching his screen while waiting, then turning back with polite attentiveness.

James felt proud, exhausted, he felt the weight of the room, probably a billion dollars in this room just in training, the best flight crew Humanity had assembled for one last cast of survival, it all seemed too much, not true, true enough, they were further away from Earth than thought imaginable in the time frame of five years thanks to the Fusion drive.

The airlock cabin door chimed, "Partners!" he said looking at the door, a communal cheer went up, Kylie Abbot was laughing uncontrollably at a comment from Anders at the back, Jason said jokingly, "We will be a couple more hours!"

James laughed, someone from behind the door said. something humorous but unintelligible. "Katie, want to do the honours?" he said looking back at Jason, who was playing naughty schoolboy again, pretending to have not said anything.

Katie stretched near Anders console and flicked a switch, four spacesuited figures, the Science team with carried helmets strode file-like through the airlock onto the bridge to a unison of cat-calls, clapping and laughter, and exaggerated bowing. Akseli Hoskinen, the Finnish Geologist, greeted them in medieval fashion, a deep bow and associated dramatic hand movements, one hand sweeping below and one perched above like a knight after conquest. Jessica Neuer, the ship's Ecologist, stood laughing at Akseli, Donghyun Han the Meteorologist with a beaming smile.

Ye Min the ship's Astronomer stood clapping, greeting the crew, next to her colleagues, her hair tied back standing six foot tall and in some ways separate from the others Katie thought, in her imposing way and brilliant minded manner.

7

Ye Min could see Jessica Neuer and her Scientific colleagues, the crew, including the ever present now parked AI survey drone, gathered in the clearing like always. Several energy tents were spread around the area. A low lying grass type spread mat-like across the floor tufted in places with tendrils poking up with two stems stretching like arms from the mid-section containing tiny blue flowers. Seven petals of fine fibrous down-like cells, waved in peculiar motions, twirling in the wind like miniature blow-up figures of disturbing car sales advertising.

The enormous forest was raised above them, the canopy around them stretched like a hundred arms as if trying to close the stone littered cleared space and fill in the sky. The trees, an ochre orange trunk, mottled grey patches, rough and warty stretching to hefty boughs and smaller arterial branches containing spore laden leaves, part green, part orange, which had deposited a heavy forest floor of decaying damp litter, smooth to the pressure of foot, the smell of musty dirt and cellular humidity.

She stood and watched the others mill around the containers with their gear and the communications mast like some priesthood waiting for delayed sacrifice on an altar, ready for the brief and any news of the dying Earth, who was dead, who was not. They always came together like a dying tribe, happy to be alive, "That was an underlying strong feeling" she admitted, they were all that was left, they were pretty sure, Earth had descended into another Geological Epoch,

Briefing was made to hear any news, get a report on the possible Cryo date for thawing the passengers and problems to attend to, their office meeting, brief, plan, approach, Science schedule, sampling relay to *Ate* for analysis, injuries, ailments, supplies, planetary status, weather, discoveries. "Not much opportunity to get depressed here anyway," she uttered softly.

She summarised their situation thinking like she had so many times before noting, that most had family here in Cryo-sleep, still the passengers were left to wait, as they had to make sure the planet was safe for habitation beyond AI reports and technology saying it was so, tests, retests, patrolling, ascertaining studying, living in the environment, taking a risk.

Also the challenging factor of another eighty six mouths to feed over a staggered time-frame of awakening the passengers, in lots of four at a time. *"The sleep of potential portents is almost over for their passengers"* she thought. *"The dangers of Starship travel have diminished somewhat now the journey itself was completed"* she said to herself. *Now we await what the planet has for us,* Looking up to the dawn sky above the misty clearing.

Her pondering was sharply aroused, with a "Morning Ye Min" the ship's Ecologist, Jessica approached with the usual smile carrying her morning coffee Jessica, like her was almost six feet tall, she noted, longish hair tied back in a ponytail, looked fit like all of them, a flight officer in her own right, wearing a green skivvy and tan cargo pants, a good badminton player, she had discussed the game with Jessica who had played occasionally, loving the cardio workout it provided, like squash or hardball but depended on all things in varied flight, namely the feathered shuttlecock shaped ironically or not, like a space capsule.

"Morning Jessica, how did you go yesterday?" she offered, rubbing her morning eye. She approached carefully through the grass, looking down, being careful not to trip. "Very well, some samples and interesting insect life, how did your analysis go up on Ate with the celestial calculations?"

"Yes, fine, fine, I have been watching the, er twin-suns and the three moons, as you know, oh, she briefly looked skywards to look for the moons hidden by the forest canopy. "No, I can"t see them here,"there is much to do Jessica, the tidal pull is quite amazing you know, very, very exciting, but trying to be practical also, you know, in terms of where is the best place for a settlement, a warm place hopefully, but anyway apart from that, very beautiful isn't it,...", she said examining Jessica's coffee mug; a picture of a black crow with yellow eyes.

"You have found more life, Jessica?" "Oh, yes" she replied, "More ants, ten instead of six legs," Jessica said smiling. "Wow, ten instead of six eh?. Ye pondered. "Ahhh, so what do you think? Better stability, maybe?" Ye stared at her in concentration, "Yes correct, probably stability as they move faster,..."mmmmm," she silently said over her speech. "But time to conduct this type of research will come later I'm afraid," Jessica offered, smiling while picking up her coffee.

"Your strong Italian coffee, I remember Jessica" She thought for a moment, Jessica had brought some items not on the manifest and had to fight to get them included, she had lobbied to bring on the mission for three weeks. She remembered several discussions with Tanya and Tom, the ship's Logistic Officers about it.

"Speak of the devil," she murmured softly, glancing over to Tom waving *good morning,* who gave her a knowing nod, a slight smile, turning to talk to Donghyun Han, the Korean Meteorologist, his brimmed cowboy hat perched already awaiting the twin-sun. "Sorry Jessica, Tom was saying good morning" She turned and waved also, Tom and Dong-hyun acknowledging.

Jessica turned smiling and continued the conversation with a modest tone, she thought, *"Not to mention her amazing scientific ability and her famous Father, inventor of the 'Neuer*

Shell', our sips anti-micro-meteorite barrier. she remembered from the Human Resources newsletter during selection.

"So Jessica, to finish my comment about the calculations, we are not sure yet of the elliptical changes, winter may be too cold here, you know, I am thinking, you know, the orbit is quite far, around the suns, she looked at Jessica nodding, Jessica looked at her with interest., "This planet has, and let me get this right, a   P-Type orbit, circumbinary" "Yes, circumbinary, we orbit two stars instead of one, she said smiling, Jessica nodding, "We think it will be ok, climate wise, in some parts anyway, then the effect of the moons, you know, I got to say I never get unamazed at them, you know Jessica, I found out yesterday the smaller two, orbit the large as well, so,.."

Jessica laughed in surprise. "Oh dear, it's a complex planetary thing going on out there" She grabbed Jessica in a friendly manner with her free arm, placing it on her shoulder in happy surprise, bowing in laughter then withdrawing to take another sip of tea. She could see in Jessica's eyes the excitement of the mission but also a hint of trepidation and thought for a silly moment she looked frightened as if her demeanour had suddenly changed.

8

All his flight crew were aboard the lander explorer on the plateau readying for a supply run up to *Ate,* the Sentient Artificial IntelligenceI *Anastasia* and Jason Findus, his Navigator in stable orbit awaiting their return. He had just been dropped off and had chosen to walk the three kilometres to the Scientists camp, through the sedge plain and eroded mineralised boulders, to get some fitness and muscle tone back.

He took in the magnificent view out to the Western range and an almost three hundred degree view back around to the distant sea, the black swirling river winding a hazy path. Stiff breeze gusting warm, then bursts of cold the katabatic wind grazing the top of the high plateau and sweeping over him.

The plateau sloped down forgivingly, his path alternating mineral and mats of purple lichen, wet slate-like stone, bits of yellow amber and ochre shards of weathered rock, the sound of water dripping off the slopes and lips, an after dinner lament, the taste of tart oxygen and a little ammonia smell as he descended to the plain proper, rain clouds dumping afar and the ocean in the distance shining, salt-pan like, a green-blue pancake. *Not bad.* Looking up and out to the mountains, having stopped to assess, *Pretend I'm on holiday,* he mused, the massive range, scissoring across the horizon like a child"s paper cutout, "Tanya Gery will go nuts out there at some stage", he uttered to himself.

His path wound down in gradual steps, segments of flat rock lips like melted dinner serving plates stacked unevenly on one side from the plateau. *"The Captain, out alone, on a walk across a yet to be declared safe planet"* he remembered Kate Arnold"s words concerned but overruled, *"No, Kate, I"m going, if anything happens to me, you have the helm"* he had said jokingly, smiling, picking up his pack, Kate unimpressed, arms crossed, looking at the ground with a face of ordered obedience. *Considering risk is a part of adapting to this place, he thought.*

Without risk they would fail, without some considered daring they would not win. A part of the final throw of the die, *staying inside* was not an option. *This is part of the approach to success. He* thought reinforcing his Mantra, *All crew would get a chance of a Walk in the Woods,* he had said, the crew craving the outdoors after hearing the Scientists stories, seeing the landscape, the life, *the wondrous life,* he thought. *This also will restore some sanity to the Captain,* he lamented quietly climbing down the last rock plate tier, a stretching grapple backwards, both feet hanging then a small drop, his feet thumping to the surface, boots to stone, which edged to the sedge plain and beyond the *Scientist"s Forest*, as he called it.

This mission would have been impossible, if the Linear Acceleration Gravity created by the Fusion drive had not been developed. He found himself reviewing the structure of the ship, still marvelling at its design, ironically, as he noticed some small gliding bees fly past him and disappearing into a small crevasse in a boulder field, buzzing and then gliding the alternate tone like the sound of breathing in then a of a small drill whirring. "The linear gravity is created by the ship"s elongated design," he stated to himself, the Fusion drive powerful enough to accelerate at one G denoted by the symbol (gn), he visualised from the professors chalk-board, not marker board, old school Physics with old school white-haired guy. The ship's gravity presses the occupants against the hull in the opposite direction, in effect *sticking* them to the opposite surface, a fast ship, the *fastest ship made*, their flight taking only four years.

He awoke from remembering his lesson and started across the sedge plain, adjusted his pack after the jump down, lifting it slightly from behind at the base of his back to straighten the weight. The radio hissed, *"Katie calling boss, how are things on the plain old man?...* " Looking to the side with suppressed humour, he twisted around to face the rock ledge he had climbed down looking at the layered igneous layers in the stone, answering with a deadpan tone, "Old man ok, how old Woman?" *"Found any alien maidens yet?"* Katie quipped. There was a silent-laughing pause, they became adults again, *"Just checking, I have a question also though"* Katie said, the radio clicking, "Yep, go for it," he replied, eager to continue the walk.

"Did they replace those Fusion batteries on the Explorer?, the ones that had the defect, you know...," she said searching for the name. He interrupted, "The Sentinel series, no, no, they didn't have time, why?" *"Oh, the readouts are a bit hot at the moment"* "Right, well, remember the Explorer was in vacuum in the hold here to extinguish any possible fire, so we got to be careful, so, yep maybe we got what we got, keep an eye on it, actually you know who you could ask when she has time, Ye, see if she has any insights and get Kylie on it, alright?, anything else?" *"Ok, No, all good, ahh, Jason has been getting the supply-drop ready, Anders is sitting here doing very little...."* her comment drew an unintelligible response from Anders in the background, *"Pretty regular day on board I guess."* "Ok, got to go, Scientists to meet" he said, *"Copy, out"* said Katie and the radio silenced. *"Those crap batteries"* he remembered a fusion drive was one thing a fusion battery another.

Within the forest proper, he filled his nose with a fresh breath, tasting the oxygenated air. The massive rough-barked trunks ablaze with the orange-tinged nettle-like leaves around him. *This is one dense forest.* Making his way around the ancient trunks passing some Bromeliad plants attached to the bases of the trees, multicoloured, red, orange, light and dark greens, yellow mottled stems and patched pastel ochres. He noticed a slight buzzing sound and some black species of beetle flew by, several blurred wings and slight vibration past his ear, they drove away into the gloom, the forest silent again. *"That's odd"* he uttered, the tone in his ear changed like releasing salt water after a swim in the ocean, his mouth went a bit numb and it smelt like acetone for a moment. *"I feel a bit low blood sugar here,"* he said out loud, stopping and taking his pack off, setting it down. He leant over in a bow and put his hands on his knees, taking a moment. *Ohh, it"s passing, a little better, getting old,* he thought.

With the pack on the ground he took the water bottle, drank deeply, stood, composing himself, holding the aluminium bottle cap in one hand the bottle in the other. and replaced it, at once grabbing the pack again and hefting it through his arms. Raising his head, he checked his tracking device for the signal, the camp about one kilometre away. He looked around and up to the canopy where more bromeliads were growing on the trees high up, moss and fern like plants around them, the rough trunks patchy and looking like they had been sandpapered by giant hands.

The wind swept the nettle leaves from side to side creating a gentle lament, a hiss of sorts, a small branch fell among the heaped untouched piles of nettle leaves at the base of the tree decaying in stages the mound discoloured in graduated parts. He spent a moment examining the light squinting to get better focus, the photons filtered this way and that, puzzle-block patterns and small rays, pillar like cathedral cones of light and movie like teleport beams arrayed around striking the plant and trunk catching the contents of the air within the forest, a misty light carbon particle haze swirling in the light like embarrassed entities.

A small bead of sweat ran slowly down his temple, which he brushed across his skin, his breath felt a bit hotter but the *low-sugar moment* had passed, *"I'm ok, but fuck me, how does this happen?* he thought. *Is this finally old age?"* He thought of all the training he had been through, the flight training, fitness training, escape and evasion, decision making, endless assessments, mental ability, problem solving, ditching training, survival training, navigation, hand to hand combat, weapons training, "The multi-million dollar asset has become vulnerable, ladies and gentlemen," he suggested out loud. He made a mental note to get Andreas to look at him when back on board, *"Probably the space-flight effects"* he thought. *"My balance is out of some inner ear thing or Cancer, Ha!"* He continued to speculate, thinking of all the close calls flying, ejecting after an engine failure on a Carrier into the sea, the blinding, vibrating jet propelled force from sky to water, parachute barely opening but enough to catch his fall onto the wall of water, clear of any unmoving metal, a certain death.

With a quick look at his direction heading, he commenced again to walk the path he had in mind past the rough tree ahead and through the gloom. Another ten minutes or so brought him to an area funnelled by the rocks, *Small valley then Scientists campsite,* the terrain narrowing into a large gully as predicted. The sounds of the camp confirmed his navigation skills and his footfall described new terrain as the edge of the forest subsided, among small clusters of stone and fallen debri. He emerged, and could see the encampment ahead and the Scientific crew, the clearing contrasting the forest gloom.

He thought for a moment on Jessica Neuer's state of mind, remembering why he couldn't see her with the others. *She is ship-side with the Doc, Polkinghorn, I must remember to get him to brief me on her condition. This is a real concern. Did we get her selection wrong? Why did she panic, wanting to get back to the ship so badly?*

9

The ship's Doctor Andreas Polkinghorn looked around Jessica Neuer's door in careful check-out mode. Jessica sat reading a small book on the finger-like sleeping pod, *Car's* lighting on, red hair tied back into a tail, still in pyjamas. Age 37, One point eight metres in height, 68kg, green eyes, former Curling champion and ships Ecologist. Prolific reader, archivist trained and Zoology mad. One small scar above the left eye and Father who designed the ship's radiation shield, the *Neuer Shell*. Trusted like all aboard of course but calm, pilot calm, good decision maker. Plain-Jane looking, but attractive in that way he thought, much like women who wore makeup but looked better with it off than on. *'Good dancer too'*, smiling inwardly. A hologram showed a mountain vista on the far wall, clean ship board lines defined the chamber in its sleek clinical look, lit well with light designed to comfort not irritate.

'Light on board was designed by a Scientist Kurt Cars who invented a new gamma light wave emitted from a series chamber and adapted to light sockets' Andreas thought on the technology while sneaking a quick look at his patient before she noticed his presence. He remembered the explanation of the technology, *'The light was commonly described as a new source of vitamin D colloquially but the wavelength was designed to placate tired retina cells using a direct relationship between nerve fibre and wave type.*

Ophthalmologists he recalled called it macular massage or technically 'Calm Isomerization Protein Transfer' It was later discovered that (CIPT) delayed macular degeneration in susceptible patients' remembering his lectures and light booths designed like photo-booths that people sat in in the city.'

Jessica looked up wide-eyed with a greeting like an interrupted parent about to eat something forbidden briefly then smiled as Andreas entered. "Sorry, may I come in?" 'I didn't realise you would be in your PJ's' he asked, straddling the door frame. "Don't worry, I may remain like this all day" she replied, "Many things are not realised in deep space Andreas"…She looked at him with intent, he chuckled as he entered."Dancing *Doctor Livingstone* I presume?" she added. "Hah!, I wish Jessica Neuer," he sighed, "no more canned air in the Jungle" he intonated to a higher pitch.

Andreas remembered the last dance-off on the ship. They had teamed up and won after their pairing with a certain amount of attraction residue in the aftermath, '*dancing does that he* mused', '*it's probably essential*' he thought, smiling, he drew her gaze. "Indeed," Jessica pursed her lips, long enough to elicit a smile from him. Andreas sat down next to Jessica on the pod bed and smoothed the sheets as if examining the fabric, staring across to the Hologram then back to her, a friendly posture of "Look at me" "I'm quite nice" Jessica stared straight ahead but smiling like an uncommunicative child would, chided by adults with silly humour. There was a short impending pause, a conversation waiting moment between the two parties.

So how about a Tango?" he said, matter-of-fact, breaking the timer.' Jessica laughed, "Not in the pyjamas Doctor" she replied with serious dryness. "Ha!" He smiled looking up to the ceiling "I'm not going to continue on this line…" "Ha, ha," Jessica uttered, turning to look at her physician, still smiling. "Well, still a sense of humour I see," he inquired, eye-brows raised. Jessica stared ahead again, an "almost-smile" on her face.

Andreas continued, stating much like a read report, "So, I am here to enquire, er, well ask what is going on, I heard that you rapidly left the planet's surface yesterday. That's what Jason said and the others couldn't understand it. You're going, that is.

And, ah, we are dancing friends, remember, you can tell Doctor Andreas" They both smiled, the tension broken.

"Yes, well not implying, it's true, they are right." There was a thinking pause, a *'I have to get this response correct pause'* Jessica blinked and consoled the floor in reply, moved her left foot over the right, "I had to leave yesterday" Jessica turned to face him, her perplexed expression seemingly indicating a mixture of fear and confusion. She closed the book, *'Dry Sclerophyll Forests of Australia'*, placing it on the bed. Hands either side of her head she moved her hair back, scratched her nose while slowly shaking her head at him.

"I can't really explain it, it's not fear, more like an instinctual desire to run, run fast away. I've never experienced anything like it except…" 'What?' He stood and faced her looking back and forth at the light, concerned stance, with a studied look at his patient. She looked up at him with a puzzled expression. "It's like when I was on a Primary School camp and we had just arrived, and then I got this longing home sickness so severe I almost went out and started the bus to get home. It's like an inner desire so strong you have to satisfy it, an addiction almost" *'Fuck me, don't say that!* she thought. "Ok"

Andreas dragged a chair from the wall and sat facing her, hands on his knees. Jessica's hands pointed to an apex around her nose, seemingly embarrassed. *Flashing diagnosis went through his mind, then thoughts of events that may have occurred on the surface, arguments, assault? With this team?, no, possible but what about…,* She continued looking up at the ceiling,

"I was ok before I went down to the surface, excited, ready for work, Ecology on another planet, I mean what a coup that is to get to do that, then I get there and then I'm all teenager, like I'm not experienced enough, inadequate, ugly, in the wrong place. Wrong Ball"

Sighing, she looked away to the Hologram and back at the floor, back to him." It's embarrassing, I know." "It's not embarrassing twinkle toes," he crossed his arms while widening his eyes. "What's happened has happened, we just need to understand it a bit more" She smiled more broadly, 'You are supposed to be serious here..." "Sorry, yes I am, but remember humour never hurts anything between friends, nor between Doctor and Patient for that matter." He looked in her eyes, both of them still aware of the harmless attraction that would never go anywhere. "So did something happen on the surface with the others? Is this an argument, fight.."No," she shook her head puzzled. "No, no," she shook her head slowly side to side. "I wasn't even with anyone at the time, I was on the Forest floor, within safe range but collecting samples" There was a silence as they both looked in different directions, thinking about it.

"Sooo.., if I said to you *get out there again tomorrow,'* would you go?" "I feel like I have to, well yes, I do have to but it's like, It's like, ummm," she looked straight at him, her demeanour a serious Scientist, like a researcher that had found something terribly important, she shifted on the bed, adjusted her arms straight down to lift her slightly, bringing her legs at an angle as if to soften the next explanation, "Look, I got back from there like I escaped from Prison or something, escaped death,..."

He could see tears well up in her eyes, she looked away embarrassed, shaking her head. "I'm supposed to like fucking plants! Now I'm all nervous, fearful, hesitant, scared" she wiped the tears from her eyes and walked to the drawer, collecting a towel to dry her eyes further. Arms wide apart she faced him then returned to the bed. "There's something biochemical going on and *"no"* I am not pregnant." "Never occurred to me to ask," he said tongue -in-cheek. "However, we will examine your blood anyway, for any changes" Jessica rose from the bed and walked in Philosopher fashion to the wall and back staring at the floor, reseating again, one leg folded under the other. "So, what about infections of some kind? What about brain function? Can you do scan's?" Looking at him more concerned, the humour eroding her demeanour. "Yep, we'll take you through the ringer, we want our Ecologist back"

"So is it fear of the external environment, do you think?'Like the descent to the surface, the risks of infection, accident? I'm just ticking some boxes here ""No, no, no I never had this in training ever, how would I pass this flight test? We went through a gruelling exam, remember?" Jessica started at the floor like someone who had just been beaten by a better competitor.

"Any recent injuries?" "No." Shake of the head. "Any medications?" "No, nothing" She shifted again about to say something, looking upwards at the ceiling. "What?," he inquired. "It's a mental thing, I'm still really fit as I can be out here, and I don't like saying mental because of all the stigma that will probably bring when you file a report" He looked at her widening his gaze, "We are all *mental,* Jessica in our own way, you know what I mean, and there will be no report unless I say so." "Of course there will be one" She tilted her head to him to emphasise the point. "But I will tell you one thing, I am not looking forward to going back down there and I want to go home as silly as that sounds, but that's the truth, I want to go home like a spoilt child, that's how I am feeling right now" She turned to look him in the eye. "Five light years from Earth for fuck's sake"

10

As Captain James Williamson emerged from the forest, the twin-suns were lighting the camp slowly. A small cloud bank dotted the sky above the clearing he saw, as he looked up to stretch his neck, the trees swaying slightly to the breeze, the sound of small pebbles to his footfall and rustle of grass. He could see that Tom had seen him and had an arm raised in greeting from the throng of Scientists. He waved back, adjusting his radio, and strode toward the others milling near the Comms tower in the clearing near the operations energy tent, walking with the knowledge that things on Earth were worse, much worse. I thought that three klick walk would be just the ticket, *now I just feel strange*, he thought.

As Captain he constantly assessed the Scientists progress and balanced his decisions with the information from Tom and Tanya as to where a settlement might be established, what external hazards they would have to cope with and assess a good landing site for when the majority of supplies and personnel arrived. "Learning as we go," he murmured, the main unknown at the moment was the effect of the twin suns' elliptical paths in terms of potential seasons and climate. Doctor Ye was collating a large amount of data of which was impossible to obtain pre-flight. "We want to avoid a -200 °F winter. For that matter, a hundred and forty degree Fahrenheit summer" he added dryly.

In the time it took to hear the greetings from the Scientists he suddenly wondered, "How many briefings had he been to, he wondered in his life-time,several thousand? Combat flight briefings, space flight briefings, disciplinary briefings, briefings about briefings, "ahh," and he thought, "my favourite type of briefing, the, *"It will all blow-over briefing."* He had chosen to wear his one piece grey flight suit. "Always had to look the part" he pondered. As he approached the others he recognised his two mission *wildcards,* those selected as non-flight and non-scientist personnel to be part of the crew, Tanya Gery and Tom Auer.

Both had been equally invaluable already, with organisation and logistics, good team players, no family connections, single and content, "Tom, formerly a Sailor and Tanya a,...... "Well, let's say, Adventurer" he thought to himself. He saw Akseli Hoskinen, the ship's Geologist and Donghyun Han, the ship's Meteorologist talking, thick as thieves. He scanned around and saw Ye-Min the ship's Astronomer standing by some terrain crates. "Well, at least they are all here minus Jessica, that's a start," he thought as he approached, one by one the Scientists raised their gaze in his direction in anticipation of the news.

The briefing was a tense sombre anticipation, he explained the situation on Earth, there had been multiple Tsunamis, wiping out the Eastern seaboard of the United States, a massive Volcanic explosion in Iceland that had ejected several million Gigatonnes of debri over Europe and widespread fires in South-East Asia, quoting the transmission that had taken just under four years to arrive, leaving the *Elephant in the room* for the gathered Scientists to speculate on.

He held the light paper printout heavily, wanting to quote the direct communication at the end of the message, glancing up to his throng from time to time, Tom Auer looked at the ground, sweeping his right leg in a pendulum like motion lightly touching the small stones in a searching motion,

Ye-Min, held her tea like a statue about to be removed from its pedestal, at the back, looking skyward as if searching for Earth itself. Dong-hyun Han and Akseli Koskinen exchanged some quiet exasperated comments, backdropped against the green grey forest like two lost explorers. As he started to narrate, the paper rustled to a slight breeze as if in portent, some nettle leaves falling around them with the wind.

"Transmission outbound is unlikely from this date as infrastructure is compromised Worldwide and the situation critical. To be clear, we face global annihilation. Several World leaders are missing, population devastated, Sentient Intelligence has limited capability due to network failure and complete power grid destruction. The atmosphere is becoming increasingly toxic, several high mountain centres have been established, above at the moment, the toxic lower atmosphere, in Chile and Switzerland, but this is expected to be a short-lived scenario. Tsunami events are devastating, magnitude ten earthquakes are a daily event. Several cities destroyed by massive earthquake activity - terrain waves seen on the terrain's surface.

Those of us left hope you have made it, returning to Earth under any circumstance is not an option. Hold yourselves high and embrace your new world, unmanned resupply vessel was launched two years ago as planned. We also hope that this mission is successful and reaches you. (See Appendix for supply details and Geological information gathered before major Earth events)."

End of Transmission

There was a silent prophetic pause as the group digested the terrible news in communal solemn unison. He folded the paper and put it in his trouser pocket, looking around at each of the Scientists. "The crew have heard this as well, it's what we expected but...nonetheless it hurts us all."

Pausing he blew-out a cooped up air from his lungs. "We of course will continue on, we have been lucky, but well prepared to get this far and everyone has done a great job. Transmissions inbound will continue, *Anastasia* will try and get another response, but given the delay..." "Poor devils, I am sorry everyone," Akseli Hoskinen the mission Geologist said, looking around clearly upset. Tanya Geary, the ship'

Logistics Officer poked the ground around her with a stick, shifting the small stones.

Dong-hyun Han the Meteorologist looked straight ahead with a puzzled expression like he was searching for the right word. He continued getting increasingly uncomfortable for some reason, suppressing it quickly, "News like this makes us want to get our loved ones out of the freezer, I know, and everyone is working at that, I am sure we can make good progress this week surveying a suitable site, Ye, thank you for your work on this I know you have been very busy with the elliptical calculations." Ye, nodded, the others looking appreciatively around. "Until we get an idea of what we can grow here in what climate, the supply situation has to be maintained with another eighty six passengers at the table soon, as you all know. As always, it could be worse, and yes I am serious, the climate is comfortable at the moment, we have Earth-like air here, which is very amazing." There was a unison agreement from the gathered.

He paused. "And, we, um, excuse me," coughing, a strange sensation overcame him. *"And from this point on I have a new mission,"* he told himself, thinking of how to wrap this all up quickly. "Anyway, look all, I am sorry I won't bore you all any longer, I am wanted Shipside, something has come up, nothing serious I assure you but Captain's duty" Tanya Gery stared him with a perplexed expression, as if to say *"God-damn Captain, you only just got here, we wanted to talk about the next supply movement, ...anyway, duty calls I guess"*

She looked at Tom Auer the Ship's Supply Officer who seemed resigned to the decision, adding "Ah, that's a shame Captain, speak soon though" Akseli Koskinen, shuffled impatiently, "Captain I will just access that Geological report if you can release it, what has happened is incredible, it may give us an insight to the cause and help us here, you ah, never know...." "Done, Akseli, I will send it over, ok sorry folks, gotta go, happy travels, speak soon"

With a wave and distant look behind the Scientists as if searching for some unseen danger he turned and walked as fast as he could back across the clearing, the paper in his pocket dislodged and fluttered down to the grass and blew slightly away with the wind, unconcerning him. Once he had entered the Forest proper he started to run over the nettle leaves at pace with only one thought, *Take the Ate Succession back to Earth at any cost.*

11

Donghyun wondered why he had been chosen Altar Priest and why he was a leader and knowing that Hexibarber had chosen him, for sure, after he had taken the initiative to craft the helmet, but what was his method? He tried to recall what had passed, his early life, but this time was vacant like a hollow shell, but he was sure he had always been here, among those of the tribe. He had dreams sometimes of weather and rain, he was typically standing in some field releasing strange alien objects and marking data in a leaved apparatus, sometimes he held a small round object, marked with lines spaced evenly and the most frightening thing, a floating fabric container on a rope that he held aloft then released, the thing skirting quickly to the sky and away, the rope dangling with a small box at the end. This gave him an unsettling feeling afterwards. "There are many unknown things, Hexibarber," he said to the helmet, the orb still and looking out to the plain.

He glanced down at his hands that seemed to have receded, smaller he thought, the flakes of sleet hitting them and dissolving upon his reddish palms. He was desperately hungry, the Pineapples were sustenance but only just, and their Unbeliever food had dried up, the long things in unbeliever fabric were deemed ok to eat by Hexibarber. He had stood one morning in front of the area where the boxes were piled, a light freezing wind blowing through the stick fence, his eyes weeping, his skin dry and red, hurting from the cold, and quickly asked Hexibarber if it was ok, and stood for a few moments like a stilted statue in a freezer, then flew the first box open and tore a wrapper from the food and ate with large bites and wholesome chewing, looking around to see if the others were watching, but now the strange boxes were nearly empty. He would ask Hexibarber about the food situation.

I am very happy though, he thought, *I have a great responsibility, I must keep the way open and the crux of the wicker cane temple secure, Hexibarber will show me. There must be discipline and rigour, the tribe must brace and smash, cut and twine, the burnt temple allows us to remember the evil cable-culture, the things that flew like in my dream and the shining square metal faces that were found in the sand, scaring us at one time,Ha!, it glowed it did, and showed shapes, mmm , then Akseli smashed it, the Mineral Master was alert to the danger.*

"So, Hexibarber, what do thy say?"Donghyun turned to look at the helmet, a cold gust of wind slightly rocking the perched orb upon the rock. "Ah, so you say my friend, I am of the similar thought, the unbeliever must be taken from the tribe as the infection would seep into the others, our lovely gathering cannot be wedged or cut. What do you say at the end? Will it be skinning or stoning?" Another gust rocked the helmet slightly sliding it on the uneven rock surface, a small piece of dry sedge grass flying out of the cavity and away with the wind, the helmet now facing him a little as if turning to discuss murder.

He smiled and continued to converse with the helmet, the placed mineral eyes staring malevolent and with seemingly smouldering portent at him. He felt a little unsettled like Hexbarber was angry with him and kneeled down in front of the effigy, looking up to the helmet with sincere piety. "Great Hexibarber, I thank you for this chance to discuss the tribe and the judgement upon the unbeliever, I kneel before you to accept the skin of tribe and blood of union, oh great Hexibarber" The helmet remained still, the wind abated momentarily, the flakes falling now in greater numbers speckling the surrounds with white on green, the weak suns light fading but arrayed and haloed still, the plain a dancing slanted confusion and beauty casting a set-like vista in an unknown play.

Donghyun remained silent, thinking maybe he was not worthy for a moment, his head bowed and obedient. Another gust of freezing wind swept the plain and over the effigy turning the head further to be facing him and looking above him and away upon the rock. "I understand Hexibarber, you want an indication of my connection with the temple and sacred understanding" He unsheathed his stone knife, the Mineralised Master had fashioned it for him from an important sharpened stone, bound with string twine to a wooden handle, and within the grain, small gems placed in cut depressions and glued in with fresh amber as an indication of his standing as Altar Priest.

He rolled his grass smock arms up to his elbow while looking up at the green sky, and placed the knife atop his naked arm, the blade turned toward the skin and sliced a portion out of the top of his arm, the size of a small stone, screaming with the pain, the blood welting and pooling in the wound then running down his arm and past his hand dripping and sliding onto the ground in long dribbler partly congealed airborne strings. He placed the portion of skin in front of the helmet, still clutching the knife with the same hand as if discarding the skin of a freshly peeled apple on a table, the limp skin dripping blood and smearing the stone in front of the effigy. He breathed out with concerted control, his head still bowed and pious, the wound starting to hurt him with a sharp cold pain and aching intent, the helmet shifted again with another gust slightly away from his straight on level below, Donghyun, smiling with the recognition, the blood pooling from his arm into a small well in the dirt floor, reflecting the sky in crimson and darkened shapes.

"Thankyou Hexibarber, my skin is your skin, I thank you for the mightiness within you and the forgiveness that you exude from the tribe, and …yes…what is that you say?, yes, yes, I understand, yes… the unbeliever will be cast from the plateau and bound according to the ritual way, I understand, thank you my Tribe, my saviour, my casting light of discipline and tempest, there is only one Hexibarber, one almighty, one light, and yes, I understand, yes, I may have two mistresses for pleasure, oh, thankyou, yes, thankyou…they can be taught the strain of desire the Altar Priest has to be satiated, yes, my Tribe, I thank you."

The flakes fell heavily, the helmet now with a frost of white cover and tiny pieces of sticking ice like a welder had cast a frozen arc weld around the soft snow on the orb to accentuate the illusion of hair. The twin suns had reached the horizon red and seeped fast into the plains horizon. He rose and held his arm, still seeping blood heavily, backing away and bowing still to be sure the respect was certain and the task had contented the great Hexibarber, the mineral eyes sparkling reflected grain a little with the dusk. "My Tribe" he rose, standing and collecting his knife red and streaked on the grass floor and sheathed the blade.

He leaned and collected the helmet, some grass whirring away through the visor opening with another gust, then with the strength of the wind, it slipped from his grasp falling heavily on the ground on some stone, the wooden frame within sounded dislodged, "Hexibarber!" he cried, as a single mineral eye rolled out, wheeling across the space between the sedge tufts. He jutted his foot out to try and stop the eye but it expertly hit a small pebble which diverted its path and circumnavigated his stride and continued over the river bank and sploshed into the river shallows somewhere beyond his sight.

"Fat Unbeliever!," he blurted out in error, "Forgive me Hexibarber, I… " he put the helmet down on the ground, then picked it up again, momentarily forgetting his continuing unpious error and replaced it back on the stone, "My tribe," he uttered, bowing at the stone turning to look where the eye had gone.

Another gust whipped suddenly, the area, now increasing with torrent snowfall and sending the grass sedge flat with the strength of the wind, and unbalancing him, as he leaned to the stone placing the helmet, "Ahh!," he fell like a sack of plain pineapples, trying to break his fall with his injured arm, which crumpled at his weight, the momentum flinging him over the edge of the bank, "Ahhhh!" The water exploded around him as he hit the freezing shallows, sending a spray up the bank, in a semi-circle pattern, *"How could this?..I'm in the water, comprehensively wet!,"* he thought. He moved in a comical late turn to try and avoid what had already occurred. "Fuaaaack!," he blurted again.

Red faced and freezing, his arm bled profusely, the water had seeped through his pants and he sat facing the river bank in the water, Hexibarber he could see on the stone looking Eastward above on the bank, with one mineral eye, and a protruding stick, part of the frame within, jutting where the other eye had been.

The effigy presented a miserable sight, like a dead Captain on a ghostship bridge, long dead and decayed and waiting grounding on a distant reef.

He rose from the water, the wind now he noticed a storm rated strength, gusting as if unhappy with his presence. He struggled up the bank, he slipped again and his good arm collapsing under him and his face falling straight into the bank on a gap between the sedge grass like someone had thrown him flat, "Unbeliever Monkey, and dead dogs arse!" he shouted, fuming at the fall, his face was imprinted with small balls of miniature pebble stuck to his face, he felt as he brushed his cheek in rage, quickly wiping it off in forceful strokes, too forceful he realised cutting himself again with a sharp piece, feeling the stripe of warm blood on his cheek. "You star-studded minging two faced clown!" he roared, at himself but hoping it had been someone else, and continued up the rise, as he looked over the top feeling an incandescent rage boiling up within.

Hexibarber had rolled off the mantle and was prostrate upside down, neck hole showing, the grass inner blowing out, and wobbling to the force of the wind. "My Tribe" he bowed apologetically, and picked Hexibarber up and placed it again on the mantle, the timing perfect for the next fierce gust, which hit him hard and making him steady his legs, sending the effigy flying with the frozen wind like a featherweight beach-ball away towards the river. The helmet revolved fast turns, the helmet bottom catching the wind like a cave-like sail sending it whirling above the grass and gaining momentum until it landed madly wobbling in the sedge like a fallen severed head, hard and soft at the same time bouncing up over the river bank and into the middle of the river proper. The head splashed then turned to face him, the mineral eye glaring from the gloom of the visor gap as if to say a *"You wait, you fool"* goodbye to him, continuing fast downriver with the current until it was out of sight, bobbing and inert.

Donghyun Han stood watching, a bunny in the headlights moment, like a person at a petrol station belted in a car the moment something had suddenly exploded in front of them in a ball of flame.

His mouth, he realised was open and his arm felt like a frozen grater was rubbing off the skin, a small blood trail reached his mouth from the cheek graze, stopping at the ridge of his lip as if asking to enter. The freezing wind continued to rise in tempo and the sky had gone black with the dusk casting the plain into a grey-white haze. Stalks of grass were flying past him and each gust of wind swept the river surface he saw looking around alarmed, sending variegated patterns where the wind was trying to push the surface tension, buffeting the running tide.

Suddenly he felt his grass trousers rip away. A mighty gust of wind-searing snowflake and grass seeds flying in a terrain driven tempest, one leg tearing up exposing his buttocks sending a freezing weight against his thigh. The rude fabric flapped madly exposing his naked leg with the wind suddenly sending the grass stitched cloth flapping legless pant fabric cracking like a whip against his face. "Unbeliever pestilence!," he yelled, he fell again, twirling, and fell on his back, the grass and dark sky perambulating a mottled blurred motion as he fell hard on the pebble. "Ohhhh! What do I have to do here!," he roared, legs momentarily up in the air, the trouser leg at right angles to his prostrate body in the stone, the feeling of wet ice on his bottom and numbness in his arm.

"Ahhhh!" He raised himself up quickly but realised he was standing on the blown off trouser fabric leg, camouflaged on the ground which unbalanced him, making him feel like with broken stay, hitting the ground suddenly again. As he tripped, he landed on his injured arm. "Oahhhh," he sat up again, half-defeated feeling suddenly very tired, and wiped his eyes. Now the grass plain was in a deep darkness, he noticed unable to get a pattern out of his sight of the horizon or the ground, the wind howling like a mad trumpeter, the snow driving hard flakes against his face. He sat breathing hard, then shifted up again, tearing the blown trouser leg off his right leg, unable to see properly, in a strength driven rage, and letting the wind blow it away.

He set out, like a scarecrow awoken, his buttocks seared cold and aching, his arm feeling like set infected mud, to where he thought the tribe was, a foreboding feeling within him at Hexibarber's passage and what the Altar Priest would tell the others. In a final humiliation he tripped on the trouser leg which had wedged on a low small rock at the start of his path, "Skin and bone!, you, you ahhh!," he lamented angrily, furious with the wind and continued through the blackness.

12

The Captain sat at the terminal they used to access *Anastasia* when she was in safe mode, the interface used to configure Sentient Intelligence settings like personality, voice or command changes. He quickly and stealthily exited the Explorer after docking and made his way up to the Bridge, passing Jason Findus, his Navigator while he was busy at the docking terminal, the radio buzzing with the Explorers crew and Katie prepping the craft for the return supply journey. He had radioed Katie while setting off back along the path taken to the Scientists camp and made it in time to the Explorer, on the way making up the story. Only the Captain could receive Emergency messages from Earth relayed by *Anastasia*. Katie was surprised but not overly to cause suspicion, she was used to him contradicting her and an order was an order, *"Let's get topside, I have a message from Earth, must have been sent soon after the last transmission, some secret stuff in there as well,"* he had said, smiling. The fact that secret messages had to be viewed on board helped his case, *Anastasia's* terminal was the only way to access them, originally a pain for him, now a boon.

He needed a key, a code and the First Officers consent and their door key to get access. Having all three now. It was for the Captain's eyes only, secret, covert. "A little white lie, Katie, but I know you won't mind, I think actually you will thank me when you can be free to take command..anyway, I got to go, so that's that," that is certainly that and this is this, I need to get moving here,.." he uttered softly. He paused, looking at the screen, feeling a little odd, there was a swirling sensation in him, a giddiness of sorts, his eyes were a bit rusty-scratchy, a picture of him looking at himself in a mirror flashed across his awareness, the mirror self yelling at him, something he couldn't hear, couldn't understand.

He looked around again to be sure no crew member had snuck up on him. The small enclosure around the terminal smelt like metal and tart lemon, the standard ship smell, the gloom punctuated by the bright terminal interface and a few lights blinking above his console. He could hear the internal cabin fans feeding oxygen from the greenhouse filtration system. He leaned forward in the bulky starship seat designed for G-forces not terminal commands. Jason Findus was at the other side of the bulkhead in the command area, Jessica Neuer with the Doctor so he was safely alone. From the left portal he could see the planet, green and grey, massive and new, primordial, and unsettling. The day side of the giant orb reflected a brilliant light into the ship casting silver shadows into the interior silence, contrasting the faint ground communication filtering through the open channel speakers and the clicking of beaming buttons of engineering in the upper consoles.

"Time to go" he thought, "Time to go" he called softly. "It's the right thing to do" he spoke again to himself. He got lost in thought for a moment, staring at the terminal screen, the blinking cursor awaiting command like a silent sentinel, powerful and burdening him to input ruin and delight at the same time. A momentary change came over his demeanour, he felt a bit hazy and for a small amount of time thought, *"What am I doing here,"* the thought soon passing, his mind set on leaving, the consequences, he was quite aware of, but somehow denial seemed right, *"Mmm, there are other concerns here at play, other concerns,"* he thought. *"Having Anastasia in safe mode meant that she was effectively ready for enquiry from him, a human, although she still monitored the ship's systems"* he thought, starting to type, not speak, the terminal also was a fail safe method against improper or hasty spoken commands with great consequences, it required computing command literacy, after authentication. The terminal login awaited his input.

Captain@Ate Succession - Anastasia: ~$ su -

He requested root access, the administrator, Superuser login. Human input, his ticket home.

Password: *********************

Root@Ate Succession - Anastasia: ~$

Authenticated he now had root access, meaning full access to all of Anastasia's menu command options, with the command:

Root@Ate Succession - Anastasia: ~$ ls

Intelligent-Conversation   **Life-Support**

Gender-Parameters   **Communication**

Download   **Media**   **Boot**   **Root**

Passenger-Status   **Anastasia**

Life-Boat   **Heat-Exchange**   **Power**

Fusion-Drive

He changed the directory to Communication, and listed the contents,

Root@Ate Succession - Anastasia: ~$ cd Communication
Root@Ate Succession - Anastasia:/Communication$ ls
Root@Ate Succession - Anastasia:/Communication$

Interstellar-Pathway   **Radio-Transmission**

Internal-Dialogue   **Language**

Military-Encrypted   **Dish-Antenna-Coordinates**

Emergency-Command

He changed directory, within, the option to change from Sentient control to human control, effectively take control of the ship, a failsafe to avoid Sentient Intelligence malfunction.

Root@Ate Succession - Anastasia:/Communication$ cd
Emergency-Command
Root@Ate Succession - Anastasia:/Emergency-Command$
Emergency-Command
Root@Ate Succession - Anastasia:/Emergency-Command$
Interface ready for enquiry:

He looked with satisfaction as Anastasia's interface listed the
contents of the **Emergency-Command** directory and a short
explanation of the additional options that could be added to
the command, *"Good,"* he thought, *"a usage example"*

Options:

Human-Control	**Evacuation**	**Life-Boats**
Passwords	**Life-Support**	

Usage: example: *Human-Control -c -s- initiate now*
Options:
Human-Control : Take Human control of Starship
Evacuate: Manually control ordered evacuation
Life-Boats: Configure Life-Boat AI
Passwords: Change passwords and security options
Life-Support: Manually control life-support options
Options:
-c: control
-s: control all systems
-f: override any existing parameters
-t: take control after specific time
-a: abort last command
-d: disable onboard announcements
Root@Ate Succession - Anastasia:/emergency-command$
Human-Control -c -s -d initiate now
Password: *****************************
Root@Ate Succession - Anastasia:/emergency-command$
Successful

He leant back, and clipped his dual seat-belt around his arms, *"This is great,* "going home at last, can't wait," he said softly. He felt for a moment like a lost child, his limbs tired and his memory erratic, his parents lost, his blanket gone. His nose was moist and his throat dry, and his mind seemed dull, but sure, misty but certain. There was no movement in the area Jason Findus was occupying, *"On the radio to the camp it sounds like,"* he thought. "A few more commands should do this," he softly said to himself.

Root@Ate Succession - Anastasia:/emergency-command$
Orbit-exit: initiate
Root@Ate Succession - Anastasia:/emergency-command-$
confirm new coordinates please.........

Anastasia asked for the new vector, "Where are we going," he asked himself concentrating on getting the next input right. "Something I have learnt of by heart in case of your failure Anastasia" he said looking up at the AI's blue and red decorated room as if she was looking down at him.
Root@Ate Succession - Anastasia:/emergency-command$
<u>*2233434noad-3 Earth-sector7-Milkyway*</u>
Root@Ate Succession - Anastasia:/emergency-command$
successful
There was a worrying pause, the terminal for a moment seemed to be stuck at what to say, the screen blank, then a listed command syntax appeared tearing down the screen as the ship calculated and prepared, checked and initiated.
Prioritising.....please wait......
Engaged Fusion-drive...
Successful...please wait........
Parameters agreed.....
Sentient is down...yes
Life-support stable..yes
Authenticated...yes
Please wait.....
With the ignition of the Fusion drive he leaned back waiting for the inevitable discussion with the others. "It can all be

explained quite easily" he softly said, "No need for argument or conflict, hah!, after all, we are going home, they should be happy, ... shouldn't they?"

13

Akseli Koskinen, climbed the base of the large rock finger which jutted out of the forest like an accusing judgement. His tall frame strided upward in wiry ascent, a thin studious face like an ancient archivist, searching for stone and fossil, lava and sand, a wandering seeker, lost and found. He adjusted his floppy hat on a close-cropped hairstyle, thinking of his blue favourite that had seen many suns, and some moons. He had chosen to wear his patched cargo trousers, another favourite item of clothing, khaki, left blue denim patch, five pockets. His green tight fitting skivvy, enough proof against the coolness, with enough room to flex around. Instead of sunglasses he wore light safety goggles, wrap-around, with an elastic green cord around the back of his head.

His primary role was to discover some information about the planet's climate past and for that he needed his drilling core sampler, an item yet to be ferried down from *Ate Succession*. In the meantime he was a lone Ranger, free to collect and discover and assist Dong-hyun with the drone and his weather mapping from the orbiting satellite that was in place above, launched not long after orbit was established. Dong-hyun, had given him time today, *"To go and piddle around"* as he recalled him saying, wishing he had never taught him that phrase. *"What is piddle?"* Dong-hyun had originally asked, looking at him with suspicion, one time when they were wading a stream, the freezing water coursing around their legs, alert for another joke at his expense. *"When you waste time, doing things of little importance,"* he replied. *"Piss around," pelleilla, in Finnish if you like,"* he said. "Byeollo jung-yohaji anh-eun il-eul hago issda," Dong-hyun replied. *"Huh?"* Akseli said with a screwed up joking face. Dong-hyun laughed, *"Korean translation, ok, so what is it again?, piddling around, I like it"* He thought therefore, the old volcanic plugs were interesting and a look into the planet's obvious volcanic past but also no doubt had influenced the climate during its Geological history, justifying his "piddling around."

The base sloped upward at a forgiving angle so he was able to access the layers higher up. The stone tower rose at a peculiar angle like it had flexed down to allow him an easier route above. The twin suns hovered in the midday cast, with a cool wind and some dotted clouds shifting in the breeze. His pack contained his samples, his Geological hammer, the old steel, the destroyer of a million rocks and driver of several hundred tent pegs, a small lunch of *Starship hash* as he called it, dried health bar, noodles in a can you could heat and some dried orange pieces you could add water to and they expanded into juicy wedges. His old compass was still inside, his water can, a GPS tracker, emergency beacon and a spare pair of shorts, socks and underwear.

As he climbed, he thought of Earth, watching the rock as he walked, the stone pebbles, some small bizarre protruding shrubs with white flowers shaped like cones splitting the rock to wedge a root hold in different sections. His dying world, it seemed to him an affront in some respects, he a Geologist, Earth dying as a direct effect of Geological effects, his lost friends, resurrecting made up scenarios where they survived, thinking of the mighty events at play there, the misery, death, hopelessness and at the same time glad he was here, alive, too busy to mourn, too dedicated to his new family here under twin suns and three moons who pulled their minds it seemed with gravity at night at twice the pull of the Earth's moon.

The angular shadow the volcanic plug cast sent him into a bluer world on the lee side from the biting wind but away from the sun's rays. *"Why does my left ankle always feel sore?"* he thought as his surface boots scratched and drove the gravel away as he stepped up to the small rock ledge under the enormous basalt-like feature. "Is this planet's Geology much the same as Earth's? Do we have Plate Tectonics or do we have volcanic activity because of meteor strike, "I wonder Akseli" he said out loud, adjusting his stance so the weight was off his bad ankle.

Looking at the rock more closely he noticed the grain was fine, "Crystallisation in magma not lava" he noted, "Weathered slowly, harder to erode" he lectured himself. "Much like myself," he smiled. He looked around from his lofty position, the forest canopy was about ten metres below, thronging around the base of the plug and shifting in the breeze. The nettle leaves whispering their strange lament. He heard a distant crack below, a branch falling, then suddenly saw Dong-hyun Han's drone in the distance mapping and skirting like a bee looking for flowers. Away in the distance the sedge grass plain graduated from the forest pattern and he could see the blue-green river twining a long way to a hazy mirage horizon. He turned around and looked back to see his position relative to the base camp, the small valley of rocks giving away the clearing position, although hidden in the throng.

"Dong-hyun was quite a comedian," he thought, they had got on well, and several practical jokes had been played already, notably finding his Geological pick under his bunk-bed pillow and chilli on his deodorant roll-on. In response Akseli had recorded his voice and downloaded it to the drone on a timer so when Dong-hyun was working in the field it *spoke* to him, telling him that he was doing it all wrong. Radio chat had jibing gags like *"Tornado coming in from the West..."* or *"I think I see a volcanic eruption to the East!"*

Smiling, he took his pack off, shouldering it to the ground, the sample cans clanged. *"That's why we were selected, we can get on, and oh, well, lets not forget no family ties and children,"* he thought to himself. He removed his hammer and looked at the rocks surface for a suitable gouging point. *"A small sample will be sufficient"* he thought, analysis of the grain structure possible through a microscope later in the camp's lab. A small fissure provided a striking point, an eroded rivulet of Igneous stone for his hammer to wedge between. Striking the mass, he dislodged a piece that broke in a flattish shape and fell to the ledge floor. He bent down to retrieve it, grasped it and held it to the light, the mineral surface like new, unweathered glistening. He searched for a patch of sun that the ancient volcanic plug had not blocked and walked a few paces ahead where a ray was filtering past the far edge of the stone to get the direct glare on it.

There were two distinct veins through the cut surface, a green sparkling mineral and a lower fine grain silica type arrangement. Turning the piece he accidentally dropped it, sending it spinning like an asteroid bouncing from the ledge and down into the forest below, "Perkele!" he exclaimed, angry at his mishandling, a Finnish profanity that he seemed to use much more these days. Looking down, he could see nothing of the trajectory, the forest canopy covering its tracks like a camouflaged interloper. As he continued staring down in silent annoyance, he noticed another rock formation that rose just above the canopy, like a small hilltop that jutted out slightly, almost totally hidden, but the rocks fall had meant he looked longer at the area than he would've done otherwise, a hiding formation from a searching Geologist.

Staring at it he noticed that the top of the mound was flat and had a smooth rock pile five rocks perched upon it, one rock atop another graduating upward to a smaller size in pyramid fashion, much like a bush-walkers marker placed sometimes on places where the track was lost to guide the walker. Two spiky shrubs either side seemed evenly placed and each of their overhanging branches reached over the formation in an arch to touch the other, like someone had done some deliberate landscaping and pruning, He snorted, "Bizarre," he mused, *"natural enough,"* he thought, *"but then again, looks sort of made"* He could see that the formation was connected by a small raised land bridge to another rising older more weathered volcanic plug, now more a plateau feature, flat,

73

with a depression from the centre like a carved river bed reaching the top of the base where the seemingly arranged rocks perched.

"That, Akseli, looks like Sedimentary as well, my old friend" he uttered silently, scanning other areas to see if it continued, fell away or rose again. He looked to see if there was a shortcut down rather than climbing back the original face,, stopping momentarily to gouge out another sample, a larger splinter this time, placing it in his sample container, carefully marking the quadrant, and scrawling, *volcanic plug 3*, on the side of the tin.

The side of the plug's ledge fell away too steeply where he was, looking down, he saw it angled towards the base as well, a rock-climber's face, not an old Geologists route. He investigated the other side of the plug from his height, sliding around the stone on a small ledge to view the side the sun was warming, noticing the difference between the cold and warm rock, as he carefully took hand-holds and slid his feet in a sideways direction keeping contact with the surface, feeling the mineralized sandy grate against his boots. Sliding to the other side, in a human pose, arms and legs forming a large cross like a spider, he noticed the temperature change, the sun-side of the rock bright with the twin sunlight, here, the face had several tiers, where he calculated he could scale down manageably. Looking down, he could see the continuation of the Sedimentary formation from the other side, a fallen tree had unmasked the section of forest and uncovered the rock face, scything some now rotten branches that sat upon the top of the sediment. In the revealed section he thought he recognised a "Clastic Dyke" he thought, a narrow vein within an existing rock formation that had been filled with sedimentary material.

He scrambled down to the next tier, turning around to face the formation, another ledge allowed him to rest, now closer to the forest floor and within the top of the canopy. *"Now, this is*

74

nice," he thought, *"up in the trees,"* he muttered climbing down a bit more, shuffling to a lower foothold so he could see below, the forest floor, a puzzle-shaped, green-grey gloom down below, fallen branches, litter, a yellow light penetrating the canopy in shards mottling the sea of leaf below. He must have been up about thirty metres or so, from his position he got the full orientation of height, the ledge providing him with a safety net of sorts, the flat surface and tiered graduating step-like holds below. The wind had picked up and the tree's upper branches swayed in dancing roughness, the day still fairly clear, he noticed, looking up apart from some long cirrus cloud above his perched position. He started the descent, scraping down backwards, his pack clanging, feeling the Geological hammer's weight, a constant friendly weight.

After cursing and getting the pack stuck on a branch that was touching the tiered rock face, he stepped onto the forest floor, looking up to his volcanic plug path down the steps, satisfied and a little relieved as it was higher than he was comfortable with, the sound muffled in the leaf litter. *"Cooler down here"* he thought, searching for the formation looking in the general direction of the rock he viewed above.

A short walk around the rotten stumps from the tree that had fallen, brought him face to rock-face, the dyke running in a eighty to seventy degree angle from the top of the formation, filled with coloured crystals, mineral sands, larger pebbles and bits of orange amber. Its colour changed from striking red at the top, the sun highlighting the rock silt then a grey coloured variation streaking down like capillaries through the vein like an ancient arm, a satellite view of a river delta, a Geological advertisement. He ran his fingers over the lower layers, the accretion of the silt trapped in the vein long hardened and set to conglomeration of mineral and organic kilned debri, the effect of time, compression and chemical acidity. *"There must have been a funnel of sorts from the top"* he thought, driving the sediment into the crack, then filling and setting, sloped flat rock a running depression where water could be directed to the crack and form a vein.

He took some photographs, set the small ruler against the surface to indicate the scale on close up and set the Geological hammer resting on small holds for larger photos, also taking a selfie, standing flat against the dyke to get a human scale relative to the size of the anomaly. Cracking the surface he dislodged several pieces with the hammer, some crumbling, some like a set small pancake conglomerate-like adhered pieces breaking away. He dislodged a larger section which fell away scattering and shattering in the process near his boots. The scene in the vein was initially hard to register with him thinking it was a mineral formation but soon he realised that he had uncovered something else,*"A drawing?, a rock painting, what is this,"* he softly said to himself, still trying to register the object, at the same time several theories were swirling with his thoughts.

The drawn diagram reflected the forest light that had moved with the sun's path, mottling the vein with patches of light like it had been painted with a substance like fluorescent dye or marker paint. The wind dislodged several sticks from the canopy, sending them crackling to the ground nearby, making him jump with fright for a moment, looking where the branches had come down, a misty debri mist where the rough bark had scraped off hanging in the forest air. He turned back to the find, *"Certainly painted,"* he thought, inspecting it closely and rummaging through the pack for his small torch. *"Definitely metamorphic,"* he thought, *"that has no place in this Dyke, unless it washed down inside,"* he hypothesised his hand feeling for the torch.

The light revealed a small square-shaped plaque-like section of stone, a light mustard colour, fine grained igneous rock. The drawing depicted an insect, a Beetle, blue-grey in colour smooth and shiny, its carapace facing the viewer, but turned to the right side a little, with ten legs extended outwards, standing upright a little or like it was climbing something, two antenna upright and, beside it another much larger form, seemingly in intended scale, a machine, a robot figurine of basic design, standing, four appendages like a human but shiny and angular, with no other discernible human-like features, smooth painted gold and extending an arm to hold one of the beetles legs.

They seemed to be drawn to the orientation of looking at one another and clasping hands in some alliance, behind the figures, a finely expertly crafted sketch in the background, a detailed map showing a route, a path, a terrain walkway , a river, a desert and a formation of rocks. Above a planet five stars with two interacting galaxies intertwined, the fine dotted stars coloured and depicted with an expert illustrator's hand. Dotted beside the beetle the artist's hand had depicted a fine mist, intricate and seemingly moving atop the rocks surface a slight hue of pink and purple. To the side were three figures like a gingerbread cutout side by side. The right figure was a figure made of stone, the second a figure swirling like wind or cloud, the third a figure with tree limbs as arms.

He stood motionless, mouth open, eyes squinting, blinking in astonishment, amusement, a kid at a carnival, a serious Scientist. the torch light reflecting back the beautiful, crafted painting, momentarily laughing to himself, thinking, ,"This better not be Dong-hyun" 'no,..... no," he looked closer adjusting the torch light, he smiled, he could see from experience, not an elaborate joke, the sediment was encased naturally around the plaque and old, he suspected, very old, being in the lower part of the vein. The extraordinary beauty of the image was enough to take his breath away, "An Anthropologist's dream," he mused. "What created these colours?," he thought, reaching for his lupe among the pack's contents. Laying his lupe close to the surface but without touching it, he looked through holding the torch steady so he could light the scene. "So, somehow this was done using the natural grain of the mineral, including the colours of the mineral" he lectured to himself. He reached down into the pack again and retrieved his tin which contained his Palaeontology kit, a small paintbrush, vinac solution consolidant, two chisels, his army knife, labels and plastic bags, opening it on the ground, an open satchel. Using the paintbrush, he carefully wiped the sand grain from around the plaque, careful not to touch the drawing surface until he could ascertain the durability of it, using the torch in unison, the ancient painting reflecting torch-light brilliantly back at his face, like a god unearthed.

The twin-suns had moved higher in the sky above the forest canopy and a beam of light was dissecting two trees in the distance through the nettle-leaf canopy, striking the painting for the first time, like a show about to start. His first thought was that the light seemed no coincidence, the forest floor behind him was actually a smooth stone formation that stretched between the two trees distant, not allowing any other saplings to grow, a made orientation to allow the light to strike the painting, now unearthed. He turned and walked across the flat forest floor stone, walking to the two massive trees and standing between them looking back at the plaque, small in the dyke, but shining a larger message, punching above its weight in the twin-sun glare. He looked back through the gap in the canopy, holding his hand up to the warm suns to block the light, to see the orientation of the suns more clearly. He turned around looking at the painting in the distance casting a long shadow in the morning light that stretched almost to the dyke formation, the wind blew through the gap and piles of nettles gathered the sides of the flat stone.

"What.... is......this," he softly said out loud, walking back to the dyke and looking around to see if he had missed another feature of this forested area, the gloom of the distant forest floor giving no further clues. Walking back to the trees again, he stood silent, for a while, the wind blowing a little harder, some nettles falling, the sound of the tree branches blowing in the wind. His brain took a while to register it, realising, and thinking, "This is a gallery, an art gallery in a natural picture frame like a rock painting in a cave" "Yes. Akseli," he said out loud to himself, "Yep, the dyke vein, was the sheltered concave section, the painting protected from the elements," he continued to hypothesise. *"The sedimentary material flowed in afterwards, from the top, the land bridge above and covered the drawing" "Its too much of a coincidence, and the formation above is a marker, like a beacon, advertising something,"* he thought, his realisation, exciting him, at the same time his sceptical Geologist self wary of speculation and non-existent gods.

14

Dong-hyun Han sent Karl, the drone AI, up to three thousand metres to assess the moisture content and report back, in half hour intervals. He had established that indeed the planet had excess clouds and a vigorous Stratosphere uptake effect to confirm Ye-Ming's data of a slower planetary rotational spin. This theory ran concurrent with the fact that there were more storms due to the moisture in the atmosphere and increased turbulence of the troposphere.

"I wish beer was available," he thought. Looking to the sky and the distant storm, now grazing the tops of the mountain range to the West. *"Weather aside, this is not a bad vista,"* he mused as he sat on a raised grass section of a former river bed an ex oxbow lake marsh, still with water, small gnat-like bugs flitted around the surface of the reflecting pool, the twin suns low in the sky. He unfolded the piece of old paper he had found in his pocket wondering what the hell it was and looked at the writing, *"Ah, yes , the advertising blurb when we were assembling the toilet system at camp"* he thought.

The Bee-Brown Dump model 65A, is a stand-alone fusion powered portable Bio-Toilet. An oblong portable energy tent fabric over a super-tough Universal molecular steel frame constructed entity that can be assembled in about half an hour, which includes special Sentient controller instructions. Sentient cleaning control is always in place, monitored and implemented by a complete sanitization after every visit, and assisted by the maxi-fan exhaust system completely replacing the interior air within a few seconds. Human waste is broken down into a usable gas for cooking, automatically bottled in recyclable containers that can be reused three hundred times or rethreaded and reused again by placing in the engineered rack or reprocessing as recyclable metal. As part of the Bio-toilets hardware, one only has to open the toilet door and walk to the rear. An array of small gas bottles, ready for *standard screw mount only on Bee-Brown heaters, cookers, and terrain bikes, quad bikes, Bee-Brown adapted vehicles and accessories. **"Screw and Go,"** is our motto.*

But that's not all!, The remainder of the waste is super-freezed and desiccated, bacterium removed and destroyed with Ultraviolet searing technology, the completed product available as an agricultural fertiliser, use as desired or get a cash back recyclable refund and free collection, which is also produced as part of the Bio-Toilet hardware, small sealed bags of fertiliser at a handy five kilo size, stacked in a handy rack at the rear of the toilet, or how we like to say it, "Dump and Grow."

"The Bee-Brown Dump Model 65A.
A perfect intervention for a Third World and a New World"
Flexible-Atom-Acrylic-Glass Industries and Interstellar Design Systems Inc.

"Let's Screw and Go, Dump and Grow together"

The light grazed the surface of the sedge grass beaming through several cloud banks, then getting obscured, the shadows casting new colours, the light paling the hues of the diminishing day. He would spend tonight out in the open, his energy tent set up as he ate some re-hydrated apple pieces, thinking of his wife Hwa Young who was still in Cryosleep, *"My wife no longer loves me, and here we are on another planet."*

He thought of separating before the trip but it was all too much, there was no time for arguments and bits of paper, his young son, Beom Seok, only eight, badly disabled from birth and finally passing away, the sadness and loss something he still could not describe, only remembering the service, all the clocks had seemed to stop and all the clouds were grey in unison lament, all the trees swaying to a strong wind, all the people crying and knowing it all really meant nothing, he was gone, and that is all that mattered, never to return. He returned to his fantasy, his way of soothing his grief.

He and the young blonde in one of the dirt buggies from the Explorer charging across a desert plain, her hair flowing, he smiling and turning to her.

"Ahh, one can dream, one can dream," he mused watching the lake and the small gnat insects hovering and then diving into the water in pairs and then emerging as pairs from the surface. *"Interesting,"* he mused, *"I must tell Jessica"* He gazed East where he knew Akseli was working on the Volcanic plugs, the old piddler was always up to something, last night having hidden his Kimchi, eventually finding it in the Bio-toilet, sitting on the toilet seat. "You are disgraceful, you Finnish menace," he said in a mock seriousness. *"Sorry, Dong-hyun, I thought it was something else.."* he had replied, glancing sideways, chewing his pineapple energy bar, while reading a Geological paper.

Karl would be taking readings all night and warn him if a storm was approaching. Camping alone on another planet sort of made him more nervous than camping generally, he was used to set-up command tents like at the camp, but he had stayed out too long and rather than walk back in the dark he had decided to set his camp, Tom checking his position and giving the ok. *"There have been no sightings of large animals, no savage planetary tigers, giant insects, killer birds,"* he smiled, *"Maybe I will be ok, ...still lonely though."*

He thought of his home, his Dad a fisherman coming through the channel past the Military barbed wire beach and concrete emplacements a reminder of humans that can't get along. They loved Sashimi, his Dad used to catch the best fish taking some home after market, which they enjoyed with Kimchi and veggie wraps, a lettuce leaf with some fish and soybean chilli sauce, chilli-ice noodles a favourite winter dish, Barbeque beef, vegetarian sushi, his Dad drinking rice wine alcohol and his mum tea.

His Mum ran a cafe and eatery from their home, remembering she loved the business, the customers like the regular fishermen and soldiers having lunch and the American tourists and English travellers with their nattering English conversations and polite manners, and the local kids saying strange things in their newly learned English. Her workers were her friends and she went to the market to negotiate prices for the store.

He remembered the poor old ladies selling whatever they had in the marketplace, the smell of fermented rice in the drains, and the sound of jet fighters constantly patrolling in the sky, displayed on the old ladies blankets and old rugs, green vegetables, radish, cabbage, beets and potatoes. One seller stuck in his mind, a destitute old shrivelled woman, a blanket spread on top of the cold road, a withered turnip, her sole product, in the middle of the blanket like a forlorn broken ship amid a confused sea it seemed. He stood for a while, she looked at him and smiled at him, her poverty gone for a moment, his realisation as a child that the world was a harsher place than he realised. He approached her and asked her how much for the Turnip, she waved him away smiling, his Mom came and talked to her for a long time, treating her as if she was one of her friends, and she bought the turnip, the old woman was delighted and he was still sad.

He had thought school extremely boring, thinking in fact the time he had to go there was unnecessary; a state driven prison. English classes after school, it was all exhausting. He was relieved to be accepted into University, something he did enjoy. He remembered his Military service, the badgering of the Instructors, carrying tree trunks in the snow, standing out in the rain as punishment, and then returning to his life predicting the weather and not standing in it. He smiled, civilians now signed up for the military boot-camp punishment buying special package deals in order to lose weight and get some discipline.

He continued to take in the vista, the suns were sinking lower, the afternoon benign, the gnat creatures were still alive on the lake diving in pairs, the wind had subsided a little the Western ranges alive with high sun, striated elongated cloud and unseen wind. He unpacked his gear for the night from the fibre-crate, lifting a surface suit helmet from the crate, its visor reflecting his face, a dark Donghyan, unreadable and with poor definition. He thought about the technology they had while looking at the helmet, *"Here we are on another world which seems so benign, surely all this we have will be enough, the planning, the flight, the Cryo-sleep success,"* he mused. He considered the Cryo-Sleep an amazing outcome, they had been told something like, *"There may be changes in brain chemistry after such a long haul flight, and people may feel, lets say, maybe depressed or cycle through moods'* *"I actually feel better,"* he pondered, *"Not so indecisive all the time, I feel like I have turned a corner"*

A cool gust of wind buffeted the lake surface sending a waverly ripple through the surface tension, the gusts blowing the sedge grass to the leeward side, the gnats momentarily blown to out of diving position, only in symphonic mastery, to return to the same positions and continue their tandem vertical paths. He put the helmet down on the rock beside him, the visor reflected the weakening suns and a distorted view of his camp and his unpacking. The energy tent was glowing slightly, getting brighter with the diminishing light. He grabbed the radio headset and set the small receiver on, "Karl, how is it going, do you have the first readings?"

"Yes Donghyun, first reading are completed, readout is available in my report, nice view from up here, the Western range extends far into the North West, there seems to be an arid area to the North, a cold dry desert, weather for tonight, mild Easterly winds, gusting to three knots, ten percent chance

84

of any rain, temperature, range for this evening and tomorrow, 7°C - 24°C, I must say the benign weather surprised me a little given our twin-sun scenario and elliptical path, I must consult Ye-Min's report. No other land based animals sighted, various insect species apparent at two thousand metres, black green beetles with remarkable flight ability and yellow backed bees, there is no storm activity in this area."

"Thanks Karl," " look forward to the report, have fun, out." He took the headset off and placed it on the rock beside the helmet, thinking "Why did I bring that thing? *"Ahh, yes regulations for now, an alien planet after all"* He noticed that the visor was slightly open and reached to close it, noticing that there seemed to be something inside. *"What is that?,"* he thought, lifting the visor up to its full extent. He leaned back momentarily in fright, startled by the appearance of a face within the helmet, then smiling, *"Akseli, you clown!, this has to be you,"* he said softly with annoyed intonation.

The helmet with the visor open revealed a face, a crude wooden framework within the helmet head-space had been fashioned and two eye sockets made, a makeshift complexion but slightly frightening face confronted him, within the eye sockets two fake rock eyes gazed at him, the minerals within the rocks glistening with the twin-sun rays making the creation even more life-like, the face was a thin set make-shift skull of sorts two sticks fashioned in a vee shape and the flesh made from stuffed dry grass, the slightly open mouth a smiling grimace of sorts, teeth made out of two rows of metal comb one above and one below, a grin which instantly unsettled him, the grimace resembling a look of *"Here I am, now you will pay, with violent force if necessary,"* the whole effigy a wholly unsettling looking construction as if it had been fashioned at some sudo witch-doctors convention, or some beachside paradise where hippies and the fashionable had lost their way in boredom and drug crazed madness. He imagined them dancing with their fire poles and doof music pumping out at a deafening disturbing volume, the effigy held high on some beachside altar.

The light danced on the thing, casting even more menacing shadows in the afternoon light, he thinking, *"Akseli, for the stars sake, how were you brought up I wonder,"* he smiled, looking at the face, unsure at that moment whether to pull the head out and destroy such a horrible masterpiece or to preserve it to show the others of what he had to put up with. *"No, I will keep it, get him back somehow later,"* he mused. He left the helmet perched upon the rock and continued unpacking, looking up at one stage later at it, the fading light casting directly on the face making the thing look alive and even more animated. *"Maybe it will protect me from any nasties,"* he thought, as a small swarm of green metallic beetles flew by suddenly past his ear and way across the lake, slightly above the surface and away into the green sky, he momentarily startled, then watching them as the twin-suns hit the Western horizon casting long shadow and filtering rays across the plain.

He awoke refreshed, and could see the first light through the energy tent. The pristine air of the planet had a glazing effect, and he thought of his dream, partly delicious, partly disturbing and he stayed wrapped in his terrain sleeping bag because the temperature was perfect and reflected on it, not wanting to face the day.

The blonde was smiling, beckoning him to come and swim, her perfect body made for the bikini, and the bikini made for her, the warm clear pristine water lapping up to her thighs, just below the place that many men and women desired most, the breakers washing around her like a female goddess of the salt and tide, he smiling, looking considerably more buffed than he actually was, walking towards her in acknowledgement, tight swimmers and obvious intent, the day a perfect ten, the beach deserted, their Hibiscus patterned towels placed side by side on a fine sand beach, mobile phones and keys expertly hidden in their sand shoes where no one would think to look, on a deserted beach, palms overhanging their paradise, coconuts here and there, whales out to sea blowing and sea birds swooping, the odd crab running, puffy clouds arrayed like smiling gifts, and the breeze warm like a comforting friend or a cash-laden generous Grandmother.

He then disappointingly became a crab and scuttled through the shallow water and lamented the loss of the blonde, as he had almost reached her on the water's edge. He swam after a wave took him out to sea and he drifted down to the sand again and then jumped off the continental shelf and with ten legs splayed and drifted down into the dark depths. He reached the bottom, a sludge, a fine marine clay that rose with his legs impact and then settled like gossamer on grass. Below in the pressure laden ocean he wondered why he did not feel the strain of the atmospheres above him and he realised he was adapted to this depth. He scuttled into a small rock gully where he could see via his wonderful infrared vision and the life that was organic lit up with warmth and the crustaceans had blinking lights and eyes shaped like stars. He had forgotten about the blonde and wondered why such a ugly creature would arouse him. He found others like him that greeted him with a raising of their legs and they touched leg to leg and scuttled together into a small cavern where tiny glistening green fish swam above and then descended and picked the slime and detritus off their shells as they arrayed through like train through a long tunnel.

15

Jason Findus looked around from staring out at the green planet from low orbit,a master light had come on his console and was flashing like a beacon. He interrupted his call with Kate Arnold who was explaining why the Captain had come back up to the ship, the explorer was docked and crew readying for the next trip down, the resupply. He switched off momentarily only marginally listening to her as he noticed an information light on the console, "Hang on, Katie, ah I've got a master light here...."What the fuck, Katie the Fusion Drive has been activated, is this an error, have you?...." *"Yeah, Jason, I thought I'd fire it up while we are docked,"* she said half annoyed, half concerned over the ship's comms. "Well , you better get up here, we have an activation warning, a master caution and a, hang on.. Yes and a low-orbit release warning, Katie I think Anastasia has done something here..."Anastasia! Why do I have these warnings on my console?" No usual greeting was returned from the Artificial Intelligence, the ship clicking and whirring with the faint sound of commotion in the docking area from the docking crew. "Anastasia?" he said again, with the growing realisation of something wrong creeping into his trained Navigation brain.

"Find James!, I'm on my way," Kate Arnold came on the radio again, he could hear exclamations from the others in the dock, they knew that the Starship was moving, be it in minute adjustments in preparation for thrust away from orbit. He accessed the intercom and sent a text command message and ship intercommunication announcement asking for the Captain to come to the bridge that would be displayed on every terminal, worried now he could see the planet moving, and knowing it was actually *Ate Succession* moving. He noticed the twin suns, bright in the vacuum, cast a stark shadow across the bridge floor from the Flexible-Atom-Acrylic-Glass supports, which ever so slowly moved like they were attempting to fool him, something clanged in the dock, new

lights came on above the console indicating the beginning of the ship's exit from orbit, there was a loud thump and an alarm signal sounding somewhere.

He sat down again. He, for a moment felt like a lost child who had sat down on a shopping centre bench, after much unsuccessful searching, frightened, his brain in neutral, the situation had momentarily stumped him, his professional self in denial. Gradually, he realised that his only option was to use the ship's terminal, Anastasia was almost taken for granted, always there, voice and presence, the Intelligence made everything so easy, "Anastasia do this, do that" he thought. In ship networked systems were controlled by the AI in most cases, she had just docked the Explorer, hadn't she?" he uttered softly, thinking aloud trying to solve the problem.

"Terminal access was still available but only the Captain used it for encrypted signals from Earth, secrets, confidential information, and sensitive details. Apart from that no one uses it anymore except for small maintenance repairs if you're away from Anastasia's influence, sometimes software alteration's" he continued to lecture himself. "Fuck this" he exclaimed, accessing his terminal as he saw the shadows moving in sync with the planet outside, creeping ever so slowly, a stalking problem, a covert sign. He issued a command about the status of the ship, immediately thinking to terminate what was happening. The terminal returned the unwelcome reply, its syntax almost mocking him.

Navigator@Ate Succession~$ Orbit-Status
Status: Orbit has been terminated, waiting for ships systems
--------- *New coordinates have been set by root:*
(Captain-Emergency Command)
Anastasia: Safe-Mode
Vector Coordinates: <u>2233434noad-3 Earth-sector7-Milkyway</u>
IP: 103.212.227.163
Terminal: Anastasia
Transfer: 1065.26 MiB received, 2219.62 MiB sent

Uptime: 11 minutes 41 seconds

He quickly sent a command, to halt the vector, he had *sudo* privileges or "super user do" as it was elaborated, which usually meant he could do most things, especially Navigation commands except administrator passwords, viewing classified messages and *"blowing things up,"* he thought. *"Anastasia usually does all this anyway,"* he thought, *"What is she doing in safe-mode?,"* more scenarios flew through his mind, *"someone changed it, malfunction?"* He tried calling her again "Anastasia, status!" The silence from *Anastasia* mirrored the shadow's physical action, continuing to crawl with certainty across the bulkhead floor as he looked away momentarily to see the position of the ship relative to the planet.

Navigator@Ate Succession~$ Orbit-Command -a -r now
"Abort the orbit exit and return to previous orbit parameters immediately," he translated to himself in his mind. The terminal replied in familiar dead-pan fashion:
Navigator@Ate Succession~$ Orbit-Command -a -r now

Cannot change orbit parameters - Permission Denied {13}
Emergency Command only - you must be root and in Emergency-Command mode to change these parameters.
"Who the crap is in root login?" he thought, continuing to type. "The Captain," who else?, only he can access the root, I probably have permission to see more details of the orbit as well" he uttered softly. *Navigator@Ate Succession~$ last root*
"Too long ago," he quipped dryly, seeing the quickly listed output.

wtmp begins Mon Feb 19 01:13:07 3038
root pts/0 dev-AnastasiaAI-server Mar 13 04:16:07 3038- still logged in
The command sent his mind racing, "the user who logged on as root, was still logged on, to Anastasia's server" he thought.

"Better check the time before the altered orbit initiates" he said out loud.

Navigator@Ate Succession~$ Orbit-Status -t info
Orbit-transition - 5:00:34

"Crap in Hell," he shouted, the timer said it all, five minutes and they would be on a light speed trajectory back to Earth. "Double crap in Hell!" He shouted seeing the shadows slowly moving as the Fusion-drive was being prepped. He could hear the familiar alarm, the console engaged button green and flashing, a whirring, within the bulk-head, then a shouting booming, jolting Captain's voice contrasted the din, "Hi Jason! I'm actually in the next command centre, *Anastasia's* terminal" He turned his head in surprise and froze, straining his ears to see where the call was coming from, standing up momentarily shaken by the outcry.

Several thoughts flowed through his mind, his calm training suggesting that it was a simple malfunction, an easily rectified error, a Captain's joke, even. He crossed the floor of the Navigation portal, the planet's light slowly changing, a shadow moving on the floor, the ship turning. The crew and Captain were supposed to announce when they came on deck, *"Another worrying aspect,"* he thought, it was the Captain at the terminal, now he was clearer.

The reality of it begins to seep into his mind, like a slow hidden leak slowly approaching a live electrical circuit, in an explosive flammable environment. The ship started to emit sounds from the bulkhead, movement, talking still was coming from the dock PA, *"It's going,"* he thought. *"The sounds are too familiar, like a star ship's crew busy before leaving port,"* he mused alarmingly. He only had to hear it once.

He rushed purposefully through the door that contained Anastasia's terminal and command hatch where the AI's hardware could be accessed, the blue-red room usually secured and locked with a passkey, the door open and a shape

91

at the terminal. He had already thought very quickly what his first reaction should be, restart Anastasia at the terminal and get the AI to take control of the ship, by far the fastest solution. The Captain turned his chair, smiling as he approached, the room dimmed but enough light to see the happy expression on his face, "Fuck, is this a joke?" he thought after all. "Captain, the ship is moving, Anastasia is in safe-mode and the Fusion Drive has been activated, we are leaving orbit" he said, still in between his Captain and reason dictating his behaviour, a possible elaborate joke and complete potential disaster.

"Yes, Jason, yes Jason." The Captain swivelled in his chair and then stopped and looked at him with a strange expression of resignation and underlying puzzlement."We are on our way, look, there is no need for concern here. Look, with a lot of consideration I've decided that I need to return to Earth, I'm lonely, you know and cold sometimes, this planet, well, I'm not sure about it, I think we should reassess..." The Captain tilted his head slightly looking at the floor as if embarrassed about something sensitive, "You know, let this mission, *blow-over,* have a think about doing it again at a later date"

He paused looking at the doorway,he could see the orbit changing. *"With that speech"* he thought, *"We have a problem here"* He could hear Katie come through the bridge door, "Jason!" "In here!" he shouted, looking at his Captain. "Captain, you need to tell Anastasia to take command of the ship, we are in a lot of trouble here, the ship was not designed to return, you know that" "Nonsense!" He shouted, James Williamson shifted in his chair, annoyed and irritated, stretching like an itch had developed somewhere.

Kate Arnold came through the AI door, wide eyed. "James, what is this?" The Captain continued to shift in his seat, seemingly confused for a moment, not answering. "James!" Katie screamed at him, "What?," he looked up with a defeated look like a runner who had done their best at the finish line.

The Captain straightened, looking at her with widened eyes, rubbing his chin with his left hand, stretching out the right hand on the console.

"We are going back, it's no big deal, my lovely First Officer... I ""Is he drunk?" Katie said, looking wide-eyed at Jason. Jason replied, looking at Katie blankly, then back at the Captain with resigned bewilderment, as if he had been told a grim secret. "I don't know, but we better think of some way to stop the ship or we are going out of orbit with a Fusion Drive about to turn this thing into a flying lightspeed candle without, I suspect, proper preparation." Kate Arnold looked at him, starting to say what he expected, "Can you, abort...." He stared at her, shaking his head slowly, "Tried, Emergency-command mode, he has Anastasia in safe mode and has root access."

"Listen to me you two lovelies!" The Captain interrupted loudly, seated, arms folded across his chest, legs straight out crossed on the floor, swivelling his chair side to side in small movements, looking at them with authority and renewed confidence. His voice became soft and commanding, childlike but masculine, demented but intelligent,

"You have three minutes maximum to come with me or get off the ship, I suggest you decide. I have Emergency Command of this vessel and we are returning to Earth, there will be no further negotiation, no change of command. He shook his head, lowering his chin as if he was telling a child off. He sat smiling, confident and calm, *"like he is about to go for a swim,"* Katie thought, James looking at her like he was going to laugh about the huge joke.

She realised at that moment, *"The time it would take," "Without his password"* she thought. *We are lost at sea on a raft going nowhere, they would be fumbling around like a child that thinks they are an adult, pressing different buttons for the same reply from the terminal, no time, dictated to by an unrelenting timer.* Another loud sound reverberated through

93

the bulk-head, a buzzer sounded on the bridge as a reminder of the ship's new attitude. There was a pause in conversation, nothing but the sound of the ship, the massive entity around them like a mausoleum, all three of them in the blue and red room. Katie looked at the Captain, Jason was looking at her, her Captain had a humorous *Anything else?* look on his face.

The terminal was flashing the familiar launch warning and the ship was moving as she remembered at the last ignition. She made her decision and instinctively reached for the ships comms above the panel, the Captain shifted, smiling, swivelling his chair around and put his feet up on the console desk, like someone winning a bet or seeing their practical joke bear fruit. *"Anders, are you in the dock?"* her calm voice belying the situation. After a short pause, Anders' tinny voice returned his concern, the crew talking and alarmed in the background. *"Yes Katie, here, what's going on?"* *"Get the Explorer prepped for abandoning ship and everyone there back inside the Explorer understand?'* *"Yes"* but you... *"Anders, that is a direct order, prepare to abandon ship now, wait for Jason and I, we are on our way to you"* *"Yes Ma'am"* prepare to abandon ship, confirmed"* Anders voice changed from friend to third officer, the training kicking in.

She grabbed Jason and pushed him through the bridge door, he instinctively running with her, "Come on, we've got to get to the dock, but before we go, get on that com channel now and get Andreas Polkinghorn and Jessica Neuer in the Life-Boats, they don't have time to reach the dock from the infirmary, she said, decisions flowing through her mind like her entire training life being tested as Jason picked up the intercom phone.

She realised quickly that they had to go, the ship was aligning, the planet moving away she noticed from the portal window, Jason was talking to the Doc, *"taking too long,"* she thought, "Jason, abandon ship, tell them now, now, lets go!" Jason turned back to the intercom and yelled, concluding the call hastily and changing to a rushed louder volume, *"Abandon Ship Doc!, get yourself and Jessica to the Life-Boats"* She pushed Jason through the bridge door and ran behind him towards the dock, she noticed the sound of their feet knocking the steel, *"like a doomsday timer,* she thought.

The explorer left the Starship, a controlled drop, fast skirting the exosphere at twice the speed of the original drop to clear the Fusion Drive's possible ignition, certain death by vaporisation. The *Ate Succession* was aligned at right angles to the planet as the craft dropped into the first upper atmosphere, then the red light enveloped the Explorer, entering into the friction atmosphere, breaking quickly into the troposphere for the second time.

16

Kylie Albott hurried through the Explorer door after landing on the plateau, carefully negotiating the tiered rocks down from the plateau, running with her pack to the Scientists camp, the three kilometres, thinking about what had just happened, what had happened to her Captain, a man she trusted, trained with, was in combat with, drank with, danced with, kissed once.

"The Starship has left the system," she thought, Captain James Aegean Williamson, her friend, fellow flight officer and her Captain had had some sort of breakdown, she powerless, getting the order from Katie Arnold to abandon ship before she even got off the Explorer, the only crew member that has root access like the Captain, sitting there like a carnival mannequin, all show, but being unable to do a thing. Katie Arnold said *"Go, load it, do what you can"* when she told her about the program, Anders preparing her pack for her after touchdown, hurried, with tech gear splayed around, as if he was a paramedic working on an unconscious body. Jason doing after-flight checks and checking the trajectories of the two Life-Boats one with Jessica Neuer aboard, one with Andreas Polkinghorn, released by the AI pilots.

As she ran, She reviewed the software packet she had made. It was a last-resort program, she worked on it in her spare time, told no-one, that would have been a mistake, adding software to Anastasia's environment, an AI Developers flame-war declaration would have happened, the powers that be, namely James and Katie would simply have said, *"No, Stop it."* She thought differently, and always about the idea that there was always an additional variable, the variable that was almost impossible, but still possible, the last key to the last door. The digital packet was an encoded Trojan virus in effect, but an AI-enhanced version, the code actually had *intelligence*, the same as the AI software construct programming breakthrough code developed in late 3078 that saw the dawn of Sentience.

She felt good as she ran, feeling the super-fresh air in her lungs. Images flitted through her mind, of James, the ship, the passengers still in Cryo-sleep. *It's as if the mission planners considered this scenario, none of the crew and science team have family here. We left them to die, I hate to say it but we did in a way.* She entered the forest, the huge trees gave adequate room for her to run below and around the trunks. High on some massive trunks, masses of Bromeliads hung to the sides of the bark jostling for position and the light.

The Trojan would delete the Captains username, change the login password for *root,* and disable safe-mode, waking up Anastasia. The distance meant she did not have time for back and forth communication like Virtual Network Computing, or having access to a command-line text interface or Graphical interface like a Desktop. The packet had to enter the system via the radio transmission, enter the network traffic, and run its executable file, then run the program inside, mimicking an Ate Succession system program, in this case, the maintenance program Anastasia used to monitor the ships systems.

The maintenance program would in effect make a speech in programming language dictated by the Trojan, something like, *"Hey Anastasia, I see you are asleep in safe -mode, can you wake up and attend to these system tasks?"* The maintenance system was not a user, like a human so it was exempt from authentication, once run, the Trojan tasks would be executed.

Also she had encoded a directive to lock the Emergency-Command directory and encrypt access effectively totally locking him out of the system, and Anastasia would not recognise his authority verbally either for any command decisions. If successful, he would no longer even be a regular user of the system; she was hoping the key words for him would be: *Permission Denied {13}.* The final executable command would turn the Starship around, supervised by Anastasia, a long dangerous process, to de-accelerate then realign back to Gemmi 7a. *Good old terminal power.*

You can have all the artificial intelligence you want, doesn't stop a madman, she thought, slowing her pace to circumvent a large bromeliad thicket.

As she ran and walked over rough areas, she thought about her life, her reason for being here, her Dad and her Sister and if her Mum would have liked her to be doing this, she had gone and an emptiness was still there for all of them, a ninety year old driver killing her in a carpark, driving off, chased by police and denying the event.

Her Mum used to say,*"Why do we spend so much money exploring space and sending ridiculous probes to god knows where when people can't afford a home?"* and *"For heaven's sake, they are building another Cathedral in town, what do they believe in, rockets or gods?"*

Her Dad she knew would be pleased, he worked as a Robotics Engineer at the Thalamon Labs, a company trying to get Sentient Intelligence into a moving human like Android so it could learn how to walk, there were considerable setbacks, then the Earth decided to change like it had had enough of humans and things stopped, people died, the sky became hazy and half-built androids sat against walls.

She started working on the Sentient code that heralded the Sentient Intelligences like *Anastasia* and the hardware that allowed the Intelligences to expand their understanding of the world around them. Quantum computing had proved "clunky" and fibre-brain technology changed the odds when connected to the development code. The code ran through a control fibre and controlled commands and actions, a fluid interaction between fibre transport and set commands, the result, a thinking learning artificial brain.

98

It was almost sentient, but not quite, the code was still the key to the thinking and Human-Sentient Intelligence collaboration was required. Also, the thought that a machine could kill everyone was apparent and strict human counter-command tools were put in place, thus the Captain's ability to effectively turn off Anastasia. *"Now we are in a world of shit,"* she thought.

Her body started to object to the run. Her head felt a bit rubbery and her legs were not friends of her brain, the left ankle was starting to get uncomfortable. *Fuck, I am out of shape. That's space travel for you, Mad Captain and unfit and fat. Don't listen to the mind, the mind during exercise is like a con-man looking in a mirror or friends on social media, always agreeing with each other about false information.*

Her *left for dead* sister came to her thoughts.

Jane was in State Prison for killing her husband. She shot him three times, an abusive wife basher, she would never see the light of day, but she visited her twice every month, they discussed through glass and steel and nothing would make it right or end, and they both knew she would probably die in there and she didn't care, she said, *"If I hadn't shot him, I would be where he is now and he would be where I am now, and besides, it doesn't matter now, everything is ending"*

Leaving that place was a relief for her just visiting. She remembered walking out to the carpark passing an old couple going in, their eyes meeting, the same ruin and aching lament that life sometimes dealt and never rescinded.

Her Dad hugged her before she left and said smiling *"Well, next time you see me I will probably be a fossil"* She couldn't be angry, she loved him, she left and got into a taxi, he stood watching her go then it started to rain and he was lost in the rear window as she turned to watch him, with the droplets of rain distorting him and then misting him, then a corner turned and her Dad was gone. She turned back and sat forward and saw the Taxi driver looking at her in the mirror as if to say, *What am I driving a cab for now?. The fucking world is about to end.*

She had made her way through the small rock valley breathing hard, with sweat accumulating, and her left foot still aching from her slight jarring after jumping from the plateau, she deduced. She emerged from the forest, now a dimmer colour, the light fading, one twin-sun below the horizon the other lingering like a child that wanted more time, the sky a glorious mauve blue, the sound of insect and buzzing wing, and the ever present alternating buzzing-gliding bee sound from the creatures around the seven petal, blue flowers that dotted the clearing.

The sedge grass made a rasping sound as she ran through, the sound of the small pebble ground, some small pools of water from a recent shower, some blue-black beetles swarmed around the area she noticed, rising and falling and buzzing away across the forest tree tops, passing her in the opposite direction momentarily, then veering away with a soft humming sound.

She reviewed what she was about to attempt, running through it in her mind, making sure she wasn't on some misguided pantomime tour, or that she had missed something fundamental like some hardware was missing, like she forgot a simple thing, a cable, a usb key. As Systems Engineer as well as Second Officer, she had the responsibility of working with Anastasia, writing extra code, remote patching around the ship to fix hardware issues and was Anastasia's practical hands in effect. She and Katie had discussed their options on the way down.

She thought it was quite funny and terrifying at the same time, Katie flying the Explorer through an atmosphere, while having a technical discussion with her, she remembered Kate Arnold's demeanour, dead-pan calm, the responsibility of the crew's survival, another landing, which wasn't easy, she had remembered despite the fusion-drive's stability and capability to be able to land like a helicopter with the enormous thrusters sending coursing flame, scorching pillars of propulsion in contact with the plateau rock surface, shaking the plateaus core and making a temporary lava of the contact surfaces, acrid smoke and stone splinters rising a scattering to accommodate the behemoth.

She reached the command tent, Tom Auer had the communication energy tents door already open waiting for her, the two not exchanging any words, the situation clear, Katie's message sent, everything ready for her. She set up her laptop quickly on the makeshift desk and patched to the communications tower interface, her virtual private network tunnel to the *Ate Succession* enabled.

"I have only one small chance at this," she thought typing, quickly, expertly, inserting the coded transmission packet into the radio wavelength frequency wireless band so it could be transmitted across the vacuum, through space. *"Thank the stars that I don't need a massive radio dish for this anymore,"* she thought, the technology originally requiring the Deep Space Network capability from Earth, an array of aligned dishes on the Earth's surface that encoded digital packets of info to control satellites.

The *Ate Succession* was now accelerating gradually away from Gemmi7a at about one quarter light speed, she calculated, so she had time, a small window to get the transmission to Ate and hack Anastasia's system, in effect waking her up and giving her back control of the Starship. The ship would reach one G acceleration soon, then de-accelerate from halfway through the journey and arrive, *"Well,"* she thought, *"maybe arrive, as it was never designed to return, and if she was successful, it would return here instead"*

Kylie Albott continued to type, preparing the transmission coordinates based on the ship's position given to her by the orbiting weather satellite. The light of the laptop screen highlighting her face like a lost artefact in a dawn light, the Scientists outside in the Dusk, talking softly, amazed tones, exasperated voices about the situation, and the sound of the Explorer's drive winding down on the plateau. The twin suns had set and the sky was now azure-green with the fading light, the energy tents lighted, small domes casting a filtered light on the clearing like some ancient lantern festival with no one attending. The night instilled calm, no wind, the buzz of insects, warm stillness, allowing the river's path to be heard across the pebbles more than a hundred metres distant. There was a hum of the com tents walk-in cool room, the tapping of her keyboard and a clicking of the communication tower server. She stopped typing for a moment, ready to send the packet, the cursor in her terminal window waiting for the executable command to send the message:

albott@anastasia-remote:~$execute-transmission-packet? Y N

An odd feeling came over her, distracting her typing, a tingling in her right arm, feeling like she might be having a stroke, grabbing the edge of the table with both hands, then the feeling passing, replaced with a fuzzy hazy sight which immediately cleared.

She closed her eyes, then reopened them, making a fist with her right hand then releasing. She turned to look at the command tent wall and stared for a moment, feeling relaxed like she was in a state of meditation, then back at the screen. Her head felt a rush like she had injected something and could feel it in her bloodstream, coursing through her arteries. That made her dizzy, then calm, her sight sharpened, then phased up and down like someone had a dimmer that controlled the light that entered her eyes.

102

Initially, she couldn't understand why she couldn't press enter, then she felt that she might press it, but then realising that was unlikely, then realising that she couldn't press enter, she couldn't physically do it, and mentally didn't want to anyway.

Then she thought, *No, what am I doing,.....this is stupid, what a waste of time, I mean this is not going to happen.* She aborted the process, uttering to herself, "Wow, that's a relief," how silly was that?" "What do you want to do that for?," she asked herself.

albott@anastasia-remote:~$ execute-transmission-packet? N
albott@anastasia-remote:~$ operation aborted

She got up from the desk, closed her laptop like a lesson had ended and walked out of the command tent, looking up at the sky feeling good, happy, very relieved, sort of reborn, she smiled, breathed the clear air in " the nights clarity of breath," she mused, looking up, she saw some pillow-like cloud still visible in the sky, she felt younger almost, like a teenager, stronger , more raw, untouched, like a demi-god.

The stars were glistening with the first dark sky, the light of the three moons behind the trees yet to rise up above the forest height. Tiny little galaxies were visible in the corner of the quadrant of the star laden sky she could see. She looked at the ground and swept a tuft of sedge grass with her boot, then walked a short distance out to the clearing.

Someone was laughing, there was a hiss like an air compressor, a loud clunk then, a clang of metal. She walked over past the Communication tent over to where she heard the sound and the Scientists, in time to see Ye-Min the Astronomer chasing Akseli Hoskinen the ships Geologist with a tree branch. Momentarily lit by the energy tents, both of them laughing like gibbering monkey's, sprinting through the alternating light, silhouetted then invisible.

Donghyun Han, the Meteorologist was perched atop a pile of storage containers, a weather balloon in each hand, arms raised outwards and up like a starlit god, Tom Auer and Tanya Gery were nowhere to be seen. Donghyun Han had a cone shaped hat made out of grass perched on his head, she noticed also, he stood clapping and turning as he watched them, and she, thinking it was a little out of place, and softly uttering, "but eh, "I guess they can do what they want after work"

17

The Beetle's wings shimmered in the dew light in arrow formation as the small swarm landed in flight sequence on the stem structure and entered the Bromeliad flower. Five beetles, encrusted purple and lime-like green metallic and shining, sparkled in reflection, sheening like new, with a surest stride with intelligent candour. The Bromeliad was nestled in the jewel coloured forest floor among the rotten logs and weeping mist and scattered leaves and strange shapes that cast confusing vignettes. The canopy was immense, a blue and green hazy exo-skin, the odd flying gnat and drip of carbonated water prompted the light. The forest grew high from the moss and lichen slime, the Bromeliad understory vast and clinging to tree, rock and lichen conglomerate to fawning bark and tanned husk lamenting upwards to the grey trunks and ochre leaves out to the bright azure sky of the non-forested exo-skin.

The beetles remained chemically silent for a time. A ritual of evolutionary paganism, a scent of temple and altar within the known boundary of reality and conscious knowledge of the Universe through transmitter pathway and alchemy of spirit. No need for false gods and created demons, neurosis synthetically adjusted to Universal reality. *"Is our pheromone adaptation not magic enough?"* They collectively pheromoned the must of humour, content in the Universe, within the wing, the sure-shell exo-skin, a natural prophecy. The past was always remembered via pathways of ancient enzymes and misting fragrance, the perfume of primordial vastness. In unison the parked beetles connected to the planetary memory almost in time itself, there but not there, here but within the pathway was super-awareness and contented modern history.

"Past of ocean, current and crust, soup of dream and chemical dust, winged and life, the barren shore, stem to rock and magnetic core.. " The chemical dream opened to the beetles

slowly and raised the clear image within the synthetic permeable transfer...

The forest floor had been covered for millennia with ashen leaves and rotting twigs, the humus of time descending from aired branches for eight hundred million years, reaching through the moist gloom and carbon dioxide mist. The behemoth continent micro-sailing like a lofted zeppelin upon the planet's oceans connected by magma and plate, driven by core and clock, parsing eon-climate of frozen tundra to rich plain, desert dune to rainforest water-world majesty, the natural bioforming transition from hostile-consciousness to intelligent ascension.

The ancient insects had parlayed among the soft detritus, rising with winged buzz and hazing fleeting flight for eons as microscopic descendants using the chemical communicators, undisturbed by the weight of limb and scrape on the forest floor. Five billion years had passed since the accretion of planetary dust and Argon-rich gas within the planetary cycle. The planet started with three moons, two suns then two moons one sun , then three moons, two suns. The smallest potentially fourth moon had lost its orbit and was pulled away to the distant twin-star to be consumed, ending the quadruple tidal pull of the planet.

The ancient quadruple moon tides of the primordial rich gas enveloped planet had already served the uncertain master plan. Their legacy had created vast exposed tidal flats of steaming pools of bacterial life, shimmering under the ultraviolet protected upper atmosphere, the twin suns staring like a pair of examining new-born eyes in the green sky. The multi celled organism biachondria enveloped the nucleus within the tidal pools and rock fissures, synthesising hydrogen and argon, oxygen and carbon, a chemical celebration, intrusion from time itself.

From ancient water-life nymphs, consciousness developed as an evolutionary adaptation to counter the murdering environment, the harshness, unpredictability, a gamble of the foothold of a species within planetary development, like climbing a near impossible route on a near impossible mountain with likely severe conditions predicted. The nymphs were for millennia a bottom-dweller with ancient calcium eyes. Originally asexual and hostile. From gossamer cocoons on sea lichen, protected by adapted twin-parent dedication, the nymphs crawled from the lichen trunks to the dotted and mandible grip-friendly surface stem-specific-adapted marine trunks and grasped the atmosphere, permeable skin and ancient gas, bio-transfer and accretion of fluid.

The first small wings slowly dried and parted with moist patience as the skin casing split and wrinkled loose like a pimpled seed pod in the wind. The ascension to air, first flight, atmospheric awareness. The rise from the channel between two breaking continents where the water was warmer and turgid with strong current and plankton rich, small creatures within the twisting currents and harsh debris. The first beetles to hum, shimmering and vibrating from the sea onto a terrestrial dimension, approached.

They shifted to a first wind to wing with the magnetic aurora gleaming green, blue, orange and azure-red in the distant horizon. Flying above the shimmering foam waves, buffeted by wind convection and moist salt plume they lofted to the sand and stone. Already conscious of their world before ascension, shadow-searching for long-lost archaic parents and embracing danger, the chemical ability ancient but potent, boiling and synthesising within the exo-skeleton. The beetles awoke from their transitory dream and scented their winged companions,

"Ready for negotiation."

Above their forest Cirrus high altitude clouds and wisps of orange tinged alto-Cumulus spotted the hemisphere, the greenish half-dome sky. Large outcrop ancient magma flow remnants covered the landscape, enormous pillars and jutting of rock crag. Three wide aggressive rivers carved forest and tundra through the planetude, weaving ancient free to roam out to the semi-frozen sea, past moss and stone, epiphytes and eroded smoother stone, and multi coloured sand from reluctant parent rock. The immense ancient volcanic remnants ejected from the windswept crag and white top ocean high above the sea, the tempest current and driving foam mass surrounding the pillars and spraying white squall. The short Meridian latitude, short of day, quicker of night, dawn and dusk rotational dependant on slight planetary tilt seeping into cold night and dark hemisphere, the dark side.

The beetles collected around the submerged portion of the central flower, a striking red, orange, ochre blue majesty rising to the apex above the collected water. From the main central stem, the flower radiated upwards into the distorted water-air transition zone. The beetles were arrayed upon the stem edges, half-floating like radiated flower pearls themselves awaiting the dawn. Small flecks of white caressed the aqua mire, swirling around the forms, black and blue, wings glistening and jet, sharp lines, ten legs, three appendages, the head portion with two azure-green antennae, jutting above the silicon-compound eye.

Minute misty pheromone particles filled the chamber. *"Greetings, updates, kindness, sorrow, inquiry, confirmation, status, injury, swarm status, deaths"* The beetles moved with the scent, slowly swaying the lower abdomen side-to-side, antennae searching, slowly turning in small circles like intricate cogs within a liquid clock. *"Scent agreement, Bipedal infestation, counter has been emitted. Uptake will be slow and patient, sure"* A beetle adjusted a fifth leg to rest upon the central stem, the others, arrayed around flexed their

108

appendages in various fashions, a mandible ajar, legs flexing at intervals.

"Exit of starship is desired, Captain is sure, system interrupted. Female identified and marked, Agreement scent" The beetles seemed to dance a rhythm, turning half-turns to the left then one hundred and eighty degrees to the right, then a full three sixty turns, to face the stem again. *"Genetic Insecticide not detected, no weapon scent required"* The dance continued, reversing, but containing a slight hop and shuffle, the winged one's content, evolutionary, effective, with instinct and chemical time.

The water swirled as though alive, the sun's rays reflecting from above down the green stem of the flower casting now colourful shadows and delicate shapes like a secret puppet show. One of the gathered adjusted their wings, the fibrous underside exposed and wool like a red pastel colour with specks of green tinge, the black-green silver wings folding again in place and scented. *"Dangerous, bipedal survivors, with consciousness, ecosystem conflict, pheromone persuasion only, the exit will be sure. There are five however that are off-world suitable, shall we wait and see and consult the Gardener?"* Antenne, bent, mandibles sharp, the Beetle's came together around the stem closer touching the tips of their communication twigs together.

The five emitted from the flower spread like windy small leaves and made a trajectory across the forest floor. Each honed to a marked plant's, drilled rock and pattern shaped colour to spray the mist. Reactionary pheromone was strong, strong for large neurons, large brains and erratic behaviour. The Beetle swarm fleeted across several forest sites, past the meridian and far dark side, through the colder crystallised forest and rocky frozen lakes. Pheromone controlled species assisted dispersion, four, five, six, seven, eight and nine legged versions spread via long miniature stony trails, grassfields, forest paths, potential landing sites carrying the transport scent to small crags, wildlife trails and leaf litter. Winged species dropped scent on the shore, the waterproof aqua pheromone drifting, unseen, insoluble, inert and timer-awake.

18

The plain seemed to shrink with the cold, the snow falling at a moderate pace, a million flakes a minute and the forest seemed to watch silently and wait for the canopy to grow old and white. The plain set white now and permanent, the sedge grass dotted with snow that no longer melted and creating white tufts like bizarre hairstyles to accentuate the sky, black and leaden. The mountains were no longer visible, the low lying mist and portent ice a grey cover that seemed to be a colluding outcome. The woman was covered in a grass coat and shambled along, stopping at a tree and looking skyward, then around as if lost, then to the tree and looking as if to see a piece of heat or warm gift.

She had a feeling of strange portent some days like she had almost done something really important but not quite managed to pull it off. She had saved someone or got close to saving someone but then she failed or gave up. "That's a really annoying thought", she said out loud, her breath sending warm to cold in a large breath cloud. She rubbed her hands and tried to get them to work, the cold seizing them under the inadequate gloves she had made of unbeliever fabric. She had originally been wearing an unbeliever suit before it had shredded off with wear and the Altar Priest had disallowed any unbeliever items to be used. The suit had *"Kylie Albott"* attached to it and she didn't know what that meant but she liked it, and it was warm.

She was frozen and felt like a skin was on her skin, and wondered why her arms had a strange red area and her nose ran all the time. The tribe had retreated into one hut now, lighting the flame with the unbeliever fire, but the small protruding device was sometimes failing now, sputtering , and no flame was coming out to light their sticks. They slept in there, the Altar Priest making strange noises and the Mineral Master sending the wind from his rear constantly, a terrible stench, she thinking, *What a most displeasing idiot he is,* knowing that he desired her and she avoiding him, knowing at some stage the Altar Priest would present her as a gift, something she found repulsive and foreboding.

The Altar Priest was bad enough when he came to her, but she had to perform, making him think he was desired, otherwise she suspected the Priest would grow angry and even consult Hexibarber, the punishment could be harsh. *No, better to smile and get through it, it didn't last long anyway,* she thought. They could collect the water from the river to drink but it was icing over and she wondered if they could heat the water like she had seen the sun do and make it melt, then she could wash in that. They had placed dead grass on the outside of the hut, to stop the now constant wind that blew from the high area and drove the snow across their exposed area with icy intent.

The Mistress pulled the pineapple fruit off the spiky plant and wondered why it had a spiky trunk. She looked at the pineapple, turning it, looking at the skin, a rough texture like the bark of the forest trees but more shaped and seemingly patterned, the pattern repeating around in the shape of a triangle, *triangle,* she thought. *Now how did she know that?.* She knew what *shape* meant, she just knew, and she knew that the Altar Priest did not, when she asked him to pass her the round shaped rock, he looked at her then back at the pile of stones, passing her an angular one.

She asked him later, secretly testing him, *"What do you prefer, the square shaped unbeliever bar or the round shaped unbeliever bar?"* He said nothing for a moment, she knowing he had no idea what she was talking about, he turned and said ,*"I prefer the bar that is both round and square at the same time, an unbeliever bar is an unbeliever bar"*

She looked around the plain, the sun's low and the light fading already, the morning and day receding with the white stuff falling and the sky leaden and casting the forest dark and green. She dropped the pineapples into her bag made from Unbeliever fabric, she had five already and she was cold, her hands starting to get hard and aching. The trees were getting thin, they had stripped them and she had to go further out to collect the fruit from more distant trees. She would have to go soon, too cold, back to the smelly hut and charred fire, something she thought wasn't quite right. *"Hexibarber has said there would be relief from the cold, the Altar Priest had relayed from the effigy in 'Long Service Leave' He had been gone for some time,"*she mused, the Altar Priest adamant he would return soon. Her mind wandered a little, she was cold but she remembered her dreams and sometimes they made her feel better.

She picked a snow encrusted pineapple then she felt strange, like her head was lighter, like the white stuff that was now falling softly around her. She grabbed the pineapple stalk and steadied herself. She noticed her vision was split in two. The top half of what she could see wasn't connected to the bottom half correctly; the two images were not aligned. The image went bright, then black and she descended, all the while hanging on to the pineapple stalk. The vision cleared again and she was somewhere else it seemed.

She was on a grass plain and she lifted her head from the ground and stopped eating the grass below her and she saw the other creatures next to her, she looked at herself and she realised she was like them and had a coat of marvellous finger like soft fibres that had a tough vein through the middle that splayed outwards with the soft fibres and were arranged in lines on top of one another so it made a covering, it was warm and compact like a coat and she could stretch out her finger-like things and then fold them back to her sides, the fingers falling into place.

She looked at the closest creature and it had the same fingers and two legs and was bending pulling at the grass and seeds within. It had a magnificent covering of brown fingers, like the grass, black fingers, white and grey and some of the fingers were blotched and mottled. The creature's nose was hard and formed their mouth which it was using to eat the grass. On top of the long hard mouth was a display of more fingers, but coloured and rising then falling at the top like a funny hat, but it was striking and glowing and every time the creature turned its head it flopped around and she smiled at that wondering why it was beautiful and funny at the same time.

Then she realised she had one too and she could feel the weight of it and she shook her head and finely coloured fingers arrayed around her head. The creature next to her breathed in and out with great breaths, the grass in front of its mouth swaying with the breeze.

Then she realised that they were very big and tall and they were raised off the ground about ten metres high and their legs were enormous and they were tall enough to be as tall as the trees lower canopy and the small hills around. She raised her head and the others raised theirs, every time they ate some grass looking up and around for danger and looking at each other, with their eyes, yellow and glistening, their great three-toed feet making indents in the grass as they walked their weight evident.

She stepped forward like the others and enjoyed the grass, tearing it and pecking it, the lower section and the roots the best part, now and then she saw small insects and she pecked them too and occasionally a thin worm like creature was exposed and she relished those, tasted wonderful and she was always searching for them. She saw some younger creatures, half her size, adolescents and a Mother with tiny creatures running around her in the grass buffed and whose fingers were fluffy and crazy looking, her young elated to be with their mother, to be born, living on the plain, adapting, trying.

114

She realised she had exceptional eyesight, she could see things in the grass with high clarity, tiny small grains of sand, sections of worms hiding, tiny ants that skittled and danced around the fine grass lower world, small mites and scuttling spiders, their ten legs allowing high speed and fast stop. She could peck at what she wanted really fast and her movement was aligned with her mouth and eyes, a coordinated perfection, she never missed a meal. When she looked up and away into the distance it was the same, she could tilt her head and see with her right eye up to the green sky and discern the patterns of the clouds and the fine colours of the sky and see dust and mist and particles of rain and swirling detritus, fine grass stalks and torn bark almost invisible against the exosphere, and flying things with small wings, bugs and gnats that glistened like water through light, and glare through the fibrous mats of their wings and the reflection off their carapaces and the tilt of their combine eyes, looking down on her as if they were in celebration and performance, swaying in great swarms with the wind and eddies, rising up and bellowing below like lost smoke reflecting a hesitant mirror of the great hemisphere.

She turned her head further around realising she could turn it so far around so it was pointing backwards and she could see her end fingers at her back displayed upwards, a yellow and black green and orange, purple and blue colour with white stripes. Behind her, the plain was filled with her creatures, probably a hundred or more stretched out together feeding on the grass on the plain like a million jesters that were performing for a forgotten King. The expanse stretched vast and immense, loosely arrayed here and there were rock outcrops and sections of heavy marsh grass and pools of wash and debri, and small rivulets dancing between and connecting the pools reflecting a bright twin-sun sky.

They grazed most of the warm day, sometimes resting in lots of ten, arrayed around the plain like groups of terrestrial clouds driven down to meet the dirt. They came and sat together, forming a circle facing each other, their hard mouths now used as tools to clean their fingers, each finger stretched a scoured with a rubbing of the mouth down the length, the arms open to drill beneath and root out pest bugs that sometimes liked their skin and got below to itch and compromise their covering.

They ruffled and touched mouths together in comforting preen and enduring bonds helping each other clean their fingers and root out the pestilent gnats in parts they could not reach. Their eyes reflected group and flock and herd and clutch and they stretched their necks, sometimes stood and stretched one leg like a dancer on the plain, splaying arm fingers, then moved around the others searching for bugs and pecking the backs of others in jest, some emitting squeaking sounds and disgruntled warnings and laments and contented snorts. Sometimes they sneezed and the others chortled in surprise at a high pitched sound like a small ball emitting air when squashed flat, sometimes mouths open in sneeze anticipation, then emitting the ball sound with displeasure and surprise.

There were several lead males and the flock had strict hierarchy, parts of the plain were favoured most and the lead creatures ate there, the others pecked away if they encroached in friendly, not friendly manner., reminded but not injured. She had many sounds she could emit to her brethren, "Stay away," "Move over," "This is my area," "That feels good," "Beware, I am watching you," "Last chance before I peck you," "Where are you?", the flock is fractured," "I am not happy with this situation," "It hurts," "Come, find shelter," "Danger!, find cover!"

The males jutted and pouted around, keeping the females in check and mating with them as they desired, and chasing them in anticipation and in punishment depending on their mood, their magnificent fingers stretched high on the tail, more than the females and they were stronger, bigger and had a nasty claw that was a weapon at the base of his heel. She wondered

116

about the claws, "Why and when would they use them," she thought.

When the suns got lower, the creatures exited the plain via a vast valley, momentous stone rising above the path worn with glistening green and blue minerals sparkling the sun's rays, and the creatures stride, side by side females and point guard male, the hundreds impinging on the gap like a coloured tide of fabric funnel and cloak liquid that was alive and channelling a distant dressmakers lament.

Through jutted rocks and small shrubs, the creature tide ran sure with arid spiky demeanors and broken shale seemingly a directional floor searching for clawed feet, small grass islands and broken basalt, fine grained rivers of shattered sand and faces of exposed sediment fissures rising and descending angular and dome like, showing strange shapes and creatures of the past that had been trapped and ended and within and around the granular finery, small intricate shells, tubular and twisted mathematical spindles of an oceanic past and sandbed murmur, and stalks of plants dotted here and there, small winged insects frozen in the time trap, some with wings preserved and others of broken carapace and detached antennae, set hard like thrown sticks within a slushy mud balloon arena. The boulders were smooth and resembling ancient statues, with monoliths and columns, and rotund enormous batholiths rising beyond the valley gaze and a vista of the valleys strike down below, oval balancing hats of fractured forms on confused conglomeration bending and twisted, some pointing in eroded stillness as if touching a concerned sky.

She exited the massive valley with the others running side by side, hundreds of running forms, their legs like full steam ahead machine pistons, flexing with powerful strides and heavy thigh muscle, their fingers rustling with the movement, their breaths more constant and whispering strong, their head displays wildly flaying and quivering atop their skulls. She watched the movements of the other creatures, their pace and unique anatomy determining the slight tilt of their bodies from side to side with each stride, as with her, her pace a delight and celebration of speed and dexterity, with flexed thigh and tempered femur.

They spread frantically and finally from the exit point that widened, like a bee hive disturbed, spilling in certain lines of finger and dirt grain highway sections of creatures following each other to secured spots and cratered depressions on the ground, the creatures running and creating an enormous dust wake on the now sand-dirt surface, a vast contrasting plain of grassless fine dust and eroded micro-shell a billowing upwards in a rising section of concentrated updraught, twisted current convecting skywards, a twisted pillar hundreds of metres high, then dispersing high with the upper wind, and right-angling like an anvil motionless from the ground and hurricane from above. The mass of creatures spilled like water on a dusty surface, dispersing wide and far, as if to soak in a desert, then groups settling into the dust shaking their arms and settling their rumps into the primordial dust.

She found a depression that was vacant and settled with fifty or so others dotted around in similar holes, the vast flock churning as far as the her sharp vision could discern through the fumigated haze, settling her breast and kicking dust with her grounded legs sideways and pecking the dust, shovelling wads on to herself, she instinctively knew to rid herself of the pestilent mites and microscopic gnats with wrinkly facades and stubby antenna that liked to burrow in detached skin and moist enclaves.

She could feel the small beasts scuttle for safer cover on her skin like fleeing soldiers in rout, to be threatened again as she filtered the dust expertly through her finger covering in scouring fine grain sifting and like a miniature sweeping sand tsunami across a dry skin desert. A desiccated bug and broken mite succumbed to the tide, shaven and rubbed, flayed and sanded. They fell ruined and worn down to basic shells, their hideouts scathed clean and rampaged through. A rough ruined fibrous leg, antenna useless, as the sand sea consumed them, mummified opportunists now, a part of the dirt ocean of the creatures conglomerate baths.

The afternoon suns shone warm, lighting the dirt plain with vignettes of dust particle streaks, the creatures nestling and content, some falling asleep and some grooming others, pecking their backs and bottoms with due care and attention, pulling fingers that fell to the dust in wait for a new one, kicking and scratching, pouring dirt on their necks and sitting sideways and using the free leg to grade dirt over their bodies like an organic lever, others set still and motionless staring across the plain as if they could see a better dust hole through the haze and warmth.

After a time when the suns were low they rose and community shook, their fingers arraying with the oscillation dust billowing, ten thousand disruptions on a dust bowl, dead mite and sand grain falling like terrain rain and settling in fine carpets of debri around their cleaned coats and glistening eyes. She bathed in luxurious sift, the sand-dirt cleansing her dermis and soothing the itchy lice bites and reclaiming the surface for her coat. Twenty others sat with her arranged together, shoulders leaning on shoulders, fingers intertwined, like a mad ritual of settled portent, dirt flying in arcs and sand a rye, their candour halted for a time, their gait a farcical posture and comforting regard.

She followed as the males clocks seemed to tick and they raised their heads and strutted sure, gazing at the sky and sensing the lux of the exosphere and set off, back through the mineral valley with the shadows cast long and the hue of the mineral gaze lighted on the sun-side still sparking but with softer warmth as if accentuate the slants of the twin suns in their daily unwind, the females following like a thousand magnets to the core, the great train of coat and finger. The

119

heads were forward and jutting with the gait and stretch, the setting dust rising again and stretching across the hundred million years aroused soot grain carpet and up to the clear and sleepy day sky awaiting the refinement and calm of night.

She funnelled through the valley with the mega-flock and onto the grass plain once again, some creatures stopping to obtain bugs and scuttling meals, the creatures stretching their line and milling in certain linear directions like a broken spoke wheel. She noticed the day was subsiding and the frantic pace for settlement in the undergrowth became apparent within the grass ecosystem, some winning, some lost, some insects she wounded and consumed as she rustled and pecked, flaying her legs with every rise of her head to scratch the grass and scuttle the insects from their hides.

The other females raised their heads to check the male's compass, still arching East on a line for a distant outcrop of enormous trees, an oasis within the boundary of the grass plain, rising two hundred metres into the sky. She looked at the island outcrop, the distance near, the trees getting taller and the vast trunks rough and some arching, some broken with hundreds of limbs and fallen nettle. Around the huge forest oasis were rocky outcrops and lush grass fields, she could see some haze like flying gnats and the shadow lines from the stone starking darker on the ground, the tall trees still bathing in the direct light with their view to the West as if standing on tip-toes to catch the sun. The massive flock assembled near the trees, and scattered around, grazing in the last light of day, always opportunists, she found a lush patch and fed on the abundant life crawling and milling. There were small shards of fibre on the ground and she ate that, it had a husk and tasted wonderful, she searched for more and then realised that the husks had fallen from a certain tree and she approached and grazed below, the smooth trunk rising with assorted branches, the leaves orange and shard shaped with hanging packets of seed pod, opened and falling to the ground, some in whole wads, the stem detached and scattering within the grass.

The last light was fading, the twin suns gone to a Western meeting and the last light a murmur on the plain, patches of warm mist were rising already and curling in white haze shapes into the colder sky. The wind was nowhere and the grass stilted and spiky statue, the vast shadow from distant rocks dimming further. The timer within her rang, a primordial tenant, the others filed into the forest with much pomp and sounds of position, the sound of toe on nettle, a soft wishing and scour, a grumbling and hierarchical direction and warning of proper position, the lead creatures showed the way, she followed and the canopy darkened, the flock slowed as the first creatures jumped to the lower branches of the first trees, then jumped further and further from limb to limb until the the safe perch was reached high up, other creatures ventured further into the forest all jumping and rappelling upwards, the senior creatures taking the higher branches, the male's first, the senior females, then the others, the youngest below, still high but checked in their place by peck and chortle.

They released their bowels and great clumps fell to the forest floor, settling as they did, the trees seemingly glad of the gift with the shift of branch and broken sludge fall, she did the same as a ritual for the evening sleep, the sound of a thousand clumps falling in a mighty digest, then silence, as the trees halted their soft sway and the branches set statue. There was much lament, position arrangements and reposition arrangements, younger and less senior were checked and discipline marked the weaker links, with muffled annoyance and contented seating. She raised her left arm and buried her head under it, one hundred others aligned with her on their branch, an abacus of creatures rising and striated in similar size coats, the soft fingers of the pillow, her legs sure on the strong steady branch a small leaf covering above. She could see some others in the gloom, the same head under arm position, silent now and a slow breathing apparent like a whistling through a fine shelled cone drifting and rising through the trees, and the hint of the three moon light ascending and sending the plain aflame with blue tempest.

The day anticipated across the plain, she shifted little during the night, brace of limb on limb, the others breasts rising and falling softly, the drop of leaf and ache of tempered wood, the roughness a soother upon the perch, the grip of rest and tired scratch. The moons cast and traversed their line sending forest patterns in moon shadow across the branches, revealing other creatures asleep, a hundred heads tucked and lamenting under the fingers, the massive trees immense and mighty pillars laughing at the creature's weight. The long night eventually cast cold within the twelve hour crucible of melting time, the creatures bracing slightly protected wholly within the clutch and flock two bodies side by side the fingers attached with fibrous warmth, small striations of exhaled breath fuming and gaining other clouds to ascend through the canopy and away in puffs to the night dome. The three orbs danced above the horizon for time casting strong tide on the plain grass and mineral sands, the creatures yellow eyes, glistening with the anticipation of day and reverse reflecting the three on moist cornea.

The first light she noticed was above as the mighty flock stirred and reversed perched. The rays struck the upper canopy, the light like the suns were unhappy with the forest dinginess. The explosion of bright reflection wakenned the flock, creatures descending and milling discussing turns to jump, hunger at the top of the agenda, plain below with the booty. She jumped down to the next branch, her legs stiff but still sure the drop considerable, some creatures half flying their arms stretched to parachute the fall. The exit was a sure tempest, the flock sprinting over the nettle floor below the behemoth trees, debri spinning and churning twisted paths around the trunks like water around a fast deluge.

She exited the forest, the plain alight with floating reflective haze and fine grass stems rising from the heated ground. In the distance a vast rising rock wall rose to the sky, below she could see openings, caves and Clastic dykes that had been filled then washed out by marine tempest, the dark openings alive with the creatures and their young. She fed hungrily, consuming as much as she could, raising her head with every scratch to view the massive stone walls and the small infant creatures milling with their Mothers, miniature and frenzied. She approached the caves and entered the darkness, the deep enclaves mighty hollowed caverns with dirt-grass floors, the dry detritus having been blown by the wind inside and collected by the Mothers for their nests, spotted thickly across the floor in sitting poses some with young others tired from the long lament for their clutch. The roof cavern was not whole; some rays descended and struck the floor with oval striking contrast to the dark dirt. She saw newly hatching creatures, breaking the large ovals, some white, some brown, some purple and some yellow, their small beaks cracking and gasping their exosphere breached. They rolled from their half shells and pasted yellow the yolk placenta securing them from cold until the Mothers fingers enveloped and warmed, running under her and disappearing, their life started under protection.

The day cast windy and she gazed skywards, the upper clouds charged like racers, the grass blown and whipping, the flock still among the mini swirl feeding scratching and set dotted hundreds, the males interspersed watching and patient. The vast walls distant where the Mothers sat shined mineralized grain streaked with running moss and spotty lichen, fissures apparent and large cracks where sediment had been trapped wrapped around like an inverted bowl and she was drawn to this place, grazing steadily towards it during the day. When she reached the stone side it was in shadow and the floor of the wall was broken shale and bits of slivered stone that had been cast by cold and heat and it lay scattered and carpet-like, but lumpy and sharp. She scratched at the base of the wall, intimidating her with stone and immovability. She followed the line of the base and came to an indented section curving inwards, the wall a stone curtain bending inward, she followed the terrain and other senior creatures followed making sure she had not found exotic food or falling fruit, the males astride and searching as if in the same mind as her instinct.

They came to a massive cavern, the domed walls pristine clean, shining with reflected sun that sourced from the white mineral walls outside the cavern entrance, with recently running water that fell between the wall and the smooth stone floor and ran away down into the earth. The middle of the cavern had a natural well and water flowed from a stone channel and poured slowly in from the source at the wall which flowed hugging the wall in a transparent stuck waterfall.

The others approached the well, and drank, surrounding the bath with delight and murmur, their eyes looking upwards as they drank seeing at the immense cavern ceiling, a patchwork of fractured and set stone together, the surface smooth then progressing jagged as the walls were revealed in the light. They tipped their oval beaks, filling and raising their heads back with still, cool pristine water from the pressurised Aquifer below and from the filtered mineral sieve that supplied the Hydrogen and Oxygen bond.

There was silence for a time as the hundred drank, then another hundred took their place, the hierarchy strict, the younger made to wait with peck and charge, the males filling first then allowing the older females their due. The yellow eyes reflected in the pool and were disturbed by the ripples on the surface, sending the small portraits wrinkling and waverly from the drips that returned to the pool in circles.

She ventured past the well after drinking, feeling the cool water and exclaiming silently the delicious portent of the thirst she had now satiated, she felt stronger the water's blood and current within her, her legs seemed to agree the tread sure and the gait balanced. The cavern floor she noticed was a collection of the same shaped stone forced together by some beak she assumed, *"Had they done this?,"* she mused, *"Who made this place?,"* she thought as she walked, the beautiful place was a crafted area, not like the jagged stone and valley beyond. The reverse Batholith cavern opened at the end to another just as large, she stepped with many others on the stone, their claws striking the slate in a collagen symphony, the sound like crackling shale shards or pieces of broken wood she had heard in the forest.

She looked upward, the cavern was lit by the twin sun's light above, two openings carved from the roof where the two suns were set within perfect alignment. The space between the orbs was even around the rock circles. The light shone down, like channels of fire, striking the floor in two beams, a performance silent and powerful across the stone.

She noticed then the walls were lit, showing massive murals, paintings, coloured lines in the rock to reveal shapes and creatures and she looked closer, recognising something and realising that many of the shapes were her kind, the two strong legs, the coat of fingers, the beak and gait. There was a drawing of their kind drinking from the well, arrayed like the others now, but the well was a little higher, the creatures had multicoloured fingers like they and the yellow kind eyes she now loved and understood, the vein of it coursing through her system like a conduit of time, always known and sure but not fully comprehended, the chemical delineation of it set but undescribed.

The small images showcased the large, there were things she could not understand, like a shape of a being that was a silver colour and four arms instead of two standing near the well and upon the wells circumference small beetles, black and shining a hint of reflected green the painting expertly crafted with drawn lines then colour fill, an ochre pastel collaboration and striking depiction, the beetles carapaces seemingly still and waiting or talking to the creature. On the outer rim of the vignetted masterpiece there was a strange shell, curled and rotund, metallic green and sitting, its legs splayed on the surface of a cavern much like the one she was in. From the drawing of the space a long stripe descended through a hazy brown pathway, strange plants she had not seen adorned the way, it seemed long, the stripe ending at the bottom of the mural. On the opposite side a green stripe and other different plants and a river she thought, a blue winding line. The sun's light was shining off the floor, the painting starting to glow , the colours now highlighted, the texture apparent. Slowly as she gazed a different image appeared it seemed so because the light had struck a certain grain and texture and an object appeared that was not there in the lower light, a small stick-like thing that glowed gold and looked like nothing she had scratched up, a material like the strange figure near the well but smaller and smooth.

The others milled around like clients in a gallery, the newly hatched running in fluff batches, the younger birds herding and aligning the youngsters, casting right eyes skyward to view the cavern and the masterpiece with innate curiosity and calm instinct, knowing there was something there that had glad portent or benign tempest, their yellow eyes reflecting some understanding of the ancient planet, time itself dwelt within them, the ones grown from egg and exo-skin shell, scratch and perch aloft, the flock of the plain.

Cast by the light like an ancient mould revealed, the object shone and mesmerised, a glowing relic and constructed entity. The cavern slipped into calm with the light and the creatures milled, in the majestic space, pecking here and there at the seemingly perfect stone, immaculate and almost sentient-like, the texture enhanced by the fine drawings from a master hand and directional hand. Some of the males stood still turning their heads this way and that as if searching for lost keys and dropped scrolls. The mothers and newly hatched were feeding on dropped seed from the tree above the ancient cavern roof gap which had scattered down and channelled by clever level and slight decline in places deep and still dry and untouched by fungus or mould and seemingly cooled by the cavern's own temperate still climate.

She almost fell, and the plain once again revealed itself, she stumbled from the pineapple stalk and fell into the snow like a log that had been propped against a stick hut and blown down by the wind. The white hurt her and she shivered from the cold and the damp.

The light fading fast, the snow increasing with intensity and the suns now unseen, only the low grey mass of covering cloud dispersing a weary light and meandering billowing state. Crossed her arms and braced against the cold, the temperature falling fast, *"Oh, it's too cold,"* she thought. She gazed out towards the outer pineapple trees, somewhere Anders was out there, the Encroacher had the far scouting task of collecting, she hoped he would be ok, the snow now in a driving state from the West, frost forming on her grass cloak and face. She turned and set out, back to the hut and the others she knew would be warming by the fire, the Altar Priest consulting Hexibarber, the Mineral Master with his stones and gaze and the Templar Wife who she knew had doubts about their situation, the cold, the food and the leaders ability within the Tribe.

19

"Katearnold," she said softly. *"What does that mean?, "she* mused while repairing her grass skirt. She was cold and uncomfortable but she was the Altar Priests property and he would make her warm again tonight, again. She was also very hungry and sick of the pineapple plants, and only got an Unbeliever bar once in a while. Her arms were thinner and she had to keep adjusting her grass skirt to fit around her waist. She had talked to the Mistress saying she was going to cover her top, it was too cold, the Altar Priest had given permission, grudgingly, she said looking at her two protrusions with disappointment for a moment. Strange words came through her mind from time to time, day or night. *"What was Kate Arnold?, "* she thought, was it a spell? Something Hexibarber wanted her to remember? *"No problem there, "* she thought. She thought of the Altar Priest coming to her last night and waking her.

He pleasured her, but she seemed to remember a feeling that she had done the union before with other Altar Priests and that lasted a lot longer and the feeling was a whole lot more satisfying. *"Was that a dream or real?, "* she thought. She had a memory of it, it was a lot different, the *other Altar Priest* did other things, a lot more *other things.* *"Ohh, my Tribe, "* she said out loud as she visualised it, looking around feeling embarrassed, and smiling, remembering the feelings as well, them lying together, after, satisfied, then embracing, he twiddled her hair and she was laughing. *"When did this happen?, "* she thought. *"I want some more of that, "* she smiled.

That Altar Priest was very handsome too, she smiled, blue eyes and curly hair, more handsome than this Altar Priest. He was sort of rushed and he wanted it all his way and she sometimes felt like she wasn't there at all. She twined the string through the gaps in the grass skirt, closing the hole and tightening it off, sitting for a moment, thinking.

She had a very strange dream over and over most nights. She could be like a cloud, and she set off stretching her arms wide and pushing her legs away from a mighty cliff out to the ocean, gliding then moving her arms which gave her speed and adjusting her legs which gave her the ability to move this way and that way. Over the ocean she would go, her hair tied back and her eyes strangely adapted to the wind. There were other creatures with arms too that flew with her. They had strange faces and long noses and were beautiful and graceful.

The ocean she could see in the depths was blue and foaming with the breakers and she could see small creatures that swam below, in great numbers and that turned this way and that way as she flew above them. Sometimes one of them would break the surface and she saw it had two arms as well, then it crashed back into the waves and was gone, a silver streak down below. She gained height and went up further where the air was thinner and the water below seemed curved and she could see great land masses clearly, like they were swimming in the ocean, shifting slowly.

Up in the thin streaking clouds she flew, and other creatures with bigger arms and bigger noses came and joined her and they made a shape like an arrow head and she flew at the front and they flew behind in two lines. They flew a long way, many days and nights not stopping, getting buffeted by wind and rain and hard bits of something and clouds that were bright then dark, but they didn't break their line and they were exhausted. After a long time, they descended, finding a remote craggy Island in the ocean. It seemed very remote, with a huge rock wall hundreds of feet high and a low rock platform just above the sea on the bottom.

They descended buffeted by the cliffs high wind, the last of their strength ebbing like the rock platform tide. They landed on the vast stone platform, pooled with low tide reflections of the sky, with crab and barnacle and the wash of the ocean receded, but seemingly wanting to try again with spray and swell, and nestled themselves where they could rest, on dry stone, some of her companions dropped to their sides and went to sleep, the others sat there, resting, on their breasts, legs folded below, their arms folded into their bodies, so she did the same and sat with them and they looked at her while the sea broke on the craggy flat rock and the salt spray rose and fell in small misty wisps, and she loved them.

They surrounded her and sat close to her, she could feel their warmth and their soft arms, and their eyes reflected instinct and calm and tenderness and contentment. They expected nothing, being adapted and marvellous, beautiful and splendid. They seemed to smile within as she wiped the tears from her face because of their beauty and tender regard, and smiled back thanking them.

She didn't quite understand what for, but then knew as it slowly came to her, and it washed over her like a soft understanding, about what they meant and were, and how important they were to the land and the sea, and she felt stronger and happy, and privileged to be with them.

She went on alone, they seemed to understand and she could feel them somehow smiling and content, and she flew directly above the waves very low and could see a large shape ahead. It was like a big table but had a smaller top poking out on one side, and it powered through the ocean on top of the waves with ease and when she got higher to see and closer, she could see people like her on the top of it and she knew she had arrived home.

She descended and she could see they were ready and she landed on the flat surface. The others came to her and the man she knew, and he hugged her, and she held him around his neck and he around her waist and they cried, and she could feel his love and his lovely smell and he kissed her on the mouth, the others standing around them, smiling and saying nice things, as the sky brightened and the sun came out, but only one sun, not two, she thought that was a little odd. Then they parted looking at one another, but still holding each other's hands, and then she always woke up feeling sad and potent at the same time, so very happy and so very troubled at the same time.

20

Anders twined his spear, sitting in the dirt by the small lake he visited each day to try and remember his childhood, but it was blank and he got irritated by it, wrapping the twine with ever increasing twirls , then folded and tied, impatient, set it aside and brought his legs up to his chest and rocked back and forth, looking out across the still water and the plain beyond. *"I am Anders the Encroacher, the Altar Priest had said, from a family of great hunters,"* he said outloud. He thought of the talk they had with Hexibarber, sitting in the dirt circle, its majesty thrilling him, the bare pole a bane and friend. The Altar Priest had said Hexibarber would talk to him, but he hadn't heard back from the great one, and was concerned, and sad, and a bit angry.

He had tried his spear throwing earlier, but had missed the tree three times, the last throw wobbling the spear to the ground. *"This was just my mood,"* he thought, he could bring down an unbeliever easily while running, he was the Encroacher after all. He thought a bit more about the unbelievers and how he *"Actually I haven't brought any of them down yet,"* but he would and could, he was sure.

"Who had his Father been?, he didn't know. *"Was this a test"?* He wondered, Hexibarber was watching from the plain, he was certain, watching his mood, his actions, testing, judging and watching over his safety as well he was a good presence, he felt it, made him calm and warm and pious. He would do his best he decided, Hexibarber would come to him in time, show himself in time. He looked down at his member, thinking that it had not worked, the females had not acted on the appendage as he had hoped. It was a little blue with the cold. He decided that he would cover it with grass pants and then they would have missed their chance. He looked forward to their disappointment, then he would make them pay and ignore them, content with feeling himself and thinking of the Mistress.

The sky was clear, he noticed, apart from some small clouds on the horizon, the twin suns now were smaller and it was getting very cold, colder each day he thought he would have to cover the appendage anyway, it was hurting and shrunk a bit as well. The lake was left over from the river, he deduced because it winded a certain way, and if it had done that it would have cut itself off forming this shape, "Yes, he thought, with some things I am very good, I sort of have a memory of it, but don't recall ever been taught about it," he mused silently.

The wind was increasing and the tall flowered blue seven petalled stalks bent long to the ground with the breeze and back again like half pendulums, the mountain range a constant, the green sky tinged with ochre pastel patches of lit and unlit exosphere. The lake reflected blue to a green sky and milled shifting strands of grass and dust particles, swirling like in conference with one another.

He stood and walked around the lake, throwing pebbles and watching them skip across the surface, sending mirrored disturbed circles waving to the edges and breaking small foams to the water's edge on the miniature beach, and reflecting the morning sky, an irregular pattern of puffed ball and high streaky lines, distorted by the oxygen and hydrogen, the twin suns red and yellow now instead of yellow, yellow as was the case a month ago.

He sat again and thought how hungry he was, the Pineapples were ok, but he had lost weight and his stomach was rumbly. He had done a smell earlier and it had come out like liquid, and slimy like the river mud and he was a bit concerned, usually his discharge was solid and like a log. The Unbeliever food was the best but it was only allowed now and then. *"Was there anything else out here to eat,"* he wondered. He looked over the grass as if he might spot another plant that he could eat in response. He decided to search for something and rose, starting out and winding his way to the edge of the forest away from the river's view, passing stones and small pebble paths between the green sedge grass, the wind a constant whisper through the stalks and blue flowers bending down to the ground and then up again as if marking his way, his path and journey for his stomach.

Inside the forest boundary he looked around at the trees. *"If the Pineapple trees provided something, maybe other trees can as well,"* he thought, looking up at the massive canopy, the branches rustling and scratching, rubbing and making a wood say strange things. He approached the closet tree, a mighty behemoth rising up he thought, *"Maybe forty sticks,"* his newly worked out unit of measurement. He peeled a bit of the rough bark off and smelt it, musty and wet it didn't seem very nice. It was mottled and lumpy, there were small fibrous lines down it and it was strong and tough. He searched under the tree, the Pineapple tree sometimes shed the things and they were on the ground. They had seen on the side of the Unbeliever food that they ate, the script, *Pineapple*, and the Pineapple trees tasted similar so that's what they decided to call them, *"The unbelievers were a problem he thought but they had good food, you had to give them that,"* he thought.

A huge pile of the tree's leaves had accumulated and sat rotting at the base, he couldn't see any things there. He walked further in, the forest gloom descending on him, he could see massive fallen rotten logs, trees that had died and fallen, resting on one another. *"Very old,"* he thought. There were vines and thickets of sticks and an accumulation of nettle and a mass of leaf litter and the wind blew through the top of the canopy he could see the great limbs stretching and hitting one another and small sticks falling down to the ground, a misty bits of desiccated bark floating in the forest air. He felt calm and the place sort of made him feel safe and tempered his hunger, the air was so very fresh and the trees seemed to talk to him, as they moved and he thought it was a beautiful place. He looked up and around to get an idea of the vastness of it, then continued through the thicket and a bit further past the boundary trees.

In the distance he saw a different thing, it was a different shrub and had round small fruits on it, about the height of him and with a stumpy large trunk. He reached the shrub and touched the leaves a furry touch and the fruits dangled in small clumps, many had fallen and lay rotting at the base. He picked one of the fruits off, a small shape like the stones he had seen by the river. He smelt it, it didn't smell like the *pineapples*, it seemed a nice smell, though.

There were small things that had ten legs, crawling on the stems and collecting something, then carrying it back down in a manicured trail through the forest floor, where they had moved the debri aside and cut any plants away for their forest way. He ate a bit out of it, it tasted nice, made his tongue feel ok, less rough than the *pineapple* plant. The juice from it tasted sweet like some of the Unbeliever logs they found in the strange wrappers. He really liked them and started to eat more, stuffing them into his mouth, realising how hungry he was.*"Wow, these are good,"* he thought, the juice running down chin. He looked around and noticed more of the shrubs, through the gloom further into the forest.

Having eaten many of them he tracked back through the path he had taken and emerged into the plain again, and past the forest boundary and towards the river, reaching the lake again and sitting eating the small fruits. He felt better as well, his stomach was calm and he felt stronger, his vision seemed to improve and he was glad he found the shrub. *"Why did the Altar Priest not tell them about these shrubs?,"* he thought, *"They were all hungry and Hexibarber had promised to find more food,"* he thought.

135

As he sat in the grass and while watching the wind blow the sedge this way and that. He thought some more about where he had come from and why he couldn't remember his Family and his friends, as if he had suddenly woken up from a dream in reverse. Now he was in a dream, nothing made sense. There were strange things like how he could add up items well, he was good at collating things, and he found he could do several things at once, he was fit and didn't get cold much, and he had secretly found the forbidden things that emitted light and displayed strange shapes, fiddling with it in a hidden place, away from the others.

He had pressed something on the flat surface like the lake, it lit up like a sun, scaring him, dropping it and running, but then realising he better pick it up and hide it. He had found a place to hide it, near the sacred fence, but on the outside so he could sneak around the perimeter and grab it and run into the forest. When he was hidden and settled he touched it again in the same place and it was a sun again, he looked at a strange pattern that showed things like funny sticks like how the hut was, or how the sacred pole area was, and a thing like a channel like the river with a stick at the end, a stick that wasn't there and then was there, like someone hiding then appearing. He visualised the stick things in his mind:

Login
Ate Succession Command Interface

A B C D E F G H I K L M N O P Q R S T U V W X Y Z

"Very odd," he thought, "Very, un Hexibarber-like," he mused, totally confused. He could never tell the Altar Priest, the things were forbidden. The Altar Priest had taken the others to the strange thing on the Plateau, the beast with a tough skin, and eyes like his, clear but very tough, he hammered it with his spear and the spear broke, stunning him, sending a piece of the shaft flying past his eye, just missing, the stone head dropped to the ground with a clack sound and shattered in several pieces, the twine releasing and spinning back into a ball of confusion which made him furious. The others were looking at him, the Mistress was smiling, he was angry and ashamed. The Altar Priest and the others then stood looking at the thing, the Mineral Master scratching it with his magical mineral-war hammer, emitting a sound like when the wind blew from between his space, between his legs., *Did the beast do this as well?,* he thought at the time, *Was it alive?* The Altar Priest read from *'The scroll of Condemnation,"*

"I, the Altar Priest of the grassy plain, who has with due rigour, consulted Hexibarber, our saviour and friend, our keeper and chant of safe passage, with concurrent regard to our situation and peerless non-judgemental demeanour..."

Anders had thought standing there with the wind high and the view to the distant river quite stimulating, he didn't understand what the Altar Priest was saying, but feigned concentration and pretended to know, nodding as the twin suns hovered above the strange swirly things that were white and then below dark and very frightening, now and then flashing like the sun thing, a horrifying streak down to the ground and then a shake of the plateau. He looked at the Altar Priest briefly, the others heads bowed in union. Hexibarber was upon the plateau rock on a small raised section of pillar stone looking at him intently with the mineral eyes, within a darkened hood where he knew Hexibarber's mind was, where the knowledge was, where he could rise to be an Altar Priest one day. *"If only Hexbarber would say something,"* he mused. He looked at Hexibarber and mouthed a message,

"Hello, great Hexibarber, I love you" At that moment a huge crack sounded in the distance, he remembered, the five of the gathered crouching with terror, the Mineral Master akimbo with his war hammer ready to repulse. He bowed down and looked away from Hexibarbers gaze with terror and shame,

sorry he had tried to address the one, which was beyond his rights. The Altar priest raised his gaze and continued, he seemed scared, which couldn't happen to an Altar Priest he had been taught, but this was probably something else he finally deduced, *"Maybe a secret stance,"* he had thought. His Altar Priest had continued, and he thought, looking at the stone, "What does *circumference* mean?"

"We are considerate and kind, yet have means of persuasion, a craft we have inherited from the Fathers and Hexibarber, who had taught us the scrolls' meaning and just circumference. Do not fear the barb of the strong plateau beast, nor the raised angular relic that is buried in the sacred dirt, each leg bound and set as it was written to enslave the high beast's lament and sour the mind-bending sun rocks its children smashed that sang horror, and made rude noises, flat and malevolent. The gathered in unison chanted,

"We have destroyed the sun rocks, therefore we are saved"
"We have destroyed the sun rocks, therefore we are saved"

The Altar priest had continued, the scary puffy thing had moved away, no doubt Hexibarber had talked to it. He remembered shuffling with impatience, it was a long talk by the Altar Priest, no doubt Hexibarber had reviewed the material, and *'given the go-ahead,'* "Where had he learned to say that?," *"Given the go-ahead",* he thought, standing on the plateau, pretending to listen. There were other sayings he had dreamt too, like *'It will all blow over'* and *'What do you want me to do about it?,'* *'Yeah, just put it there',* *'I will see about it',* *'don't know'* and *'Do you have milk?'* "What was *'milk?'*"

Sometimes there were things he knew that helped him. He knew how many sticks there were if you put them end to end to get to the top of the plateau, he calculated ten by seventy sticks, it was very useful because he could calculate how far in the sky things were and how far the forest was and time himself by how many *"Hexibarber's"* he could say as he walked and compare that number to the same size sticks he had made. He calculated that there were seven sticks to every Twenty *Hexibarbers*.

He wondered, as he looked out across the grass, now lit with the sun's light, making it look wiry and like the twine horrors that the unbelievers used. He rose again and set out toward the river, passing over the pebble and the mineralised sand and among the sedge grass blowing steadfastly with the wind. He could see the water distant, and the sound of the current moving over the rocks and a tiny view of the stretch of water winding away to the ocean. The seven petalled blue flowers were dotted around, the ones with the high stems, he noticed. *"These are different to the blue flowers that were in the clearing in their village, but now had been scraped away to make way for their meeting place where Hexibarber adjudicated. These ones have higher stems,"* he pondered.

There were ten legged bees, quite large and fat with orange backs and golden heads, and wide wings on the blue seven petalled flowers in between the sedge here approaching the river. *"The flowers are small but the stems are pretty high,"* he mused, stopping and holding the stem so he could see how high it was. He noticed that it was about one and a half sticks high, so a little higher than him, *pretty tall.* Releasing the stem, the flower raised a little then blew down with the wind, a bee gliding down, gliding down near the flower again, the flower raising after the gust of wind had died down, then the bee gliding back up with the wind. He noticed that the bee was very good at gliding back up with the wind, catching it and using the force of the wind to circle around and rise to catch the top of the flower again. He also noticed that it timed the glide as the wind gust abated. *"So, it uses the wind to gain speed so it can glide to the top, then, can buzz when at the top of the flower within the blue petals,"* he thought in concentration. He wondered why they just didn't buzz all the time.

139

"Why glide down to the flower?," he thought. *"And why glide back up?"* *"Why not just stay on the flower and continue what they are doing?"* he thought. He sat down to watch them, *"Yes, every time, they do the same thing,"* he thought, *"Buzz on top, glide down, then glide back up"* He watched for some time, noticing that there were other flying things as well, a small red thing that flew and a green thing as well, the green thing was a little bigger. They both buzzed around the flowers but they seemed to have trouble landing on it and got blown away a lot. He laughed as he watched them struggle with the wind, some eventually rising then drifting off and way out towards the river and into the sky as if in frustration.

After a while only the bees remained, repeating their cycle of buzz, glide, glide. Buzz. He sat fascinated and wasn't sure why, but he was, and continued watching. He then noticed that when the flower reached the point of almost hitting the ground after a gust of wind, the petals closed in an arrow shape like his spear. The green and red thing flew down to try and get on the flower but it was closed and then when the flower raised and opened again, they buzzed to the top but the wind was too strong and they got blown away.

The bee, though, was able to glide to the top and stay on the flower, using its larger wings to counter the wind. *The red and green things,* he thought, *tried time and time again to get to the flower when it was closer to the ground where the wind was softer, but were faced with a closed flower. And why do they try to get on the flower in the first place?,* he wondered, "I will have to watch them more, the next time I am here.," he uttered softly.

He sat looking, watching, in a dream-like trance, he felt warm and happy at that moment and had a short feeling of relief as though Hexibarber had spoken to him and said, *"Anders, you are Anders the Encroacher, you are wise beyond your years, we are great friends and we will together satisfy the Tribe"*

The river ran hazy blue and mottled its surface with small debri of grass stalks and some blue petal, there and there, swirls of trapped water in the shallows, revealing sand and alluvial conglomerate, washed twigs and nettles from the forest, clinging together in shapes like rafts and circling in patterned shapes and then drifting to the fast section of flow and rushing over the shallows and through wedged rock awash, and cleaned. The twin suns hovered like warm sisters knowing their ascension was already achieved, the warmth slowly radiating away from the early day, like a climatic vacuum that was hidden somewhere and sucking dry, and dictating the season. The wind was moderate and constant, the blue flowers thickening near the river edge and the plain awash with steady wind and sure direction, the bees and other insects conferencing quickly to access the nutrient and opportunity, flying in small masses and rising to the next flower head, pilots of the plain.

He rose, as the wind seemed to drop a little with the late morning sun, and walked the final few sticks to the river's edge, peering over the blue-cast rippled water that was running fast and beating stone and passing smooth rock. He walked down on the bank towards the sea running towards the bank. The waterline was pebbly and awash with logs and branches and sticks, nettles filtered the boundary in small masses.

In the distance he noticed a white shape, "Probably a white stick," he thought. The white object was on the other side of the river bank. Moving closer he tried to make out the object, oval shaped with some branch looking thing protruding out of it. It was nestled in some loose stone, about one stick's length from the water, surrounded by debri, it had a vine wrapped around it. He moved closer to the water edge, looking and focusing, still unable to define it properly. The wash was strong where he was so he decided to cross down further where there was a pebble shoal and semi-landbridge. Crossing, after walking and looking at the object with

141

increased interest along the water's edge he fell and cursed in Hexibarbers name, embarrassed and wet he continued.

He reached the mystery object, knelt down and then realised what he had found, not a stick, "Hexibarber! My Tribe!," he bellowed, and turned the helmet to face him, one mineral eye looking at him, the other gone, a small stick from the frame within the helmet poking out to mimic the other eye. "My Tribe, my tribe," he said, lifting the effigy and placing it upright, crawling back and bowing, his head on the sand. He slowly lifted his head, Hexibarber still and seemingly waiting for his next action. "My Tribe, I ...what has happened? Why are you here? Have you been attacked by unbelievers?, I will help you and carry you back to the sticks" Anders noticed the missing eye and the state of his Mighty effigy, thinking *"How was this possible?, the Altar Priest had told him that Hexibarber was immaculate, and could not be harmed by anything, a timeless Tribe leader."*

The silent helmet seemed to disagree, the pebbles providing a quiet base and the mineral eye reflecting the light, within, the visor space a darkness as if a myriad of questions were answered there.

Anders looked around, distraught, stood up and scanned the surrounding area, Hexibarber below him, still and seemingly waiting, like a buried prisoner, his head above the sand. He squinted at the river's reflection, gazing past the bank and up the river wash searching for a cause or unbeliever danger, the answer was nothing but the river, the wind, and the blowing grass. He knelt down and sobbed.

"Hexibarber, I will help you, " he said, all choked with tears and the stress of the moment. He looked at Hexibarber, the mineral eye looked at him. "Come my Tribe, I will take you back to the sticks and safety," he said, at the same time thinking, and pausing carefully, taking his arms back to his sides. *"Maybe he wants to be here?,"* "Am I intruding,

142

my…have I disturbed Hexibarber?" "Great Hexibarber, have I disturbed you?, are you wanting to deliberate on this river wash?"

The helmet stared straight ahead. He thought for a while, looking up the river, turning his head thinking that maybe the answer was somewhere around as well, a sign, a crumbled rock, a new plant, a stone maybe, could it be even the Altar Priest hiding, watching, testing, even all the tribe watching, the Mistress, the Wife Templar, the Mineral Master, all arrayed in judgement, in the grass, lying down, listening. He thought for a while, then started to smile then stopped, knowing Hexibarber was watching. *Yes, this was a test, yes a test, he had chosen to be here so he could test Anders the Encroacher, his skill and decision.*

"Ok, my great Hexibarber, I know you are relying on my skill, I will not disturb your contemplation, I see you great and wise and you are here for a reason, I acquiesce. *"Acquiesce"* , he momentarily thought, where did I learn that? A bee buzzed by his ear and away to a river bank flower in the distance poking up on the bank, the wind was a constant sound, *"It is getting colder,"* he thought, and his appendage ached a little.

The semi-naked man bowed and turned away from the helmet, walking back across the river land bridge of pebble and over the alluvial wash that had breached the middle of the natural dam, a collection of wood detritus and nettle mounds, and a tree branch with three limbs stretching upwards to the green sky, beached on the pebble, on one limb, a black and blue beetle, sitting camouflaged upon a dark section of the wood its ten legs splayed and still, the compound eyes seemingly a thousand eyes, processing his image in some ancient strategy and primordial inverted daguerreotype. As he passed, the beetle lifted its carapace shining, and swam in the air expertly and caught the wind flying over the river and through the grass beyond like an invisible drone and masterful sentient kite, then was gone.

The man's head was bowed and his spear was in hand, his small cape was fluttering and he stooped like a forlorn Batman having just been scolded by a nagging wife, with debt he could not repay. The figure walked down the far river edge and then accessed the bank, climbing a steep section and entering the plain and then was gone among the grass,the flowers bending like mechanical toys and oil pumps on the plain and the suns starting to get cooler.

21

Anders Pedersen walked through the deep snow, He had been up on the plateau and was very cold, the wind there howling across the bare rock surface like a massive freezer floor, there was no sign of Hexibarber, the stone was bare apart from the Monster that was now dead and blackened, its just reward for challenging the tribe, it was now a place of judgement, unbelievers would be taken there to taste the dessert of, ..."Well, unbelieving," he thought. The path was up to his knees as he approached the river, his breath casting in great clouds from his warm mouth, the wind abating for now but snow falling thickly. He felt stronger after his trips to get the berries but he was very cold and his skin was red raw and dry, his ears felt like they would crack off if he touched them, he thought of fashioning a hat to keep his head warm and wondered if that would be allowed, but then thought *"Well, we will see I suppose, no one knows about the berries but the Mistress and she wouldn't tell the Altar Priest,"* he was sure, they had an encounter and she had kissed him on the mouth, then flitted away quickly, he tried to half grab her but she was gone out to where the Altar Priest was, and anyway, he felt quite good after that.

The river was half frozen, he noticed as he approached the bank, snow falling on the ice and creating weird shapes, and some logs and sticks had been trapped and frozen in place, a mass of debri stuck fast with a slow trickle of water passing by and retreating under the ice. He remembered the last place he saw Hexibarber and would search there, if Hexibarber was still there then he would have to question the Altar Priests judgement, and decide what to do. He stepped down the bank, the snow drifting with him down to the waters and icing edge. Across to the far bank the land bridge was still there with extra clumps of small ice flows pushed against the dam, the water and ice had pushed around this time creating a small opening on his side, the water running though.

He walked across, seeing the pebble and ice shapes, small things like the leaves were in the forest, only white and clear at the same time, at his feet, the snow contrasted the rivers blue and clear, he thought this was very beautiful and couldn't explain to himself why he knew what beautiful was and why he thought it was beautiful, only that it was, he knew, and this place was becoming less of a worry and more of a content for him. He had no memories only dreams sometimes, things about trees and plants, strange plants that could hurt you and places he hadn't seen while awake, vast flat places and dry places, the opposite to this place, no water only sand and places that had a river like this but winded through a forest that was different with things hanging from trees and big creatures that jumped out of the water at times. He reached the far bank via the bridge and looked around to where he last saw Hexibarber, seeing the master was still visible but covered with ice and snow, a lump upon the pebble. He knelt by the head scraping the snow off and grabbing a small pebble to scrape the ice,

"Hexibarber, I am sorry I did not secure you before, forgive me I thought it was a test, but now I see you are truly hurt and trapped here, let me help you" He scoured the last of the snow, the one mineral eye was still staring out, the other eye without the stick poking out now, just a dark space. He sat for a moment looking at the helmet,wiping it clean of snow. *"Would Hexibarber talk to him now?,"* he wondered, he picked the effigy up and perched it upon a rock nearby, the mineral eye catching the light. "Please, great Hexibarber, tell me what is to be done, I am your servant, the Altar Priest said you were on the plateau, I see this is not the case, were you on the plateau?" The helmet remained silent, soft snow fell around, the wind totally abated, the quiet wash of the river apparent. He shifted uncomfortably and looked around and back to the effigy, slowly realising that maybe Hexibarber was not actually Hexibarber and that this unbeliever thing was just that, an unbeliever thing like all the other unbeliever things,

146

something they didn't like and understand."Hexibarber, I am Anders the Encroacher, I say you must reply to me, you must say something so I know you are the protector of the Tribe," The mineral eye cast cold and the vacant eye cast darkness, the slight sound of snow hitting the helmet the only contrast to the silence.

He cast a look around thinking, the blue petalled flowers were gone now, just rough petalless sticks poking up on the river bank, the white snow massed on the bank, the Western mountains covered by low cloud, the river wash winding away to his right. The snow fell on his arms and he held out his hand and let the flakes drop and melt watching the water diffuse over his skin, then closing his hand to a fist and looking back at Hexibarber, the helmet, a silent construction, sitting on the rock.

Then suddenly a voice emitted from the helmet, *"Anders the Encroacher, I hear you, I am here of my own violation, I am here for you, if you would be so kind to accompany me, I will need you to carry me as I am very tired, back to the Tribe, I can take my place on the stone Altar and address you all"*

Anders dropped to his knees in shaking shock and delight, he had finally been addressed by Hexibarber, his saviour, he started to cry and wiped the tears and snow from his face, bowing before the helmet in solemn joy, looking at the one mineral eye with astonishment, the eye glistening with the reflection off the snow in the dim light. "My saviour, of course!, I can do anything you wish, I shall pick you up" *"Thankyou Encroacher, let us journey back, me under your arm and we will take our place within the Tribe"* "Of course, oh Hexibarber the great," Ander said with intended joy and astonishment, elated at the fact that finally Hexibarber had spoken to him. "Here, let me carry you." "Thank you, Encroacher, I know I can always count on you," Hexibarber replied.

147

The Encroacher picked the helmet from the snow carefully, wiping tears from his eyes with one hand, and cradling the effigy under his other arm, looking down at the helmet. "Is that ok Hexibarber?" *"Yes, thank you Encroacher, you are very kind,"* Hexibarber said. *"Actually, before we journey, Encroacher, may I confide in you and have a short discussion about certain items on the agenda?"* "Oh.. ,yes of course, my saviour, shall I place you down?," Anders said with concern, his eyes red from crying. *"Yes, let's talk here a while, we can confide in private,"* Hexibarber said, Anders thought the voice sounded sort of familiar and didn't realise Hexibarber was a woman and was shocked, but there it was, she spoke and was talking to him, he was upset his mind was racing, he wasn't thinking properly at the moment.

He placed the helmet back on the rock, the mineral eye seemed alive, the dark space seemed intelligent and sure. He sat down in front of Hexibarber, bowing his head, waiting for the effigies command, the snow falling around him. He wiped his eyes and thought about how happy he was, finally Hexibarber his saviour was with him in person as well as in his mind.

22

Ye-Min knew the Tribe was a contrived nonsense. She had woken up from whatever had affected her, like some rebirth, aware of who she was and what the others had become, frightened but relieved, she was Ye-Min, not some warrior tribe member. Her memory was sketchy though, some things she understood, some things she was hazy about, like how the *Ate Succession* had gone. It had happened the last time she was with the so-called Altar Priest and the others, poor Tom, bound to the stupid pole, helpless to do anything at that stage, but now probably she could. Jason Findus was somewhere around she knew as they had tried to hunt him at one stage, she had heard them on the plain and spotted Jason running into the forest, so he was unaffected as well. Tanya Geary was out there, she seemed to be like her, normal.

She had to endure the diatribe from the so called Altar Priest, Donghyun and that idiot the Mineral Master, formerly the gentle humorous Akseli, but her favourite was Anders the Encroacher who she felt sorry for, as his regard for the fake leader *Hexibarber* was endearing, laughable and sad at the same time.

She had had to endure the madness of them consulting a space helmet, which she knew the name of, she wasn't sure how. She also knew that the helmet was designed to be attached to a space suit for vacuum use and understood that it wasn't some magic leader, it had no entity and was just a helmet, laughably constructed by that idiot Donghyun the so called Altar Priest. The Mistress and the Templar Wife, poor Kylie and Kate, were considered inferior she could see, but wiser than the males she thought, the males instinctively just wanted to rule the roost as far as she could ascertain, and were doing a woeful job so far.

No one ruled her, and her warrior demeanour shunned the men enough, now she had left them never to return, except on scouting missions to find the sane others. Her task now was to try and use the effigy to secure poor Tom's release, then she couldn't do anything for them, maybe they would awaken as well from this bizarre affliction, the cause she was wondering about, "Was this a Cryo-sleep thing?"

She had a concealed home in a massive cavern, a long way across the massive plain to the West, far enough, as they seldom ventured with any vigour, content with their saviour sitting on a rock. She had found the beautiful artworks in the massive cavern that shone with the light and revealed a Master Artists hand. She knew that there had been other species here on this planet previously, the drawings seemed to indicate a path to another continent, there was a signal she had located a long way away using the satellite, a beacon transmitting on a continual cycle and she had plotted the position, its origin was unknown but it was on the distant Western plain.

She had made her home comfortable with items from the forest, a nettle bed, raised off the floor, constructed of sturdy logs, a water source that didn't freeze within the cavern, a well that someone or something had constructed, and the grain tree seeds she ground down and made paste out of, then baked. She had also found a red berry that was an exceptional addition to her diet, packed with vitamins, as her OTAA had told her.

The *Organic Taster and Atmospheric Analyser (*OTAA,) or the *Ottar* as commonly called. *The Ottar, developed by Dr Allen Ottaway for survival markets, is a small probe attached to a super-tough analyser unit hand-held, compact, using AI generated algorithms paired with bio-finger technology.* She remembered the briefing. The OTAA could test anything, the probe just needed in most cases to touch the object, occasionally inserted into organic or non-organic material and provided a readout of if it was edible, dangerous or otherwise. A detailed chemistry report was accompanied with the readout. A adventurer's dream, the OTAA identified safe food, dangerous chemistry, and even into wounds to identify infection and was a small sentient device in itself able to communicate with a wide range of other medical and ship board devices. Her people designed the OTAA she assumed as it said the name on the outside and she instinctively knew how to use it. She had crafted a good knife, a sword and her bow.

The cavern air temperature was about twenty degrees warmer than outside, it would save her during the winter with the addition of a fire. She had a large collection of wood stacked for a fire she would light under the stone roof window, where the grain tree shed the seeds. She had pilfered away any items from the miserable village that they considered *unbeliever,* as these items were very useful, like the fabric from the space suits and the dehydrated food they were clueless of, having no knowledge of what it was in the first place. She also had a tablet, which they called *sun-rocks, "My goodness,"* she thought. She knew how to access the weather satellite and the weather forecasts and had a detailed mapping file on the planet's land masses and oceans. She had a memory of her people putting the satellite in orbit, but it was hazy like everything else.

She could see that the *Tribe* was heading for disaster anyway as their inability to obtain nutritious food and construct good shelters, not to mention their non-existent hygiene would eventually kill them all. *Could I be content with that outcome?,...* No, she thought. "No, the journey must be made," thinking of the directive deep inside her psyche that ticked like a precise clock and fundamental timer, something she was aware of but didn't quite understand why. *The beacon must be found,"* she said softly to herself. *"But before that happens, I will save these miserable bunch of deluded space men and women."*

She had watched the so called Altar Priest by the river last week as he lost the helmet with humour but also sorrow, she felt that she had some connection with him and indeed all the others but couldn't understand why. The directive was within her, but also something like a feeling but more assertive that was telling her that her crew needed help and she was the one to make their lives at least livable. If she could sum the feeling up it would be something like,

"To secure their safety and well-being for a harsh winter, if they are to survive, they need a competent leader, good shelter and a constant nutritious food source."

She was ready as well, her health had never been better, for some unknown reason she felt like *Superwoman*, she had good stamina, her shit had changed consistency suggesting better digestion, she could walk all day out in the open, cuts and grazes healed quickly, she only needed five hours sleep. The increasing cold seemed to make her sharper not colder and her vision and hearing had improved, her mind was sharp, content, patient. She didn't know how but thought maybe the red berries had something to do with it, she would take it though, the Winter would be a test.

She knew that the elliptical path of the planet was going to reach the outer limit of revolution in about six months, by that stage the temperature during the day would plummet down to minus thirty to minus forty degrees Centigrade, her marvellous mathematical mind, which she loved, converting the temperature to -40℃ and -40℉, noting that the Celsius and Fahrenheit readings were the same, for a minus forty degree reading, a mathematical anomaly of scale.

This was basically a death sentence for their wandering clueless minds, thinking a helmet would show them the way. The helmet would certainly not show them the way, in the way they thought, she would see to that. The ridiculous stick huts barely were enough in this weather, let alone after when the weather turned apocalyptic. She was the one to save them and guide them and she had a plan.

She had decided that the journey to the cavern as a base for them would be too far logistically, being two hours away and had selected a good site near the coast, a small cave system which was only a half hour walk from the stick village. From there, they could manage the move. Also the ocean may provide a new food source she suspected, and the Westerly winds that battered the plain and her cavern, although protected, was a colder environment, the plain beyond she knew from scouting a long distance one day, became a dry cold desert, sand and stone were the dominant features. At a glance during her mission, finding food would seem to be a difficult task in the area. Her base would be a backup dwelling in case the beach idea failed, the archeological find in itself a factor, she couldn't quite bring herself to allow the place to be inhabited by more people, she felt like a nervous Art Gallery Manager, or a concerned Conservationist, she couldn't quite understand the significance of the paintings, but at the same time knew in her core what they meant, it was all a bit confusing.

Now she saw the Encroacher from the far river bank, she was concealed expertly, on a small mound with a good view of the river, with a grass sedge hat that bent over her with the grass stems, ridiculous looking, she assumed without a mirror, but effective, to simulate the area and blend in, lying prone, motionless, she had found some green pants from one of the energy tents and caked mud on herself for extra camouflage. She was about a hundred metres from him, she considered that a safe distance. She had tracked him since he left the plateau, following him towards the river, she had a plan. If she could make him think Hexibarber was real, then she could demand Tom's release in the first instance and then work on their situation.

He had found the helmet again and she heard him mumbling to it, as she opened the radio channel. She had to suppress laughter, she regained control and listened intently while he asked *Hexibarber* to speak to him, she was ready. She donned her headset radio and selected the channel for the helmet. She had tested it on the helmet a while ago when the great Hexibarber was supposed to be on *long service leave*, whatever that was supposed to mean. By turning up the volume on the helmet a person could hear it *speak,* it worked well, the effigy now had a personality beyond silence. She knew after the Altar Priest's lies about Hexibarber, something must have happened to the effigy, and she went down to the river to search for Hexibarber, finding the helmet on the pebble raised from the water downstream. She thought about taking it back secretly but then noticed the Encroacher was going out on trips by himself to the river and thought, *"Well if he can find it, that would be better after hearing the Altar Priests lies"*

She listened to him, *"Hexibarber, I am Anders the Encroacher, I say you must reply to me, you must say something so I know you are the protector of the Tribe,"* She waited a moment and saw him shuffling looking around in a sad state. Then she replied, trying to mask her voice as much as she could with the intonation of the radio. *"Anders the Encroacher, I hear you, I am here of my own violation, I am here for you, if you would be so kind to accompany me, I will need you to carry me as I am very tired, back to the Tribe, I can take my place on the stone Altar and address you all, my long service leave has ended"*

After the shock he had, she consoled him and asked to talk in private, *"Actually, before we journey, Encroacher, may I confide in you and have a short discussion about certain items on the agenda?"* *"Oh.. ,yes of course, my saviour, shall I place you down?"* Anders' voice was clear on the channel. *"Yes, let's talk here for a while, we can confide in private,"* she *said,* smiling looking at the distant Anders.

§

Donghyun thought about what he would say when the Tribe realised that Hexibarber was not returning. "I could say he has risen afar and up to the sky and watches over us," he thought. "What about, he lives within us all and that is sufficient, he has become one with the Tribe," yes that sounded good, something like that. "Could I make several Hexibarbers?," he thought suddenly, "Yes, put a Hexibarber by the river and on the plateau, and here on the Altar, ..it could work," he thought. He sat in the freezing hut, his legs were so cold he couldn't feel them and the snow had piled high on the side of the hut, bits of grass were flying around outside and the snow was still falling at a high tempo outside. The Mineral Master was asleep in the corner and he was doing that more and more lately during the day, the Mistress and the Templar Wife were outside picking pineapples, their task and duty, he expected them back soon. The Encroacher was encroaching somewhere, he was spending more and more time away despite the weather, he seemed to be very strong, he didn't have the sores he had and the skin issues and such a weight loss problem. He gazed at his arms, they seemed to be much smaller and the wrist bones were poking through. *"I am the Altar Preist,"* he thought, *"Why the fuck do I have all these problems?"*

Akseli started to snore in the corner, the snow was abating a little. *"This stick village is a wood freezer, if only Hexibarber was not lost,"* he mused. He watched the embers within their fire, they had collected a lot of wood from the forest but much of it was wet and burned slowly, the unbeliever stick had died and now they had to keep the fire burning all the time, it was an exhausting task.

They had tried to cut a tree down but every time they had attempted it tiny stinging insects billowed from the tree tops and chased them away, it didn't matter where they went it was the same. In fact, he had noticed that every time they wanted

155

to destroy a plant or dig something up some insect intervened and usually with a bite.

He had many sores from the bites, and some were infected, extremely itchy and uncomfortable. Now they just collected small fallen logs, usually wet on the forest boundary. The weather was getting colder and colder and he hadn't seen the twin-suns for over two weeks, the grey clouds a leaden cast and low portent. *"In fact, I feel terrible,"* he thought, *"Is this a punishment from Hexibarber?"* *"Was life always like this,"* he thought feeling very nervous, *"Is this as good as it gets?"* He coughed, and rubbed his red eyes, he felt his cheek bones, the bone was more prominent.

He had seen his reflection in the river during the warm months, he wasn't as handsome as he imagined. In fact he was shocked, a haggard face, grey bits of hair, swollen eyes, puffy cheeks and ragged hair, in one section a tuft was sticking up. *I look like an idiot,"* he thought. *Am I an idiot? The Templar Priest cannot be an idiot, surely,* he thought. He sat up from his makeshift grass bed, his legs complaining of the movement, aching and weak. Akseli was mumbling now, asleep, and he listened to what he was saying, lying on his back in a stupor. *"Yes, Hexibarber, yes, oh yes, mmmhmm, thank you, what's that you say?, I shall be Altar Priest?, very well, very well, am I worthy?, yes ah, ah, what's that? Templar Priests come and go you say, all the time, yes I understand"*

Donghyun listened with growing alarm, Akseli finally stopped and rolled in a snoring manoeuvre to his side, chortling and then rasping, his breath heavy and whistling. *Does he talk to Hexibarber in his sleep?, surely not,* he thought. Impatiently, Dongyan put on his grass coat, still examining Akseli as if he would say something again, wondering if that was real or some dream he was having getting a little alarmed.*"This does nothing,"* he thought as he donned the ragged jacket, some grass falling from the sleeve in a clump.

What is keeping the Templar Wife, I would like her in the bed with me. The whole thing is just too cold. He stepped outside, beyond in the sacred circle he could hear talking, the snow had abated a little, he walked to where the talking was coming from, passed the vacant huts and into the sacred area, the pole white on top with a pile of frozen snow. *"Altar Priest, there you are, come and see, Hexibarber has returned!"* Anders and the Templar Wife sat near the rock stone where Hexibarber was perched atop, his arm extended in a gesture at Hexibarber with a grin on his face, the mineral eye still visible from where he stood. *What is the Templar Wife doing here?,* he thought, confused. "Ahh, Hexibarber my Tribe, you have returned, thank you Encroacher, the long service leave must be over," he said, playing the composed Altar Priest as normal.

"I have not been on long service leave"

He tried to act normal, but he couldn't help almost jumping a little which the Encroacher had noticed. The Templar Wife looked at him, her eyes raised a little, Dongyan froze, the voice was coming from the effigy, he stilted in his walk a little and clasped his hands near his chest as he approached the altar, Anders was grinning and enjoying the moment he was in awe and a little terrified, Hexibarber had never spoken, he had always assumed that role.

His thoughts raced quickly through his mind. *Fuck, if I had to be honest with myself It wasn't really real though, was it, I always thought I was actually Hexibarber, didn't I?, Did I?* he thought in alarm, now face to face with the effigy. He sat down with Anders and the Templar Wife, who was smiling, waiting for the Altar Priest to address the great Hexibarber.

"Uum, ah, Encroacher, how are you, thank you, greetings Templar Wife I, err, " he turned to the effigy. "Ah, Hexibarber, my Tribe, it is so good that you have returned, may I enquire then the reason for your absence?" The mineral eye glistened, the other socket vacant and dark, he noticed, Anders shuffled

157

on the frozen dirt ground beside him, he stole a quick glance at the Templar Wife who was looking at him much like a concerned owner would do over a small dog, the snow started to fall again and the sky darkened as a big black cloud diminished the sun.

"The reason for my absence is the fact that you lost me in the river, and I was swept downstream, I have noted that you failed to secure my rescue as I was found by the Encroacher" Donghyun froze again and looked at the ground, in disbelief and growing alarm. "I, um, oh great..." *"Silence you fool!"* Donghyun shook at the sound, now terrified, he dared not look at the mineral eye, and as if in a foreboding portent the light faded further in the sacred circle, the dark low clouds seemed to billow further downwards.

He stole a glance across at Anders, he was still sitting upright, a look of content on his face, and beyond him he noticed that a break in the clouds was showing the plateau in sunshine and the blackened monster alight in the glow, he looked at the ground again in confusion and terror, thinking his world was unravelling.

"Now, listen to me, Altar Priest, you are no longer an Altar Priest, understand?," the effigy boomed, his voice sounding female, thought Donghyun. *"Yes, my Tribe, I am unworthy,"* he blurted out with a shaky voice. *"Indeed you are, and let me be clear, you will pull your weight around here as well, no more directing the others to do what you should be doing."* "Yes, yes, I am so sorry, Hexibarber, I.." *"SILENCE!"* Donghyn shook and bowed further now feeling a terror rise in him, his breathing laboured and he was sweating despite the cold.

"Now listen carefully, I have some things to say and you will listen then carry out my wishes, understood?" The effigy said and seemed to radiate significant menace. "I am your servant, Hexibarber," he said, shaking and dreading the next reply.

158

"You will release the unbeliever, he is of no value and he needs to be given a chance to survive, you..." Donghyun interrupted, his terror making his voice stutter a little.

"For, Forgive me Gr, Great Hex, Hexibarber but the unbeliever has gone" "Gone? Gone where? He was punished, was he not?," Anders said with a questioning tone. Her heart sank with the comment, *"Punished?, how?,"* Ye-Min asked. *"Err, I"* *"Answer me you fool!,"* she shouted, getting tired of his grovelling.

"Why, Hexibarber, you took him to the punishment area, a sacred area away from here that only the former Altar Priest knows about, I think that was what you told us wasn't it?," Anders said with a tone of inquiring delight, looking at Donghyun she thought, knowing probably that Donghyun was a liar. *"I took him nowhere, so I ask you again, and I better get a clear answer, where is the unbeliever?"* "I'm so sorry, Great Hexibarber, I woke up three days ago and he was gone and I thought you had taken him away for punishment, I just assumed, I,.." *"SILENCE!!"* she shouted down the comms channel, annoyed that Tom was now hurt and missing.

"Ms Arnold can you search for him around the camp, if he is found I want him kept warm and in a safe place, give him water if you find him "Yes, of course, I will go immediately," Katie said, rising from the dirt floor and starting to walk away, then pausing as Ye-Min added, *"Oh, and Ms Arnold, Ye-Min has been given special healing powers, she will be here soon and will assist you with searching for the the unbeliever, understood?"*

"Yes, Hexibarber, I will wait for her instruction," Katie said bowing and then continuing to walk away. *"Thank You, Ms Arnold"* She thought about Tom. *Had he gotten away by himself? Maybe, but Tanya and Jason were missing too, maybe he got a helping hand.* She hoped so. *"Right, where was*

I?,""Ah yes, also, your neglect around this place is beyond description, do you honestly think that this place is suitable for habitation?" "I, er, well…" *"SILENCE!"* Donghyun shrunk further into the dirt ground at the booming voice.

"You will take the Tribe closer to the coast and away from here, with instructions I have given to the Encroacher, you will construct a new village near the beach, it will have proper sanitation and has warm caves, secure from the cold. Also, you no longer have the right to treat the Templar Wife and the Mistress as you please, as their positions have been elevated to be part of Management, this is a punishment In addition to others that will be forthcoming." Donghyun nodded in silence.

"The Encroacher and The Templar Wife will now be co-leaders and heads of the Tribe, the Templar Wife will no longer be known as the Templar Wife, she will be addressed as Ms Arnold, and the Mistress will be addressed as Ms Albott, understood? "As you wish, great Hexibarber," *"So, what are their names now?"* Hexibarber asked., the mineral eye glistening with a sudden single ray of sunshine upon the helmet. "Ms Arnold and Ms Albott" Donghyun replied. *"Good, remember them, I don't want to hear the other names again, understand?"* Yes, great Hexibarber," Donghyun replied, head bowed in reverence. Donghyun was having trouble understanding the great words, and strange names but started to mouth them to himself in fear of being tested again, as Hexibarber continued.

The Altar Priest position has been abolished, the Mineral Master will assume the role of Sanitation officer, "Sanitation Officer," Donghyun mouthed silently trying to remember the word, *he will make sure the waste is taken to a secure place and hygiene is secured, by waste, I mean when you eject from your behind and when you water, understood?"* "I understand, great Hexibarber," Anders replied. Donghyun couldn't now understand what Hexibarber was saying but nodded to avoid any potential repercussions. *"In addition, the unbelievers will*

160

be left alone, no more hunting and menacing behaviour. I will give you today and tomorrow to prepare for the move and I expect progress and that your task will be completed by the end of the week, otherwise you will feel my portent. Also, while I have you listening, the Mineral Master will secure me another eye, since you were responsible for losing that one in the river."

He began to cry, he felt that everything was lost, Anders was shuffling and standing up, he remained in his submissive pose, terrified to move. *"Now, go and get the Mineral Master, I wish to address him and brief him of his new role, go now, out of my sight, and prepare the move, I will think about your future position within the Tribe"*

23

Ye-Min watched as the so-called Altar Priest was dismissed in disgrace, Katie had already gone to search for Tom and she would be there soon. The former Altar Priest bowed and obediently fled the Altar area, Anders standing, looking quite content from her position, the image super-clear in the AISM, Artificial Intelligence Sentient Monoglass, monoscope which had a brace that she could attach to her head set so she could lie prone sniper-style and keep her hands free. She detached the lens and looked at the glasses for a moment the manufacturer's mark was shown on the outside:

Quantum Bound Industries
Thinking Lens Division - Binocular, Monocular Sentient devices

She reviewed in her mind what she knew about this type of device, the incredible advances in this sort of technology, "Pity," she thought that they still couldn't and probably now wouldn't get a working Android on the table due to the problems with Artificial Intelligence constructs and physical movement.

It seemed all so unbelievable but there was something that they hadn't seen coming, the fact that evolution had been the builder of anatomy, a billion year process and knew a lot more that they did it seemed. The device was a thinking monoscope, a Sentient-AI construct,the same as *Anastasia* who was also a true sentient, thinking like a human, the monoscope was intelligent and Military trained. Unlike a person who sits in a dark office and doesn't speak, a Government Administrator perhaps, the mono was a Military designed reconnaissance AI, highly capable. *"Able to create all sorts of mayhem,"* she thought. *"What did the brief tell us again? The mono is like a Special Forces Operator only inside a lens,"* she remembered.

She made sure the lens was clean and reattached it to the mount and realigned the view. From her hideout on the plateau, wedged between a fissure in the rock, and totally invisible from the distance to the stick village, she was now *Hexibarber* and had control over the situation, which she thought was relatively easy given Donghyan's behaviour in the past. *"Past behaviour is usually a good predictor of future behaviour,"* she thought, people are basically readable scripts despite their hippie yoga teachers telling them differently, after a latte. *"You can be whatever you want to be "* was another saying she thought. *"Ahh! such nonsense,"* she mused with a smile.

The AI scope gave her advice and commands in small text within the field of view, a ghost display like a fighter pilot's windscreen head-up display. It sent a beam signal to the target that the scope was focused on providing crystal clear images in infrared and ultraviolet also if required and had an excellent sound cast via the beam and radio and network communication ability built in.

She had salvaged the working monoscope from the charred explorer, on top of the plateau, the landing site, gaining access from the airlock, surprised to see that the systems were not totally destroyed. The command from her tablet opened the door with a wheeze and grind. Inside the craft was a blackened crypt but the fire had been extinguished by the emergency fire retardant carbon dioxide and the damage was superficial in some sections of the ship. The working door was the emergency battery backup working still, the fusion drive was spent she surmised as the fire had incinerated the controller terminal and in order to get it to work she would have to rebuild it, something that she was thinking about. Probably the lack of parts, all gone with the *Ate Succession*, would put a stop to that.

The clouds were low and the weather was freezing but the day wasn't as bad as some of the driving snow days, and she actually got some sun before, lighting the plateau like a beacon momentarily before the leaden clouds closed again, her position still secure. She had noticed the colder weather generally, it wasn't long before an end-game became apparent with the so called Tribe, and she would have to return to the cavern full-time, having collected a large amount of food and wood for the coming winter. Hopefully with her strategy, it wouldn't come to that.

Anders stood there watching the helmet and she thought about her next move with the *Altar Priest* out of the picture for now. She had already given him instructions for the move, he was the only member that was capable of rational thought, maybe she thought he had been less affected than the others, it seemed likely. With the additional trait of unquestioning regard for the great *Hexibarber*, he was the obvious choice to control the move to the coast, an area she thought would be a better option, if for no other reason, better for their hygiene.

The winds seemed to be mostly from the West and her calculations from the weather satellite's climate predictions tended towards that continuing into the coldest season. From the imagery she had selected a sheltered area back from the highest tides, which were significant with the three moon pull. The site was clear due to a heavy rock formation that had some high cliff areas and caves, perfect for shelter. The site was also surrounded by vine thickets and large trees.

"Let's hope this works," she thought, the lens scrolled a message below as she thought about it,

High definition established, sound optimal, range 400 metres, NNW, ambient temp; 4℃, wind: 10 knots, Two targets visible * <u>warning target closest to your one o'clock is armed</u>. Satellite communication established- window to dark side blackout: 45:03 minutes.

"Anders the Encroacher, congratulations on being the leader of the Tribe, it is an honour that I know you are suited for and you have the ability to carry out the task moving forward. Remember you are essentially a 'client' within the Tribe and shall be treated as such, as I am always here to help, in essence, 'My door is always open' "Unless you are disposable," she thought, remembering her last position as an Astronomer back on Earth, *"Or too old,"* she added. *"Go now and secure your team, and please search for the Unbeliever, I will give you more instruction on this shortly. The move to the caves is upon us, are there any questions?"*

Anders stood upright in respect, Katie looked pleased, looking at the Helmet, smiling. *"Very chuffed,"* she thought. He began to speak, crossing his arms in a vee shape over his stomach, seemingly a little unsure of the correct posture to address the effigy. *"Thank you, Hexibarber, I am in your regard, now that I am in charge of the Tribe, may I ask a favour?"* Her alarm bell rang a little, *"What is this I wonder,"* she thought. "I have found some nutritious berries in the forest...,." She smiled, *"Great he's found them,"* she thought, smiling. *"I would ask your permission to use these to supplement the Tribes diet, can I do this?"* *"Of course Encroacher, you do not have to ask in these matters, do as you see fit, only beware there might be some foods in the forest that would be no good for you, in this regard consult me first if you find something new."*

"Thank You, great one," he replied, clearly pleased and happy. *"Encroacher, also be aware that you might find food in the sea, the ocean, do you understand?"* *"Oh, ok, thank you, I shall look there as well,"* Anders replied, wide eyed and starting to understand other options. *"Encroacher, you must also prepare for the coming season as we have already discussed, you must gather as much food as you can and store it in the unbeliever crates and put the crates inside a cave specifically for that purpose, you remember?"* *"Yes, I remember, I will do this,"* he replied now with a serious concentrated look. *"Encroacher, you must all work together*

and also you all must gain some weight, you are all too thin, this could be a dangerous thing if it continues, you remember our discussion about this by the river?" "Yes, I remember," he replied.

She thought quickly, she better test his memory and understanding so he just wasn't nodding his head. *"So, a small test for you Encroacher, do you understand why you and the other tribe members have to gain weight?, and don't worry, this is just a kind test because it is important"* Anders crossed his hands behind his back and stood straighter to reply, obviously proud of his ability, *"Yes, because if we are too thin, we will get sick in many ways, we won't have enough energy, our thinking will get wrong and we might do strange things,"* he replied. *"Very good Encroacher, right on the money there"* "Sorry, my Hexibarber, I don't understand that last bit," he replied looking a little confused. *"It means you are correct Encroacher, well done, it is an ancient tongue, I sometimes use"*

She watched him go, exiting the Altar area shortly after, looking pleased. The dirt-scarred area was empty and she looked around but the others weren't visible, it had started to snow again, and the clouds had billowed more from the West, the light failing a little, with still seven hours left in the long twelve hour day.

Emerging from the fissure in the rock a little sore, switched her channel to the monocular AI which would keep her informed of any movement in the area via the satellite during its orbital window. *"Well, that went well,"* she thought as she grabbed her bow and handmade arrows complete with sharp stone ends, secured her pack and stretched her legs, then knelt down on one knee to make herself smaller, so she wasn't seen by some miracle, a dot on the plateau.

Rising and heading back into the Explorer to see if she could access anything else, the door sliding like an Egyptian tomb entrance complete with grind of sand but with cracked burnt metal.

Inside she looked at the Fusion controller again. *They couldn't get in here anyway,* she thought. The controller was a long way back from getting it to work, and probably beyond her capability. The ship had some good supplies, some advanced medical gear, including a defibrillator, which she took, accessing another pack that was bigger, calculating the weight, *"Twenty five kilograms, um, Fuck, fifty five pounds, well, I will be earning those berries,"* she thought, as she unpacked her gear from the smaller pack, arraying it across the deck floor. *The advanced medical supplies are gold.* She looked through the kit, everything was here for a small operation if it was required. She noticed an empty section in the kit, a small velcro strap to secure something and wondered what had been there.

The terrain vehicles were ruined as she checked the lock, the tires melted and the engines burnt out. The entire hold section was a mess, melted wiring, rubber, a charred crypt. It seemed the fire retardant had failed here for some reason, the result clear. The bridge was in better shape, including the rotating metal solar system display that Kate Arnold had near her console, still rotating.

Among the items a stock of dehydrated foods and energy bars and some good rope, some string, strong tape and another OTAA, a great find as it could be a lifesaver, maybe she could teach Anders how to use it. She stashed the device in her pack, smiling, rumaging through the remainder of the vehicle, finding another two headsets for the radio, another tablet and the find of the century, the writing shining almost in the dim backup battery light, the portable kit flat packed and stored for some reason below the bridge storage space under the floor,

"The Bee-Brown Dump model 65A, A perfect invention for a Third World and a New World"

"And that weighs about seventy kilos" she thought, a small lift in a working Explorer vehicle with a crew of five, but a heavy lift down a rock plateau alone. *"It is a game changer, though,"* she mused, looking at the crate, expertly designed for portability and storage space. *"I will think about this, it might take some time to get Anders comfortable entering the blackened monster, even for Hexibarber,"* she thought.

She rummaged more, finding more *gold,* a portable camp stove that must have come with the Bee-Brown, and fitted the gas recycling from the toilet. She adjusted the torch in her mouth, almost salivating now about what else was usable, lifting the entire storage floor panels off and stacking them up against the wall.

She looked up, suddenly remembering that she hadn't kept a text channel open as *Hexibarber* in case she was addressed by the Tribe, *"Got to keep those communication channels open,",* no doubt Anders may have some questions. Rising, she switched the channel to *Hexibarber*, so she could hear any talk, the tablet she found was connected to the channel as well so she could see any chat in text mode while she kept the headset off. There was no sound, no chat except in the background, *No,* she thought. *Not addressing him directly.* Anders seemed to be giving a lecture somewhere, *"Good, he has started hopefully,"* she mused, piling some wiring out on the floor, the backup cabling.

A dizzy spell wafted through her, she kneeled still, her head swirling a little, feeling faint. She knew this was a lack of food, the berries were good but she needed protein, the bars helped, "but a good roast would do it," she thought, salivating a little more. *Carbohydrate was a thing here, missing rice and pasta, but she did have the grain tree, which was something, better eat more grain,* she mused, her bread being in the experimental stage.

After about an hour she had scoured the Explorer, it was now officially a shell, despite the working communication system, but she had her radio and headsets. The last thing of potential use was the Fusion torch and the camping battery, but the battery was heavy, another lift job to return to.

24

Donghyun stood and quickly walked away thinking at any moment Hexibarber would strike him down, he moved quickly out of the sacred area, and ran to the hut, The Mineral Master was sitting up awake, rubbing his eyes as he entered, he sat down bowing his head, wiping the tears from his eyes. "Altar Priest, what is the matter?," Akseli said, squinting, looking concerned and sort of hopeful through the smoke haze of the fire. "I am no longer Altar Priest, Hexibarber has spoken," he said, wiping his eyes with his hand, looking at his grass bed, and noticing small creatures milling in the fibres as he looked down.

Akseli, smiled within, while looking at the miserable former Altar Priest, on his infested grass bed. "Worry not former Altar Priest, I am still your friend,"he said elated that the event had happened. Donghyun started to sob and placed his head in his hands, Akseli looked away in respect. *So Hexibarber has moved on him, I see my application was successful.* He breathed a sigh of relief and looked up at the stick roof of the hut then back at the miserable Donghyun. *Well, 'Them's the breaks'. Where did I hear that? What does that mean? I think it is a sacred phrase from my past, yes I am sure of that*

Donghyun raised his head and looked at him, after a time, and said, "You are now the *Sanitation Officer*, Hexibarber has spoken," wiping the tears from his reddened cheeks. "Sanitation Officer?" he said, "What is that?" Donghyun looked at him and he thought he detected a slight smile but wasn't sure, "You are responsible for managing the waste, it means the waste from behind and the water we dispel" "The great Hexibarber speaks and has asked for your presence in the sacred area, you must go now," Dongyun said, looking at him with a certain amount of delight and mixed fear. He looked down at the floor in disbelief and sudden horror, *"This is what I am to be?"* He thought, rising and growing fearful,

No, it must be something else. He grabbed his grass coat, and looked for his soiled pants.

Donghyun watched the Mineral Master go, and couldn't help screwing up his nose at how the Mineral Master smelt as he strode through the makeshift stick door and out into the now heavily snowing path outside.

Ye-Min entered the stick village after descending from the plateau and making her way with her pack containing the advanced First Aid kit and the defibrillator. She checked she had her Monocular-AI and looked the part, her bow over her back and her arrows. She had taken the heavy pack down to the bottom of the plateau and hidden it under a stone ledge, she would use it as a stash and carry it to her cavern in due time.

She walked fast through the valley, the snow had accumulated on the ground and her footfall crushed the slosh and ice the sound slightly echoing from the mineralized rocks, the cloud low and grey, she could hear water dripping at the edge of the forest from the massive trees into the nettle floor sounding like drips from a distant giant's leaking shower. *Now. Wouldn't that be something, a hot shower instead of a cold wash in the river?*

She thought quickly that that could maybe be a possibility, the gas containers from the toilet could heat the water from the camping stove, and there was an outward hose connection for a shower, having a dual purpose in the field. *I have to get that toilet up and running,* she thought, traversing a collection of fallen logs at the end of the valley. The driving force was still within her and she couldn't explain the enhanced motivation,

"Yes," she wanted to rescue them all but she had this force within her that seemed to course through her system, like a drug. She felt like a walking white-board of directives and plans, emotionless but a sure and exquisitely programmed

171

android at the same time. "Was that the effect of the awakening, how she knew she was Ye-Min again and not a Huntress?, was this Cryo-sleep shit affecting her still?," she thought about it, but it didn't worry her, in effect her white-board self was in command for now. It seemed to lament subconsciously,

"Secure their safety and well-being for the Winter, then you must prepare to leave"

The stick village came into view as she traversed the forest boundary, smoke was rising and the blackened Explorer seemed to greet her with evolutionary reverence as she entered the outer limits of the Tribal enclave. She and Katie looked for Tom but the village only revealed where he had been, the ground had blood on the sand and there was the smell of piss and shit where they had left him to fend for himself, injured and alone.

She checked her anger and told herself that she too was part of this debasement and continued to search beyond the village boundary during the course of the day but they found nothing and returned to stand looking at Tom's miserable hut watching the others pack and secure the surviving equipment into the terrain crates they had discovered in the marsh.

Looking around at signs that someone else could have been there and found shoe prints, exo-boot prints that were relatively fresh and realised that someone had been there, as the tribe didn't wear exo-suit boots. She knelt down and looked at the place where Tom had been and saw the prints there and signs something was dragged. *Tom,* she instantly thought. and followed the prints the best she could then stood at the marsh edge and looked into the forest. *"Mono, is there any way you can tell me if there was anyone else here the last few nights, an AI device or anything like that?,"* she asked.

"Affirmative, Karl-AI was here, the tower logged an entry as required when AI are operating in the area. The drone was above the camp for thirty minutes. Karl-AI is ten miles from this position and was recently accessed in emergency mode" She looked around excited by the news. *"By whom?,"* she asked through her headset. *"Tanya Geary, Ate Succession Logistics and Supply Officer, last logged in five days ago, 0934:32.* She wheeled around with a smile. *"So, it was Tanya and she saved him,"* she thought. *"Where are they now, can you access Karl-AI?" "Affirmative, please wait..."* She looked up at the sky and waited with nervous breath. *"Karl has replied.* The mono said. *"Tanya Geary, Tom Auer and Jason Findus have left the continent on a marine vessel. Tanya with Karls' help secured Tom from the village in a nighttime operation assisted by Karl.*

First Aid and care was given, he was in satisfactory condition when they made camp and when they were on the vessel. Jason tried to access Karl-AI and contact was made with the others, he met with Tanya and Tom and they alighted on the yacht together. Karl was made to stay for others' use and care as they had Cox-AI with them. Tanya Geary was uninjured. At that stage they were aware of the threat of the other crew members who were hostile and left to secure their safety."

"Cox-AI, what's that?," she asked, concentrating, looking in the distance as the mono piped the information and watching the sheepish looks of Donghyun and Akseli cleaning the area. *"Advanced First-Aid and Doctor AI, that comes with.. "* She interrupted the mono remembering the device that was in their aid kit on the Explorer. "Yes, I remember, sorry go on.." *"The four left over three weeks ago"*

She saw Katie approaching from the far side of the village and waited till she came and stood in front of her, she seemed different. *"Where the fuck am I, Ye-Min?,"* she said looking at her with troubled confusion, then down at her grass sedge coat with alarm. "What am I doing here? Ye-Min grabbed and embraced her, the realisation of it sinking in, she felt elated. "Welcome back, Katie," she said leaning to look Katie in the eyes, *"I am very happy to have my First Officer with me again, now listen very carefully"*

25

Ye-Min, traversed the plain in the freezing wind, but she didn't really feel cold. Through the driving sleet, which twined off her exosuit and cap and the water streaking her eyes like a windscreen, she saw in the distance like a lost city, the escarpment and the cavern that was her home, with the water pool and the paintings of a history gone and a future perhaps, and the grain tree that had been planted there on purpose above the roof with the skylight. The massive rock ledge that seemed to grow from the sands loomed high and portent, with wind swept mist scaling off the sides in eddies within the gloom of the late night.

The grass she trod on with precision was partly frozen and the pebbles crushed sure under her feet, now under her exosuit boots she had secured from the crates they had found hidden in the gully in the now defunct stick village, laying there while the past Tribe huddled in cold and hunger five metres away.

The final path to her home was a winding rock-filled area around the wall and behind was the entrance, a smaller landing of smooth stone and small cracks, a welcoming mould to the mighty cavern inside. As she winded her way at the wall's base, water dripped down from above and streaked the sides of the stone, the sound of the sleet hitting the ground arrayed and echoed against the rocks. Despite the cloud, the three moons were shining the cloud above, and strange mottled shadows caressed the rock like a puppet shadow show, cast from the low lying shrubs at the basalt wall.

The crew had been secured and part of her task had been completed. They would now be safe as they woke up one by one from the pheromones effects. The caves on the coast would be safe and warm with their terrain gear including the excellent B-Brown and now they had Karl, the AI drone.

They had tried to track her with Karl-AI but she had hacked Karl and changed his permissions. Her monocular AI was proving much smarter than she realised, the useful monocular, the military device for long-range scouting and reconnaissance. She thought about the rush to get the mission from Earth underway at the time and their equipment in some ways, in terms of its composition, resembled a traveller's emergency suitcase, stuffed with the most useful items quickly. There was gold in the deposits of equipment left and the Monocular was one of them.

She entered the cavern and her feet echoed in the Geologically scared place as she passed the rock bowl, water flowing into the pool, the water clear with the reflection of her fusion lamp that lit the area like a gallery, within a Giant's living room. She reached the inner cavern before the next more open section that contained a stone partition cut expertly in a way that the air inside the larger cavern did not disperse to the roof skylight section, the stone floor lower there past the ancient temperature controller, the cavern's temperature stable, the roof and skylight gallery more susceptible to the cold and elements.

She had set up her bed and items in a corner that was concave within the massive wall, a small tent size blister. Her bow lent against the wall, she was reluctant to discard it, her arrows in her silver container, her past on display. Her tablet was set up so she could see the screen propped on a stick base, the table, a few petrified logs of minerals from the grass plain that were laying not far from the entrance, now her ancient table, her ancient office.

The wireless power from the fusion battery set in a depression on the face of the wall was unlimited and secure and she had an uplink to the satellite, thanks to the tower. She dropped her pack against the wall, and set the monocular AI down beside her tablet, her *operations* gear, upon a fossil table. She had secured a small fusion heater and she turned it on, the ball of heat on a stand radiated and shone like a giant bulb illuminating the space into an increasing yellow light. She looked around, nothing had been disturbed, no one had been there, she could tell, and she smelt the air in the cavern, *"No human smell,"* she assessed, inhaling deeply, and raising her head towards the roof, her eyes closed like a person that had finally got the good news instead of the constant annoying. The smell was the same. *"Just me,"* she thought, exhaling and opening her eyes to look down again at her enclave. The sound of the water pouring into the massive stone urn in the centre of the cavern, the rock aqueduct feeding the urn like a marine finger, echoed slightly in the rock around her, the massive water feature surrounded by a stone bench step-up for ancient legs which had worn the stone over immense time.

The drip of water within the roof area she could hear, and beyond the wind and the plain, a slight hiss to contrast the cavern stillness and faint echo. She could smell the grain that had slid into expertly crafted stone wells that shielded the seeds and preserved them in some encrusted salt mixture at a set temperature and shielded them from moisture as they fell from the grain tree above the roof skylight, and rolled down sloped edges into the cavern.

Pondering the construction of the cavern, she had crouched at one stage, digging out the grain to see the condition of the seeds at the bottom and discovered the desiccated grain sifted when old through a series of cracks slightly larger than the seed into the stone and away to some unknown mediterranean vent.

When following the wall in her explorer way when she discovered the cavern, a small corridor that descended below, the air rising from the space below the corridor, hidden behind a another section of thin rock which opened to an oval space where the grain seeds fell, from below the grain storage wells the seed hot to the touch as she filtered some grain though her fingers, crouching to see the floor a dispersed field of a million husks.

Sweeping husks aside and felt the stone, almost hot, which was cooking the husks in a slow crock-pot fashion, the heat rising and warming the roof area, and dispersing up through the corridor, the Earth's heat below, the caverns natural heater and temperature stabiliser, the husks a smell of fibre, a calming odour that she inhaled and tested with the OTAA, the analysis showing that the husks were absorbing moisture and toxins from the air, toxins she was surprised to see that included tiny amounts of Polonium, a highly radioactive element that was also present in Earth's atmosphere.

The smell the mineral perfume of the rock and crafted stone, a slate, and basalt thyme potion, the outside sedge grass and the sleet, a frozen sure steady beat of ice raspiness and the scent from the plain proper, the sand and the coastal salt that hinted here with the winds. She knew that creatures had lived here once and an intelligent considered creature had made this place with care and regard for the occupants, and had provided water and food, and an air conditioned living space, then turned to art for history and had entered history and left the art.

Her office chair was also petrified stone, a small stool shaped rock, on top a piece of cut terrain blanket. She sat and donned her headset, the Monocular AI connected to the tablet flashed a message on the tablet screen:

INDENT   message   received   21:34:05   Satellite uplink--1224656

Jessica Nueuer, 657563 Ate Succession Ecologist
LifeBoat Drone: Iris_AI 89897
Insertion: successful: ∅   Current   Location: 152.6765, -45.874375

Another message flashed,

IDENT message received 21:38:32 Satellite uplink-1224656
Andreas Polkinghorn, 2344678 *Ate Succession Mission Doctor*

LifeBoat Drone: Gerrard_AI 89897
Insertion Successful ⊘ Current Location: 9.676654° S 8.899886° E

The Satellite's information was basic, a log that just informed whether the LifeBoats were successful in landing. *Doesn't mean they are alive, both Jessica and Andreas had abandoned ship after the Ate Succession left orbit.* She thought about Jessica's chances past the range and into the interior, a completely different challenge. Andreas had landed in the ocean between the continent they were on and the great landmass further East.

The pheromone entered her mind, she turned as if she was mad then realising the communication was coming translated through her headset, the Mono had translated. "Mono, what is this?," she asked in a growing alarm. *"There is communication incoming, I have translated the message from a chemical trace into plain English text, shall I communicate the message?"*

"Yes, of course, is it from the others?" *"Negative, the source is not from our communication systems, it comes from the chemical trace marker that is within this cavern,"* The Mono replied. She listened as the Mono translated and spoke through her headset, not quite understanding its source and looking around the cavern as if she could to see the message. *"Is someone doing a Hexibarber on me?,"* she thought.

"Ye-Min, your species here is now safe. We awoke you to accomplish this task. In time all your crew members will awake, this takes some time. Our intention was not to kill,

179

rather disable. Your Starship was the greatest threat, Bipeds in numbers are a dangerous force, your planet is a good example of what humans in numbers can do to an environment. This will not happen here."

The Fifth Universe Robots have secured this planet for now. The Universal Sentient Element, the Noble gas, protects us from the Energy Android threat. The element has been dispersed within the planet's atmosphere and alters all life that are within this biosphere. You are no exception, but time will tell us how you develop and what you and your companions are capable of. We ask for your help, as there are some things we cannot do. In return, you and your companions will be given a choice whether to help in combating the Universe's greatest threat, or leaving this planet with your own designs. Our way is not coercion or slavery, hostile we are but intelligent enough to understand the power of asking. We do however offer a trade for this choice, and this is not negotiable." She continued to listen transfixed with the entity.

"There is a network card within the desert interior. It is located on the distant plain. The hardware, when placed inside a certain type of android will activate that android. You will find the android at a location we have provided, a beacon will guide you to this device. The hardware was lost in our war many aeons ago, the androids discarded the hardware as a consequence of an organic weapon directive. Only now do we know the location of the last remaining hardware card.

This is a critical small first step to securing the freedom of the rest of the androids on the plain. The androids are lost Energy Androids that attempted to colonise our world and were defeated with our organic weapons. They currently inhabit the plain and are in effect mad and uncontrolled, hostile and dangerous. If they are made allies, then we can secure their freedom and they will work for us against the Energy Androids.

180

If you secure the hardware and activate the droid we will allow you a choice to help us or leave. The second beacon will guide you after this. The droid is needed to release the androids on the plain from their madness, the Archivist will guide you in this matter. Two of your companions are still on distant areas of the planet. Your Ecologist Jessica Neuer is travelling back to this area via the course of the interior river, we suggest you continue to her after you have secured the hardware. Your companion Andreas Polkinghorn is in a distant Archipelago within a Citadel, you will be reunited with him in time. Do you agree and understand?" The alien voice seemed to echo, the narrative ended.

She digested the information, partly aghast and partly shocked. "Ahh, that is a big request, I.." *"The hardware card for your freedom if you choose it,"* the alien piped. "Can I ask some questions?," she replied. *"Of course,"* the mono piped through her headset. "So it was you who awoke me?" *"Yes, to ensure your friends safety. They would have died in the elements otherwise, or succumbed to disease, or themselves."* "And *Hexibarber* was your idea?" *"No, you adapt well,"* the alien replied. "And the fifth Universe?. The *alloy, the sentient element,* why is this here, what are the Energy androids doing?," she asked.

"Within the Fifth Universe and beyond, the robots are able to combat their toxicity due to the sentient element noble gas; otherwise known as the alloy. This was their makers' last act before they reached the pinnacle of their evolutionary timeline entering an unknown void of time, passing to their Robots the code and knowledge. Without the noble gas, the Universe's mass will be consumed and converted to energy only.

The Robots gave us the alloy, a protection for the planet from the conversion of mass to energy. The alloy has many properties, one gives all life on this world a sentient construct and protection from the threat, but in time even the alloy, a

181

standalone defence without the power of the Fifth Universe will not be enough.

We have defeated the Androids in open combat and saved our world, they are unable to counter the use of our organic chemicals, despite their enormous energy power, so they have their weaknesses, but it is a small battle won within an ever present war waged upon mass within the Universe. The Androids rarely enter into open conflict, their way is covert insertion and infection.

We suspect that your world's mass has been slightly altered by their hand which would explain the rapid volcanism. Most of their threat comes from this type of insidious slow conversion of mass within galaxies. They have developed a sentient code within the laws of what you call Physics that is able to direct and control energy, something that we as yet do not fully understand. With the code they can physically change mass to energy in the form of whole planets and stars themselves.

That is why the Fifth Universe is the last bastion within time itself, after the other Universes are consumed, the Quantum boundary will shrink and time itself will grow cold. The Robots seed new stars in gas clouds to allow new worlds to form to slow the process but they are few, although immaculate and seemingly immortal.

The Androids grow immense energy and harvest the power to create Super-Android models and starships, and vast complexes of quantum computing power; they are in effect a Supercomputer race beyond imagining. If they are not stopped they will consume everything, they seem to have no conscious nor purpose beyond energy creation and mass destruction, literally. The only way to combat such immense energy and computing power is to step down the evolutionary ladder and use the most ancient organic weapons; their potency still untapped, this is why we prevailed.

We ask every species we can to combat the threat, bipeds have certain uses. If you choose to help us you will add to our weaponry we have. Before that can happen the hardware must be inserted into the android's brain, this is a first small step. The hardware card for your freedom if you choose it."

She looked at the cavern roof. *"Talk about being under pressure,"* she thought. "Yes, yes, of course I will do it, but what type of freedom are you offering?" *"Transit from this planet, you may access your Starship, we will help you travel to the ship but it cannot return here"* the alien replied. "Deal," she said, not really sure about anything but knowing her options were limited. *"If I don't do this then I am an alien dinner, I suppose,"* she thought. *"Very well, follow the beacon, we will contact you at that location"* the alien replied. *"Transmission has ended,"* the Mono piped. "Sweet planetary divide, Mono, what do you say, want to take a trip to find an android?," she asked the AI. "Affirmative," the Mono piped deadpan.

She was loath to leave her place here in the cavern. She walked around and looked one last time at the paintings, and caressed her fingers across the stone and ochre patterns, the images and the texture of the drawings that shone in the morning light. She looked up at the grain tree, its branches swaying slightly in the morning breeze, the pods hanging, some split and grain falling, some new and green and swaying. She thought long after she was gone there would be others here in the same place, like a museum on a different day in the same space. The water would still be flowing into the urn and the grain falling into the store and the Polonium would still be absorbed and the cavern the same temperature. She was like an exhibition moving out and then stored away, waiting for another opportunity, but she suspected that storage would not be her fate.

The land beyond the plain stretched in sand and grain to the horizon. The range in the West rose high and specific, part of a small tectonic plate grinding the terrain upwards into snow capped peaks. She walked through the rock valley, a myriad of broken rock formations and shards of eroded boulders strewn and wet from the snow that fell around, in a moderate tempo, casting white and frozen.

The wind whipped stronger beyond but she was protected for now on the valley path, a worn used stone patchwork of basalt, a garden path, a chicken run of sorts from the grass sedge plain to the Desert proper, a dry desiccated forgotten sandpit. Cast around, small boulders rested upon one another, balancing and worn like tired travellers sitting to rest but then trapped and fossilised. The sky above was grey but the bank of clouds broke scattered above the Desert in the distance and she could see sun patches striking the land beyond like torch beams and lightened sand areas.

She scanned above, the valley rising like a colosseum, the spectators pointed boulders and finger struts of wrinkled stone, the small shrubs breaking the rock surfaces where their roots had established, and wedged cracks and dark crevasses. She could see that the wind was high above as the trees at the top of the valley swayed and the snow blew straighter. She was comforted by the Monocular AI in her holster close to her chest and she wore the headset so she always had a link to the intelligence. She had chosen to leave her bow behind, a gift to the gallery but she had a black handled hunting knife that was easily accessible, strapped to her leg, a survival item from the Explorer supplies. She wore a terrain suit but felt like she could go naked and still be ok, her environmental toughness unexplained, a supreme-being, fitness assured, alert, clear thinking. She thought about how much weight she had lost, but her puppy fat was gone, replaced by muscle and form.

The Alien intelligence had told her to cross the mineral sands and follow the river that winded around the range against the flow; she would traverse the terrain by the banks and try to reach the hardware card and the android. Approximately halfway between them and then a trek further into the continent interior North was a signal, a beacon which she had saved on her tablet, the one tone location beacon transmitting every ten seconds. *"Could I change my mind about this?,"* she mused. She thought not.

26

"Greetings, updates, kindness, sorrow, inquiry, confirmation, status, injury, swarm status,deaths. Pheromone dispersed the core target molecule and infected the species. Trace chemical, the biomarker, the nutrient transmitter set. The chief target has dispersed. Lateral spread is not necessary, the virus has selected" The Beetles sang silently with the chemical.

"Core and Clock, tempered strike, combine eye, salted nymph, the Alpha mite,

Plain of salt, pull of tide, set the wing a pool of time, Tempered stem and exo-skin, fall of star and hostile wing"

Above, the light reflected red hues and darting slivers and shone down on the blue-black ten winged carapaces arranged circular and antennae attached through the water to the lower stem, their appendages casting purple hue shadows and reflected stone from the inner walls of the valley. The bromeliads spread protecting the core, a marker itself, an engineered hybrid that transfused the chemical protection with microbial mist and tangent direction, enveloping the beetles and surrounding the trunk, setting like a double rimmed water stem and connecting the pheromone, a defence marker and set a clear hostile cocktail to protect the swarm within the meeting.

The ten transversed, the array of antennae and appendage turned individually clockwise then anticlockwise, the movement a vibration and set of coxar, slight of feeler and shine of carapace, within the stem the water infused and set with the transmitter chemical, the patches of light filtering a splaying across the open flower and down to the semi-submerged fluid, specks of debri adrift and water warming with the friction of time itself. The shapes stopped moving and aligned the tempered stem, their pretarsus touching the fibre floor of the stem, tibia and tarsi bent and vibrating securely. From time to time the individual released their elytra, an opening to reveal the hind wings, superhydrophobic adapted, glistening within the fluid, ancient marine memories from a primordial pool and rare ocean current, the abdomen adrift in sediment then closing again to hide all but their Pterothorax, the green silver section near the wing shaped triangular and marker-like, a timeless beacon of adaptation.

The chemical was released again and set within the channel.

"Planetary machine, the other is aligned within the ancient cortex continent. The Bromeliad origin?" The beetles chemical sang in unison,*"Rotund pool, the ancient source, jungle vine and tempest fish"*...The chemical realigned and dispersed,*"Female and machine sentient, but adrift.*

They will find the alien path.The five are set?" The Beetles shifted and turned a slow slant, still arrayed in spiky clock fashion around the central stem. In unison the chemical voice cast the reply from the ten arrayed: *"The five is sufficient. The stone has been located. The chemical Beetle sent to the carer.*

The desert and river is a patient portent
They have a target destination. Assumption set, the spurious targets can be groomed according to instinctual movement."

The Beetles sang:

"Time the stem, the pools and pull, terrain a sphere, Bromeliad home and stone flat tide,
Species set and ancient wing, nymph of ocean salt array, the sediment ply

The robot chant and pheromone sky,
Archaeal lament, biachondria synthesis, Universe marker,
Phylotype the transfusion potent, sediment charter,

187

Species tempered, exit fly"

The ten released from the central stem, and took one pace back from the flower stem, raising their compound eyes skyward, then raising their palpus momentarily. The first Beetle released its elytron wing covers and set swimming expertly through the murky water and bursting out from the central stem portion surface tension and away to the canopy sky, foaming the surface as the others replicated the flight, one by one rising, leaving the portion and the meeting temple, the water soothing and milling with the exit, the air heavy with evolutionary portent and meandering liquid from the flower, the canopy shifting to reveal the green sky at moments the soft hazy whisper and flutter of wings and carapace descending and fleeing the tree tops in soldier swarm formation their sentinels aligned and exiting across the plain arrayed in centurion formation through the rocky fissure terrain and across the storm laden horizon.

27

She knew that the entity had given her ability and kept her wits, it had entered her mind but had not corrupted her, she still had her past knowledge of the Tribe and the mission, she was still Ye-Min, the Astrophysicist, be it a revised version Ye-Min.

She looked at the ground as she entered the sandpit arena, a vast dust bowl untouched by the snow which had stopped falling she noticed, the dust dry and a higher temperature milled within the sands and filtered dust, seemingly heated from below. Her footfall broke the dust like a moon surface, millions of years of dedication and powdered torment into fine particles that filtered upwards with each step in small clouds of plume.

Out on the dust field she felt more exposed and looked back towards the coast, the weather milling and variable, black clouds and falling snow. The mini-climate here was an odd tempest of dry air and eddies of freezing pockets of air mixed with the occasional warm monsoon wind, all swirling together like an ocean between the seasons and shallow shore waters where currents swam warm and cold together tricking the swimmer with surprise warm patches and cold tricks. The wind here was milder, she noticed and wafted rather than gusted, the dust rose sometimes with eddies and settled again as if the particles had a terrain magnet under the sand.

She stopped and looked towards the West horizon, un-holstered the AI and looked through the lens to the distant vista. Distant trees dotted the horizon and small dust vortexes rose into the sky and twirled fiercely like dancers on the plain. The sandpit broke wide and the AI had a readout of distance and direction on the heads up display.

"What's your take on this dust area Mono?" *"Very bizarre, Ye-Min, the climate within the bowl is different, it is very dry here and warmer"* She thought about how they had not seen any large animals on the planet so far, *"Were the aliens large?,"* she mused." She re-holstered the Mono, and walked on, the dust bowl she estimated to be about five kilometres round, the section behind her meandering off into the rocky valley, in front, widening to the Desert and she judged the coarse mineral sand of the interior.

The dust bowl started to dissipate after about an hour's walking, the interior was a vast sandy Desert as far as she could see, but ahead lay the meandering river that ran against her path and she set course according to Mono's coordinates to intercept its line. She noticed the distant range was now behind her and to her right, and figured it was that terrain that created the desert, blocking the moist winds in some weather construct model she didn't understand.

"The river is three kilometres, NNW, it flows slowly here after the run from the giant ancient volcanic mound that dominates the area for four thousand kilometres," Mono reported.

Her first sighting of the rodent was in the distance, a dog sized animal, covered in fur and scuttling fast across the sand, kicking sand up behind it like a stuck four wheel drive, disappearing into a rocky outcrop in the distance that was covered in thorny shrubs and pillars of straight basalt that seemed to be a volcanic remnant.

"Wow, did you see that Mono?" *"Affirmative, looks like a large alien rodent type of animal,"* "Giant rats, that's scary Mono," she said, reaching for her knife and feeling its position close to her leg. *"It ran from you though, that is a good sign,"* Mono stated. She stopped and lay prone in the sand, noticing its warmth, taking Mono and looking through the lens, the animal had stopped within the rock field and seemed to have forgotten about the danger, and was eating some leaves off the

190

thorny shrubs, its fur, brow-white and mottled grey, a pointed snout and two high ears like a rabbit.

As she gazed at it, others suddenly appeared, from behind the other rocks, a pack of them coursed through the outcrop eating the leaves and stopping and raising themselves up on their hind legs to smell the air. There were smaller sized animals, which looked like their young which followed and mimicked their parents.

She shuffled in the sand stretching her leg, thinking about the animals, watching through the AI at the creatures who were scuttling through the rock formation, perhaps thirty or so, the shrubs swaying above the rocks where they ate and were making contact with the plants moving through. Beyond the formation the mineral sands stretched away to the horizon but she thought she could see the distant river bank, some taller shrubs growing there and dotting the otherwise sand vista.

Laying prone, the wind wafted over her with the same warmer air, some broken cloud was above in contrast to the coastal malay of sleet and storm. "Let's hope they are vegetarian Mono," she said, seeing one of the animals chewing on some leaves through the monoscope. *"Four legs but uses a front set to grab and eat, I would definitely say vegetarian,"* Mono offered.

The long snout extended to a black nose, the fur grey and white splotches, the creature's feet now grasping the branches looking padded with claws extending, with a good set of incisor teeth, she could see as it desiccated the leaves expertly. *"With a frightening set of teeth for a vegetarian,"* she said, continuing to watch the mouth movement of the creature, now and then a few teeth would show through the mass of green mouthful.

The rat species moved away after the feed and shuffled to a rock protrusion in the sand which she realised, as they disappeared, was a burrow entrance concealed with some low lying shrubs. The little ones scuttled in first, the parents watching the surrounding area on their hind legs to get height in the guarding behaviour, looking as though they smelt her but for the moment content she was far enough away. The parents followed and the desert became empty again, only the wind could be heard above the river's wash. She rose and holstered the AI, and set out again for the river, content that the creatures seemed docile enough for her to risk being seen.

At the river's edge she looked towards the distant range to the right, the flow of the water snake winding away and disappearing into the horizon mist. The river was wide, *"Probably thirty metres across,"* she thought, as she stood on the bank, the semi-ice flow swirling with topped pancake ice paddies and flotsam arrayed and washing into the foaming water. The river flow had created small sturdy heaped islands of stone in the centre and she thought they may be good places to energy-tent for the night given the slow pace of the river. There was a large island about ten metres in the middle with a convenient shallow walk through the water. *"It may give me some peace of mind about animals,"* she mused, given they had finally discovered larger creatures.

Washed her hands, the water freezing but refreshing after the dust bowl and dry sand. From the high embankment she could see out across the sand, small rising dunes but mostly flat, a billiard table of sparkling sand when the light was higher contrasting the darkened sky. Taking the pack off and gently lowering it to the ground thinking it felt quite light, and expecting it to be heavier, and then thinking also for a moment that she had dropped something.

Instinctively felt her knife strapped to her leg which was secure as she rummaged through the pack, in a moment content all was there, nothing lost. Beyond the embankment was a stone formation, creating a sort of arrayed arrangement hippies would get excited about. *"A Druid's paradise,"* she mused, as she looked towards it the grey stone fractured in places, smooth in others, three large pillars of rock resembled a buried hand with fingers protruding from beneath the sand. She walked out between the river and the formation about ten metres away and scanned with the AI in a three -sixty arc pointed towards the horizon.

A faint tempo within the ground could be heard as she queried of Mono, the AI hesitating then directing her gaze out across the sands in the direction of the light thumping. She could see through the glass, at full zoom and resolution, a white plume on the horizon, small puffs of some detritus. The sound increased having the same tempo and the plume enlarged and two shapes became apparent within the glass view, the AI calculating the speed of the figures in the heads-up display and the current wind conditions that favoured travel from that direction.

They became running shapes, then as the figures became more discernible and defined with the light she realised they were giant ground birds of some type, their massive strong legs pumping the ground, perfectly balanced and striding slightly side to side with each movement of their thighs, the long necks became a massive skull and large wide beak with a pointed end that curved with species intent, the heads steady with the fast gait and looking at her it seemed from that distance, knowing their target audience.

"I suggest we find suitable cover," mono had said as the birds traversed two hundred metres distant. She quickly grabbed her pack and then it became clear they had misjudged the speed and distance and mono simply said *"Run!!"* She dashed towards the nearest formation of rocks, the three large pillars of basalt rising thirty metres from the sands. creating a sort of arrayed arrangement hippies would get excited about. She ran with surprising speed given the weight of her pack, her legs pumping the sand as she looked back, the now huge tall creatures she calculated to be four metres in height, aligned for

obvious attack, the two splitting slightly to flank any escape from the sides.

She made the formation as the birds entered the different coloured sands where the stones were protruding, a darker texture about a fifty metres away. One of the creatures gave a blood curdling screech, its jaws opened, a sound, a combination of burning tyres on asphalt and grinding metal, as it targeted her and charged, the other held back expertly, presumably to cut off any potential escape. Terrified, she looked frantically around the inner sand maze where the pillar's trunks rose from the sand. The huge bird braked as it reached the stones, she noticed its shadow as it blocked the light, its bulk too big to run through the inner formation, it wildly slashed down with its neck, with flying coloured feathers the long throat and adorned skull thin enough to access the space between the pillars, smashing the sands in an unsuccessful strike at her, the beak only about a metre away, sending a large plume of sand airborne with its mighty front ripping hook, and shaking the rock formation.

She screamed and flayed widely, running ahead searching for more shelter." *"Second pillar, the crack to the right,"* mono piped with a rasp that emitted from the headset, running in a short darting burst, crouching slightly in terror and running full speed into the space and finding the section in the fissure furthest to the rear where something small could hide.

From out of the fissure the bird raised its head again, two massive feathers coasted down from the sky that had been dislodged by the force of the strike, probably by scraping the stone. The colours belied the event a display in themselves, green, blue, red, orange, yellow and mauve striated patterns where the feathers interleaved on a thick feather stem, clear and light. The two light feathers drifted down and settled on the formation floor, one propped near some stone like a display.

194

There was a scurried thumping, and she realised the bird had run to the other side of the formation, both birds were furiously nuzzling the gaps between the pillars sending sand flying, the cling of the bigger stones striking the pillars like a demeted xylophone. She was the insect, they were the giant hunters, and at that moment she realised what being potential prey actually meant, she squashed further into the fissure as if to pretend she was a rock and wished it so.

They gave up on her after one bird smashed the rock crack with a beak strike and seemingly hurt itself, sounding alarmed and backing away, they knew what solid rock was and retreated, her shrinking like a darting and hiding cockroach within a crevice, trying to preserve its life from a kitchen giant. One of the birds attempted a few follow up searching and probing pecks on the stone, coming back around the side she fled from, the strikes a harsh chisel scraping sound of the tough beak, the breath coursing from the birds nostrils in loud rasps, the creature placing its imposing large eye to the opening of the formation and looking at her, knowing exactly where she was with a yellow orb surrounded by a green Iris, a super clear cornea glistening in the dim light and belying the danger of the beauty.

The other bird was chortling in its chicken like fashion, she assumed some sort of communication as they retreated and ran fast off across the sands again as if they had detected something moving. She sat still frozen with shock and didn't move, her safe crack echoing her short breaths, her hand on the knife instinctively. She could see outside through the formation and saw them running and swerving trying to catch something else. At one stage one of the birds hacked at a small shrub's trunk until it fell, then used its super powerful legs to dig the roots out and was turning over the sand having found something below.

They caught one of the rodent creatures shortly after and she watched frozen and terrified through the crack in the basalt as they literally tore the animal apart, about ten metres away, skinning it in effect after crushing its skull with a force from the beak she could only shake in fear from, the brain of the rodent exploding in a watermelon red misting blood combustion effect, the body going limp for a moment and then one of the birds flaying the carcass from side to side the skin peeling off and the head dissecting from the body is a sickening crunch, the head now resembling a sack of crushed crimson red berries.

The ripping power of the bird's beak seemed limitless as the innards were consumed with fast pecks and swallows as the birds tilted their heads skywards to increase the downward flow of intestines and organ parts down their gullets. Their faces became red with blood, the trails of gore running down their beaks and dripping fresh into the sand.

The true purpose of the *beak hook* which curved downward from the tip of the creature's beak, and up toward its throat became apparent as the hook tore flesh effectively from the prey like a sailor-makers darning needle applied to tissue paper. Once dissected and ripped, they ate as though food was a new discovery, bones still glistening with blood was all that remained after about ten minutes, scattered ripped fur arrayed the culinary carnage, in small mounds like scalped heads, the birds bent over the kill still pecking up small pieces of flesh that had been ejected around during the frenzy.

Still living organs were eaten whole, she saw the heart gulped like a grape, the liver she assumed was glistening in the light, slippery with blood, this was pecked apart for some reason, and bits of it shared, she assumed a delicacy. In a final display of instinctive terror one of the birds stood on the bones and scratched the carcass apart, sending individual bones flying into the sand beyond, until the bone frame was no more, only a desiccated skeleton.

She didn't move for an hour and became her own therapist within the fissure, she had been shaking like a shell-shocked veteran for a time which subsided as the Monocular-AI made light of the moment in sarcastic but strangely calming comments, such as *"Well, that's a new approach to rat control"* and *"No chance of Chicken tonight then"* She had talked to the AI for some time as the afternoon subsided, the area growing colder and the snow falling as predicted in the late afternoon, with associated flurries and later ice-prisms that floated down through the pillars of stone creating an impression of a Shakespeare play.

She decided, crouching in the fissure, and waiting out any potential ambush by the *"Terror Birds,"* she mused, that now that the birds had a name, she decided that that the Monocular needed a name. "So you are a male AI construct aren't you Monocular?," she asked. *"Yes, male, military version male I would say,"* the eyepiece replied. "Ok, so, let's see, ah, ummm, ok, I now name you, Cyclops" *"Cyclops?,"* the AI replied inquiringly. "Don't ask, that's your name now" *"Very well, thank you Min, but can I ask, it's not a derogatory term is it?"* "Certainly not!," she replied, and that was that, the AI was now a named construct and saw fit not to question further. After some time Cyclops suggested they emerge, she was glad of it and they made camp within the saving formation of stone as the three moons rose above and then were obscured in low fast cloud as she attached the fusion battery to her tent and the dome shone shadows on the rock pillars like lights from cars in a tunnel.

28

The next day it dawned freezing and she folded her energy tent away, inside the rock formation safe from the *Terror Birds*, as she had called them. The new day dispelled her fantasies of a warmer interior of the planet, the snow set hard against the river bank distant and the temperature had dropped on the desert like a rude awakening, the mineral sands now with companion ice and a snow coat. She used Cyclops to scan the area, the birds were not around.

Walking out from the pillars and over to the far side of the inner formation, squatted over the small hole as she passed her stool. The elongated piece looked like a strange sea creature all muscled and bubbly hard and set. *"That's it?,"* she thought, *"Five days of diet, where does it all go?,"* she wondered as it was apparent that was her bowel movement for the day. She rose and wiped her behind with a rag she had for the purpose, after washing it, she kept it in a small recycling container from the Bee-Brown, which was designed to assist in nappy disposal, the canister being manufactured from a molecular disinfectant, an artificial atom bond structure developed by the *Bee-Brown* labs.

Stored the rag, and wiped her hands in alcohol from a small bottle, grabbed her pants, pulled them up, securing the exo-skin suit lower section with the velcro from her coat. The freezing air on her legs was refreshing rather than uncomfortable, she knew the air temperature was around fifteen below zero Celsius, a quick calculation telling her five degrees fahrenheit.

Feeling strong and definitely changed, her mind was clear and her body felt strong, in addition she was shitting strong shit, something that reminded her of a story by an author at home about a trek across a desert on a camel. She filled the hole with a piece of flat palm-sized stone she carried with her, a piece of shale type metamorphic rock, which had proven useful as a shovel, a poo shovel, but also had a sharp edge she used to cut things after a wash of the piece in the river. *"Hygiene is paramount,"* a reminder daily. *I have to keep clean and free of infection.* The consequences, especially on an unknown planet could be the end of her.

Breath coursed from her warm interior in great plumes, vapour from a chimney and the air a shocking inhale of frigid oxygen. The river had some ice pancakes flowing but the slight warmth from the landmass she assumed kept it from freezing. There were some surrounding pools of mineral hot spring water that bubbled and foamed around the rocks, steaming in the morning air., and she could see distant plumes suggesting the area was volcanic. The cloud was low and sweeping and the desert surrounds quite apart from the river flow, a slow lament of water and stone, through the bordering steep river banks, she could see as if the river was bragging about how high it could get in flood.

The remains of the rodent creature that the birds had forgotten presumably to consume was by the rock where she had skinned some of it, the meat was delicious and the OTAA had passed it, good protein and minerals, with a surprise, the meat contained what the OTAA had discovered as a new vitamin, it classed as **Experimental, B15a.**

"So what benefits does B15a give me Cyclops?," she asked, having the OTAA report through the Mono AI. She gazed out across the river as it winded its way towards the outer desert, the flow reflecting white and foam where the water broke the rocks and washed towards her position, *"I am now attuned now to the danger of giant wild chickens,"* she thought, the images still fresh in her mind of her flight and close call. The newly named Cyclops replied,

"Enhanced wound tolerance to environmental conditions, meaning increased healing capacity from trauma due to the

199

increased production of T-lymphocyte cell types and their subsequent proliferation into a wound site. Additionally, the vitamin promotes high oxygen levels by stimulating cell oxygen metabolism during vascular disruption which is critical for healing traumatised sites. Hypoxia within the traumatised site is predicted to be of short duration and therefore healing duration is reduced and potential site infection potentially considerably reduced "

"You don't say Cyclops, what does that all mean in layman's terms?," she said, blinking with partial understanding. *"Increased capacity to endure injury, with associated increase in recovery time after trauma,"* Cyclops replied, pausing then continuing,

"Additionally, because of your heightened fitness level and efficient uptake of vitamins and minerals and subsequent synthesis of nutrients due to the unknown transmitter within your neurophysical transport environment, you present as, well let's say in layman's terms , a tough increasingly adapted organism within the current environment" "Unknown transmitter?"she said, looking at Cyclops strapped in her holster, continuing to gaze past the river bank and scanning for the birds.

"Yes, there is a neurotransmitter active that is not within known human transport systems, something that is acting within your cortex stimulating unknown behaviours, this was established at your last blood test with Karl-AI when you were at the cave settlement" "Ok, good to know Cyclops, when was Karl going to tell me that?. *"Karl tried but the report was delayed due our exit and evasion from the others, Karl-AI has made the report available via the satellite transfer protocol, presumably in good faith for your information"*

She sat down adjusting her boots, the exo-skins orange soles catching some light in the freezing air and reflecting a little within the drab environment around her. She held Cyclops to her eye and scanned the area, there were no signs of the birds, she still couldn't believe the speed of the things as they ambushed her, the only thing saving her, the rock fissure in the nearby outcrop. She couldn't see how her being *"a tough increasingly adapted organism within the current environment"* would save her with these creatures, their intensity matched only by their physical strength and adapted beaks which seemed capable of crushing large stones.

Cyclops rasped in her headset, *"So, Min, I have to ask, Cyclops - what is the name's origin?"* "A very small predatory freshwater crustacean, like a tiny lobster. So Cyclops refers to its one eye, and *Cyclops* is taken from Greek Mythology, human civilisations stories about gods and monsters." she replied tongue in cheek. *"I see, I will try my best to live up to gods and monsters,"Cyclops* replied with the same tone.

She looked out across the plain and the sands, the river and the distant range, searching for *Terror Birds* , her senses attuned to danger, her nerves not settled after the close call yesterday, *"Being flayed alive is not how I want to go,"* she thought looking at Cyclops in the holster. She stood looking across the sands, and up against the river flow, it was freezing and the snow fall had stopped and the water on the ground had turned to ice in hard pools and the grass set brown and frozen like punk hair doo's and she didn't feel the touch of the ice and she wondered her fate for a moment. *"Why had she been the one to do this?"* She turned around looking like a nervous animal scanning the horizon.

"Cyclops, I know that this journey somehow is not going to be easy given the hazards we have already encountered, not mentioning the *Elephant* in the room, our friends the chickens," she said to Cyclops

"*Elephant?,"* Cyclops inquired. "Yes, an extinct creature, from Earth, very beautiful. I saw pictures, it's an expression, *"Elephant,* the creature was big, massive, *"Elephant in the room"* meaning you can talk around something but you can't ignore facts or a pertinent point that is usually the only point," she said looking at the frozen ground, trying to get a real idea of the creature she had read about and only seen pictures of. She remembered its long snout, and the cute baby Elephants with their parents in a herd crossing a savannah somewhere. *"Now it's all gone, and Earth too,"* she mused with clarity. *"I see,"* Cyclops replied. *'Elephant in the room,' I like this"*, the AI added.

She adjusted Cyclops on the frame, her radio headset now also a mount and Cyclops her second pair of eyes. "How's that?," she asked. *"Good, I can swivel three sixty on the mount so now I can advise you better,"* Cyclops piped in the radio. They followed the river in a Northerly direction as it winded through the mineral sands, they saw terror birds in the afternoon streaking across the plain in the distance and she hid behind the far bank so Cyclops could get an assessment, the birds fleeting away in a cloud of sand and dust to the horizon. *"They are turning away, off to the West,"* Cyclops assessed as she breathed in relief and continued upright on the far bank, the ice seemingly sounding off with the cold, puddles hard set and a light sleet falling around.

In places some metres from the river bank large pools of steaming hot spring water plumed in clouds the steam rising as if in surprise at the ambient temperature which was set she saw at minus twenty four degree Celsius, -31℉, her breath mimicking the freeze steam from the pools. She bent down reaching one, the water at just below boiling point, the rocks by the side of the pool warm, and she sat and unpacked her gear to wash her things.

A scan of the surrounding area revealed nothing threatening and she placed Cyclops on a rock so the mono could keep an eye out. Her hands in the exo-skin suit gloves were warm and she still was not troubled by the decreasing temperature in the mineralised desert that stretched to the horizon, only broken by the rivers path and her path against the flow. The fissure shaped pool had green algae on the sides slime and lichen that stuck to the sides like an unkept swimming pool, the steam wafting around, in places bubbles gurgled to the surface, the OTAA confirming Carbon Dioxide at safe levels.

She looked at Cyclops, perched on the rock above her position, the mono whirring as it scanned the area on the swivel. *"Cyclops, I now have the ability to communicate via chemical transfer, what do you think about that?"* *"I think you are bragging,"* he replied. She smiled, still looking at the Mono, *"I think I am changing, have changed,"* she said looking at the ground a little disturbed. *"Your adapting maybe, nothing lasts forever,"* Cyclops piped, the mono turning to look at her with its lens. *"What is Iris's latest report?"* *"Yes, just received actually, Jessica is stable and safe, but Iris has succumbed, the drone was attacked by a river vine. Iris has downloaded her construct into the satellite and can be redownloaded when another drone becomes available. Iris was unable to tell Jessica this before succumbing to the plant"* Cyclops replied. "Attacked by a river vine?" *"Yes, it appears the plants have sentience"*

"So what about wildlife, any thoughts about new surprises?," she asked, standing and turning around to scan her position, something now she did instinctively. *"There are likely to be additional large animals beyond the coastal fringe based on our encounter with the rodents and the giant chicken-like birds, this suggests a graduated food chain."* Cyclops piped deadpan. *"Wonderful,"* she replied.

29

They traversed all day following the river bank, the snow melted further out where the springs were pooling and they followed the marshy ground, her feet were spared the ice pools and snow heaps. Late in the afternoon they found another basalt outcrop and made camp safe from the birds for another night. She looked around and decided that this was a good opportunity for a wash, the hot pools would provide some relief. She cleaned herself, using her water bottle and a clean rag inside the energy tent using the spring water, the tent warm, outside a freezing plain. She rubbed the water over her skin with the warm liquid, a relaxing medicine. Her face had accumulated a considerable amount of grime, she could see as the rag became brown. Her supplies were dwindling, two energy bars and some red berries, the rodent meat she had dried. She would have to find something else soon.

The afternoon saw some twin suns break through and she explored above the river, around the hot pools, Cyclops, was on the river bank. The view was good, a three sixty surround, she couldn't hear anything down in the wash, the water flowed across the pebble in places, a harsh rasp with pieces of ice that cracked as they hit the shoal. The pools extended in large fissures out past the river bank in a marshy area, small rush type plants adorned the area adapted to the hot water and grew in individual spiky clumps, steaming water surrounded them, the hot water current moved slowly with the convection creating bubbled paths, the steam rising into the freezing air. The pools looked too hot for any larger animals, she scanned the depths, algae and lichen seemed the only inhabitants. She examined the spike rushes and discovered small seeds that sprouted from broken pods near the points of the plant, arrow shaped and jet black, she tested the composition using the OTAA.

"Category: PR: Passed-Recommended, Safe to Eat

A high source of protein, fatty acids and new vitamin B15a, additional, high mineral content, sodium chloride, magnesium, calcium, phosphorus, iron and zinc" Also, high in fibre.

"Jackpot," she said to herself gathering the seed pods, small finger shapes about five centimetres long and placing them into her pack, She tasted one, a salty taste, fibrous, and chewy, the seed broke apart as she chewed in small shards and she swallowed. *"Oh, the salt, that's good,"* she thought, chewing like a hungry child watching the horizon. Her feet were warm from the marsh water and for a moment she felt relaxed, the seeds nourished and the water's heat relaxed her feet through the exo-skin boots. *"Spread seed. Juncus Acutus. Bipedal thanks"*

She turned around in alarm, nothing was behind her away across the river bank, she looked at Cyclops, expecting a report but the mono was silent, the swivel turned slowly, on her headset above. The voice or feeling, she wasn't sure came from nearby, the only thing evident was the spike rushes and the pools gurgling occasionally, the steam rising as before in small plume clouds and dispersing away into the cold.

"Cyclops, did you hear that?" *"Negative, what?"* "That voice telling me about the seeds" *"Negative, I have not detected any voice capable entities,"* Cyclops replied. She looked around again, the plain was still and the river's wash was all that was apparent, the wind had died and the ice prisms had returned, falling in their gentle way onto the pools of heat and evaporating like stricken balloons upon a boiling sea. She stared at the rush, straining to see if there was some alien creature within the reeds that could see her, and was talking to her. As she did so the voice piped again.

"$\Delta\psi$ / R, $\Delta\psi$ / R, $\Delta\psi$ / R, ," The voice entered her head again, she was sure this time there was no sound. She shook her head, feeling mad, but the *voice* she realised was chemical,

and that made sense all of a sudden, it seemed audible but was not. She wasn't totally sure, a channel of sorts was open similar to the tunnel she used to access Karl. The voice was a lament of sorts, a murmur, like a distant radio, too far away to tell her anything but that it was on and saying something. She knew the equation, similar to $i = V / R$, the expression of electron flow in a circuit, but she didn't know it in that form. "Cyclops, what are the other variants of this equation, $i = V / R$ as it pertains to Biology?" *"This equation is used to examine the relative movement of water through the cells of a plant,"* Cyclops replied. "Thank you." *"Yes ok, the movement of water opposed to electrons,"* she thought.

She replied, not knowing how but the trace chemical seemed to come from the opening of a communication tunnel of sorts, as if the chemicals had bonded and arrayed so conversation could take place. There was no audible discussion, the traces of chemicals created instant awareness of what was said instead of a wait to see what would or was being said. "Who are you?" *"Juncus Acutus, this would be your explanation most defined"* "You are a plant?.," she replied, thinking, *"I am talking to a plant"*

"I am autotroph," the rush replied. "Cyclops, I am talking to a plant" *"I have heard no discussion, Min, are you ok?"* "Wait..," she opened a tunnel for Cyclops, the protocol flowed through the headset so the mono could translate it. "You are an autotroph?" *"I am autotroph, Juncus Acutus,"* the rush replied. *"Yes, I can receive the transaction,"* Cyclops replied. "Cyclops, what is that name, Latin?," she enquired.

"Yes, Latin, Spiny Rush is the translation," Cyclops replied. She thought for a moment, expecting a punch-line at any moment, but the rush spines swayed in the wind and there was nothing else around, *"No exosuit helmets that I can see,"* she jokingly uttered. "I am amazed, in my world, my home planet, autotrophs can't communicate with humans, bipedals," she said to the rush. *"All autotrophs can communicate, Universal*

code is set," the rush replied."Universal code?," she enquired. *"The sentient element, fifth Universe noble gas,"* the rush replied.

Cyclops interrupted suddenly, *"Terror Birds are approaching from the North West!, 45 kph, they are one thousand and ten metres away, we have been identified, there are five of them, they are moving into their offensive flock positions…Two on point, the others in horn offensive orientation to cut-off escape."*

"Crap, …Cyclops, where is the nearest point of defence, you did some mapping last night yes?," she said terrified, looking around in a half crouching position, her eyes wide. *"Correct, run South East, there is a large hot spring lake, 200 metres, there is an island in the middle it may suffice but you will have to risk the temperature of the water, I am not at liberty to say what the temperature may be"*

She thought 200 metres would probably be too far, *"That will be close,"* she thought after a quick calculation while grabbing her pack like a fleeing child from a moving train, calculating on the fly. *"One minute and thirty seconds to get to the lake, they will be on me if I stand here in one minute and twenty seconds"* She ran pumping her arms in high arcs, her feet flew through the rushes and over the ice puddles, she could feel the ground trembling as the birds legs hammered the sand in the distance, she could see where Cyclops had indicated, a large body of water, the island in the middle about one hundred metres long, jumping in her vision as she strode towards it.

"Closing, 345 metres three from the North West two have peeled off and are approaching from the South West, distance: 310 metres"

The ground suddenly dipped and she was running downhill, the plain had subsided here as the terrain sloped to the lake.

"Visual lost," Cyclops announced.

"Fuck," she replied, out of breath, still charging as fast as she could, her pack was wildly flaying around on her back, and she thought, *"If I survive I have to secure it better,"* in a consoling moment of madness. The sound got louder and she knew they would top the rise at any moment, the other two she calculated would come from her right side to try and flank her, "Strategic Chickens," she said out loud incredulously, the water's edge two metres away.

She didn't stop, she had to swim, or be torn apart, as the two birds from the right appeared suddenly charging at full speed. She dove into the water which was agony, the springs were very hot. "Maybe boiling, boiled alive or torn apart," she cried in terror in the water.

She swam freestyle as best she could, she was getting burnt, the first bird to reach the water strode in flaying its wings in a display of attack and hit the water but then retreated in a shriek, she heard, the others had joined them and the five were running around the water she assumed, as she could hear the thumps on the waters edge. The island was another twenty metres away, she raised her head and spluttered and cried out partly in pain, partly in terror, and thought she probably would die, the water was burning her through the exosuit, the pain excruciating. It was hard to make progress in the fabric and her pack was creating drag on her movement.

The birds she could hear had tried again to enter the water but seemed to have retreated back out, screeching with pain or frustration, she momentarily looked back and two were looking at her on the water-line with the green-yellow eyes, the bird closest had a purple display of striking feathers, oblong shaped with a brilliant red streak through each feather, making it look even more hostile.

208

"Island is ten metres away, Min, you can do it!" Cyclops rasped, the tone of the mono slightly elevated.

She got to within five metres and realised she could touch the bottom, rising with her legs, now a throbbing pain, and surging through the partly boiling liquid. She thought she would pass out and reached the sand, turning back to see where the birds were, the two were still trying to enter the water, the other three seemed to have given up on the chase and were grazing near the plains edge, something else distracting them, ripping roots from the small shrubs and occasionally looking her way, in a hunter's patient stare.

She crawled up to the treeline, some small boulders and vine thickets crowded the start of the vegetation. She cried out in pain as the water's searing touch had made her exposed skin red raw. The only saviour was the falling snow and the chill of the ambient temperature, the relief of the cold sand she could feel on her hands as she clawed back the vines and through the gap, the area within was marshy and she fell deliberately into the colder water that seemed to be less affected by the island's boiling moat. *"The exosuit saved me,"* she thought as she placed her burnt hands in the cool water, then pooled the water in her hands and wetted her throbbing face.

She lay still and listened, the birds moved around scratching the ground in great strides, she could hear dirt flying and sand being thrashed which echoed across the water. They made chortling noises to each other, some sounding like the chase had disappointed them, a drawn out moan.

Now she was burnt and cold at the same time, she adjusted the headset, which had slanted during her dive but was still attached. She started to shake and thought that maybe she was going into shock, she felt her ear and some skin detached, *"Fuck,"* she moaned. She raised from the ground crouched like a flayed monkey and moved forward. "I have to find cool water," she said to herself out loud.

209

"Cyclops, are you there?, keep an eye out for cold water, I am in a bad way here," she croaked.

"Affirmative, here ready to help, cold water or other relief, scanning"

She made her way through the thicket which ended exposing a large familiar basalt outcrop, some eroded pillars having fallen with shattered age and were resting on others like drunk sailors in the gloom. She pressed forward, satisfied the birds had no way of making it to the island. *"To your left, left of the pillars of Basalt, there are larger pools and spike rushes there,"* Cyclops piped. She stumbled forward and set down in the first pool, taking her pack off and setting it down on a dry patch of grass.

The water was freezing and sedated her burns, the relief was making her pass out and she made sure she didn't get too much dirt on her skin. She pooled water in her red hands and washed her face, she felt like a hotdog in a freezer, and she could hear the terror birds scraping away at something at the water's edge beyond. She heard the rushes around to communicate, her ability it seemed set, the chemical transfer in her mind, *"Spread seed, spread seed, Juncus Acutus, Bipedal thanks, Juncus Acutus, Bipedal thanks" "I am burnt. Can rushes help me?, I can spread seed in return"" Sirrus mud, red ochre within pool"*

She looked between the clumps of the rushes, *"Cyclops, can you see a redder mud anywhere, my eyes are watering,"* she said, feeling the pain of the burns on her face. *"Standby,"* he said, the swivel whirring above. She stood straight for the mono to get a better view. *"Further up, infrared reveals a warmer surface with a slight heat signature below, it could be it,"* Cyclops reported. She strode to a large pool, and felt the water, a warm mix of mineralised sand, and briny turgid wash, below a redder mud as the rush had indicated. She sifted through the heavy clay, and drew some out, her hands felt instantly better; the clay seemed to absorb in her skin and extinguish the heat like a lit match in water.

The gloom was increasing, the afternoon was late and the ice prisms fell in greater abundance. She scanned around, the pillars were to the right, she walked to the formation and found a spot for the energy tent, the clay on her hands was a cool relief but the night afternoon was descending very cold. She worked, attaching the fusion battery, the pain was increasing down her legs. *"I have to get this tent up so I can get warm,"* she told herself. She took off the headset and placed Cyclops on the tripod that was part of the mono's setup on a flat rock so he could keep watch, then shaking, she made her way back to the pool, a few metres distant, her exo-skin boots crushing ice on the grass. She took off her suit, the exo-skin had prevented her from being boiled alive, the protected skin raw and red but only mildly burnt. Still, she wasn't sure if she would survive, burn cases she knew could change for the worse quickly.

The shock of the ambient air shook her but she continued and sank into the freezing pool, the mud below slightly warmer and she scooped the silt up and rubbed her stomach and thighs, the smooth ointment running down her legs. After she had covered all the burnt areas, she had an overwhelming sense of relief and tiredness and stumbled, and she imagined what someone would think if they came upon her, a mud-caked naked figure on the freezing island. She stumbled back, after gathering her clothes, covered in the mud and entered the tent, her headset she checked was near, Cyclops close by, her link to what was going on around her. She could hear the rushes, *"$\Delta \psi / R$, $\Delta \psi / R$, $\Delta \psi / R$, "* Lament in the distance. She laid out her terrain blanket on the floor of the tent and fell down.

30

The tent roof was light and there was sun, the interior of the tent was warm, *"The fusion battery's eternal power,"* Ye-Min thought, and imagined the waste trickle of water that exited a small pipe on its side. She felt her hands, the mud was still caked on, *"I feel like a cake,"* she mused. She leaned up a little and checked her arms, the pain had gone and the dried mud fell away as she exercised her arm. She rubbed the reddish mud, now dust on her skin to see the skin beneath, which revealed a surface that looked normal, the burns seemed to be exercised away, only a red skin remained. She reached for the headset, which was on full volume if Cyclops had anything to report and donned the apparatus, adjusting the microphone.

"Cyclops, are you there?" *"Affirmative, how are you feeling?"* "Not sure yet, how long have I been asleep?" *"Two days,"* Cyclops replied deadpan. "How did you know I was not dead?," she asked. *"You were gurgling at times, you broke wind at other times, you have had dreams I would assess; there was talking in your sleep. I could hear your breathing, in addition, the Juncus Acutus rushes have been lamenting in this area, there has been discussion about you"*

"Discussion, about me?," *"Yes, amongst other things they have told me that this area is safe, the birds cannot stand the water"* "What else?," she said incredulously. *"The Sirrus mud is a great healer and they have advised other species that have come this way of its qualities in return for scattered seed. They advised me that you will recover and in their words: "The Bipedal is not dead'*

"Good to know, I thought that might be a possibility," she replied. "What is the day like, temperature etc," she added. *"Sunny, minus twenty three degrees Celsius. There was ice formation last night, the tent has evaporated most of most of the surrounding crust, however I require some assistance, I am*

iced over here on the rock and therefore cannot see anything"
"Ok, wait I am getting up," she said a little alarmed, knowing
Cyclops was without his important sight. After releasing
Cyclops from the ice which had stuck the mono fast to the
rock via the tripod and glazed over his lens she looked around
and made her way beyond the low lying shrubs so she coils
see out over the near boiling water moat. With Cyclops
attached to her headset she could see no sign of the birds, their
obvious boredom taking them away to other potential prey.
The day was clear and sunny and extremely cold, some ice
had formed on her face and her eyelashes were starting to frost
over but apart from the inconvenience she felt strong, warm
and content.

The island moat shore stretched around in an oval she
estimated about four hundred metres and she followed the
pebble shore to circumnavigate the island. "How can we get
back across, Cyclops, any ideas?," she said as she walked and
gazed over the steaming moat, dispersing the rush seed and
shivering a little at the pain it had caused on the swim. *"There
are no trees on the island of substantial weight and buoyancy,
so I think a raft is out of the question,"* Cyclops replied. The
walk provided no answers and she sat at the campsite
afterwards and talked to the spike rushes. "Thank you for the
Sirrus Mud, I have dispersed your seeds widely," she said
feeling a little silly talking to a plant. *"Gratitude accepted,"*
the rush nearest replied. The others soon lamented the first,
"Gratitude accepted" "Gratitude accepted"
"Gratitude accepted."

"I wanted to ask your kind, er, Is there a way I can get off this
island without going through the water, it is too hot for my
skin," she said. Through her sense she could hear the rushes
and their uptake chant of minerals and water, *"$\Delta\psi / R$, $\Delta\psi / R$,
$\Delta\psi / R$, "$\Delta\psi / R$, $\Delta\psi / R$, $\Delta\psi / R$, "Yes, you can wait till four
suns, then the moons will pull the water from the moat via the
channel, then it will be ten centimetres deep, which would be
enough for your form to walk across"* "Thank You, you are a

very kind Autotroph," she replied. The rush continued, *"However this will expose the Milar crab holes and they will emerge to attack, we don't suggest this option. We suggest a covering of Sirrus mud over your skin and then swim, it will protect you for the time it takes to cross the moat"*

"Milar crabs?," she asked inquiringly. *"Yes, their claws are barbed with Poneratoxin injectors, many have perished at the low tide"* *"*Poneratoxin?"* *"Poneratoxin is a paralytic chemical, the pain would be considerable"* "Could I talk to the crabs like I talk to you and ask them to let me cross?" *"Certainly, they would require a trade of sorts though, same as us with the seed dispersal"* "What do you suggest they would trade?" *"Something that contains protein may suffice,"* the rush replied. *"Protein,"* she thought. *"What would I have that contains protein, I have one energy bar left, that has some,"* she mused.

They waited. She and Cyclops decided to stay on the island and await the low tide. Her berries were low, but she ate some seed from the rushes, careful to disperse some as she took from the friendly plants. The fourth afternoon brought the pull of the moon's tide and the moat began to empty through the channel. She perched Cyclops on the highest pillar to keep watch for the birds and watched as the water moat became a shoal and revealed the pebble below, the water steaming and milling away. From the bottom she could see dispersed holes where the crabs presumably lived and she used her mind to search for any communication via the chemical. "Please don't attack me, I would like to propose a deal so I can cross the pebble where your burrows are," she chemically voiced.

"We are listening," came the instant reply. "Well, I have what is called an *energy bar,* it contains sugar, protein and carbohydrate, it weighs twenty grams, would that be a sufficient trade?" *"Certainly, it sounds delicious,"* one of the crabs replied. "So I give you the bar, then I can cross the water at low tide" *"We suppose so, it is a small trade, but sounds*

nutritious, and besides we don't often get organisms trading with us, yes, you may pass" "Thankyou, and I have your word?" she said looking around noticing that a crab had exited a hole and was motionless beneath the milling hot water, a large red circle with angry looking pincers and two yellow stripes across its shell. Two eyes on stalks exited the water and she could see the dark pupils looking at her. *"You may cross,"* the crab replied.

Cyclops interrupted the conversation through the silent secure channel, *"I think they are preparing an ambush, several of the crabs have arrayed in what I would view as a hostile formation,"* the mono said. She stepped back from the water a little. "Thank you, I may cross in the morning, would that still be ok?" *"Certainly, you may cross"* , the crab piped. She quickly turned and walked briskly back through the undergrowth and to the safety of the pillars where Cyclops was placed, having a view of the surrounding moat. She looked up at the Mono, "Well, it was worth a try, that option I think is out," she said, looking back in a nervous sweep of the area. *"I suggest they are hostile,"* Cyclops piped. She looked back at where she had exited the undergrowth, thinking. "The rushes said they would trade, let me try again, Cyclops, keep a keen watch, I don't want to get burnt again"

It took the energy bar, her berries and some of her hair and the crabs said they would let her cross. What they wanted the hair for she wondered about."You want some of my hair?," *"Yes, we want the hair,"* the nearest crab replied. "How much?," she asked. *"The section that is arrayed downward from the back of your head,"* the crab rasped."My ponytail, ok, ...so be it" *"Ponytail, we shall remember its name,"* the creature said, the shallow boiling water flowing over its deadly shell distorting the yellow stripes with the reflective flow.

At the moats edge she had unsheathed her knife and cut the ponytail off near her shoulder. There was a gasp of amazement from the gathered crabs as if she was offering some ancient gift. *"They are not arrayed as before,"* Cyclops piped. She had all her belongings by the moat's edge, Cyclops was atop her head, her pack on her back. *"Ready to go,"* she thought nervously. She dropped the ponytail in the water, the headband still attached, the crabs instantly gathered around the flowing hair as it dropped waving onto the shallow pebble below the turgid water. They grabbed the hair and inspected the gift with their claws, milling around the strands like ballooners securing a basket in the wind. "So, are we in agreement?," she asked. "Certainly, you may cross," the crab nearest replied. The distance from the edge of the water to the other shore she estimated at twenty five metres, the day was cold, but clear again and the steam from the water rose in great clouds into the condensing sky above, there was no wind, and she could see the plain beyond the moats edge in the distance, a sandy colour to the horizon.

She stepped past the arrayed crabs and the flowing hair, feeling the heat through her exo-boots. "Thankyou," she said nervously as she passed the group, the crabs seemed fascinated with their trade she noticed, some had cut strands off and were walking away across the pebble with their new finds beneath the shallow flow. *"They have not arrayed as before, no danger on the shore that I can ascertain,"* Cyclops said through the channel intercom. Ten metres out she turned to look, the crabs were nowhere to be seen.

Stridding quickly across the hot pebble, the exo-boots were absorbing the heat and her feet were becoming uncomfortable. Five metres from the shore she realised the crabs were scuttling under the water towards her, *"I suggest you run now,"* Cyclops said urgently. "Oh fuck," she said outloud in alarm as the approaching yellow stripes grew nearer, some billowing the water above their shells in liquid mounds. Stridding out and making the shore, and running up the sand, turning in alarm as some of the crabs scuttled out from the waters edge, but seemed not to be adapted to the cold open air and quickly retreated into the boiling mass again.

216

"I thought we had a deal?," she angrily said out towards the water. *"We did, we said you may pass,"* a crab piped from somewhere within the boiling mass. "Ok, so you could chase and kill me?," she said, still walking up the sand almost onto the plain proper. *"We gave you a head start, due to the trade,"* came the reply. "That's not how a trade works," she said standing, ready to flee, and looking around wondering if she was in danger from more than the crabs milling in the shallows.. *"No, you are mistaken, you are talking about negotiation, we traded amiably, the transaction was completed. Thanks for the hair, it is a great trade, we are very pleased with the protein value, the Keratin will be synthesised to adorn our shells with additional colours."* "Good to know," she replied, shaking her head. *"Please visit again, and have a safe journey,"* the crab replied. "Sure, I'll let you know when I'm next here," she said dryly. She heard a murmuring from the crabs like a background noise. *"Was that crab laughter?,"* she thought as she turned towards the river.

"We should go and get to higher ground so I can scan the surrounding plain," Cyclops said. They set off, she took one last glance back at the moat, the steam rising into the sky, then scanned the plain as they walked up the embankment she had fled down many days ago in similar terror as she had just experienced. She donned her exo-suit gloves against the cold, the freezing plain an ice laden billiard table, she was thankful there was no wind.

Wondering then if they would get even close to the four thousand kilometre mark to meet Jessica, the whole trek seemingly an impossible task as it stood, now she was being harassed by the wildlife. According to calculations, one hundred and twenty eight hour days walking, following the river, was an overestimate, as she knew Jessica and Iris would no doubt be travelling soon in their direction. Atop the embankment she looked across at the distant river, their first objective, the frozen plain, a white desert in the shining bright twin sunlight. "All clear," Cyclops piped as she crunched through the surface ice and frozen ground mineralized sand.

Cyclops perched atop her head, they followed the river as it winded North West into the interior, the cold desert sands a white gleam and frozen carpet, the twin suns blocked like an old pipe above, trying to water the terrain with the interstellar sun. They stopped at steaming pools and ragged rock outcrops, talking spiked rush formations and ox-bow lakes, the constant the wash of the rivers flow against their path of travel. The Terror Birds were not seen again. The billowing steam plain buffeted heat and freeze, and the lamenting rushes were from time to time consulted about what they had sensed and what was what when it came to the area they adorned; telling her terrain stories. The flow of the river increased as they progressed, Cyclops consulting the satellite maps confirming a rise in the land and gravity at play. She discovered flying fish in the river and caught some after stopping for a morning and constructing a trap, a crude stick oval from river flotsam, which sufficed; her first protein meal was savoured like a child's cupcake with one hundred thousands atop, she morselling the bits of fish fried on the hot stone; a fusion battery barbeque. The rushes became increasingly helpful friends telling her about food sources for Bipedal favour, a snail that lived in the sedge grass near the rivers edge, and edible herbs on the plain.

31

After a flying fish objected to being eaten Ye-Min found it hard not to oblige and released the meal into the wash of the river. The snails also took offence she found not surprisingly, and now she had the added problem of why not to kill something although it was for food. She sufficed herself with herbs and rush seeds for a time while she worked through the new conundrum. The next fish and snails she saw, she chemically talked to. "So Flying Fish,I don't want to catch and eat you but I am hungry and need food, can you suggest other edible substances?"

"Certainly, there are several lichens in the shallows where water is trapped on the river's edge. These Lichen species are all edible for Bipeds and very nutritious. Also, If you want to eat fish there are flying fish graveyards. These can be found under large boulders that adorn the river, typically near fast flowing sections,. At the base of the boulders usually there is a deep pool, here my kind have come to die, attached to the lichen. The freshest dead are at the top."

"So snails, I don't want to eat you but I am hungry and need food. Can you suggest other edible substances? *"Certainly, soon you will find fruit trees that are adapted to the cold and now will be fruiting and flowering. This time of year the snow bees will be harvesting pollen and taking it back to their hot hives within the hot spring boulder fields. There are several varieties of varying sugar content, please let us be as we would be if we were hungry."*

"Cyclops the beacon signal is close," she said looking around towards the river's wash. *"Affirmative, the signal is only two kilometres distant, up river, following the wash should direct us there,"* Cyclops replied. She started up the river's edge again looking out for the trees the snails had indicated. The species had started to appear as the snails had said, after the river started to trend upward and the flow increased. She approached the first tree and sat resting on a flat boulder near the river's edge and watched as the snow bees swarmed over the flowers in the tree, winding their way around the fruit in the freezing dusk sky and out through the plains hot springs plumes. The tree was an approximately ten feet tall thin trunked pole, atop, an arrayed selection of banana shaped fruit attached like bombs arranged in a flower shape.

She rose and approached the trunk of the tree about ten metres away and as she stood at the trunk and looked skyward the shape just missed her head, a threatening looking spike that had four veins at the back arrayed in a feather-like mass of hairs to give the projectile stability through the air. She turned and ran instinctively, "Fuck!"she cried as another dart was released and narrowly missed her head, she could hear the hiss of the dart through the air. As she ran fast away a projectile hit Cyclops off the top of her headset, sending the mono flying into the river. "Fuck!"she wailed, waiting to be struck by another missile, frantically clambering over the river rocks and away to the safety of the plain.

As she ran, turning to look from a distance she realised the darts could only fire downwards. Realising she was out of the firing zone, she stopped crouching behind a rock, drawing in terrified breath watching the tree.. "Cyclops, are you in the river?"

"Affirmative, underwater and travelling downstream I am afraid, will keep you posted on location, no doubt a rock will break my travel eventually"

She back tracked around the tree and followed the wash of the river downstream, the water dull and green cold. Unshouldering her pack she got out her tablet, Cyclops had set his location and was still travelling with the wash a hundred metres distant. She saw that there was a flat section where the wash receded a little and thought the mono would be there if anywhere, the weight of the AI stopping its momentum through the water on the pebble.

She checked again and saw she was gaining on Cyclops, the AI had slowed as predicted. "Cyclops, I am ten metres away, hang on," she piped, climbing over the bank's boulders and down to the shale shore line. Cyclops had put his bright light on and she saw the beam from under the wash, the light swirling in a pool to her right. She grabbed him and returned to the dry shore the freezing river water a numbness on her exo-boots and her hand. 'Ok, Cyclops?' she said, holding the AI. *"Affirmative" no serious damage,"* he replied. *"Also, be advised, the beacon signal is only two metres away,"* Cyclops reported. She looked up and around searching for the source.

As she rose something caught her eye, a glistening piece of metal-like material or a glinting rock, she wasn't sure. She couldn't reattach the mono as the swivel had been sheared off she noticed, her headset bent from the blow and quickly clipped Cyclops to her belt. As she approached the object became clearer a rusted metal figure, green, blue and red rubbery sections like small flexible pipes massed out an entrance of the figures side where it had seemed to have been broken by the wash and the force of the water and the rocks surface, where it was like moving like a pendulum, hitting the nearest boulder, its limp arm wedged within a crevasse higher up.

She stepped carefully closer and saw it was a Robot or an Android, long dead she assumed, the rust encroaching on the oval head. *"The beacon source is here, within three metres of us,"* Cyclops replied. "Cyclops, any sign of communication from the device?," she said looking down. *"Negative, the Android is not electronically alive, it seems to have no power due to its age or injury,"* Cyclops replied.

She reached the Android and looked up at the cascading water moving the figure like a broken puppet against the rock, seeing whether she could release the figure from its literal death throes. She saw that the arm was wedged in hard and tried to pull it out of the water's way so she could examine the find, grabbing the torso and dragging the dead weight out of the cascading water. As she did so the hand released, sliding out from the rock, and the Androids weight crashed to the ground on the pebble wrenching her hands off the waist of the figure. Askew, the Android fell face up, the trapped arm raised like a cry for help, the body lying prone on the ground staring at her. The oval face and humanoid figure was white and where she thought it was rusted was orange beneath the white which had been scraped off from the rocks of the river. The eye sockets contained two green eyes staring up towards the sky. The seven foot figure still looked imposing dead lying on the shale, the arms encased in a hard smooth white surface material, the joints a red malleable substance like rubber, the soles of the feet the same.

She hesitated in thought. Scanned the river. The cold water was milling around her exo-boots. From time to time warm currents eddied around her ankles. She took a moment to blow out breath, examining the machine.

"So, I assume this is the android in question, now we need to find this hardware," she said, taking a glove off and feeling the smooth surface of the prone figure. She looked around the surrounding rocks and immediately saw the hardware, a small card about the size of a credit card was held aloft by a wedged android arm that was raised to the sky. The arm was between two boulders, wedged securely, the river's wash was moving around the boulders. The card was within a hard glass enclosure, the android arm was weathered and old, lichen had grown on the surface and it was missing a finger. She tried to grasp the card but it was stuck fast and the arm seemed concreted in some way.

All attempts to dislodge the card or the arm failed and she sat frustrated watching the water rush around the raised arm like an Emperor that had been drowned and was below the stone. "Cyclops, that is not coming out. Can you tell why?," she asked. *"Wait, scanning.*

There is a code protected field that is disallowing access. It is an atomised bond, similar to flexi-steel. My calculations have determined that it will not break without the code. To attempt to break the bond would probably destroy the hardware," Cyclops replied. "Wonderful, what do you suggest?,"she asked, looking to the river bank's edge, getting nervous about any more threats.*"I suggest we try and activate the droid, it may tell us how,"* Cyclops replied.

She panned Cyclops around over the form so he could see the new find. *"Wait, pan me slowly over the form, I will do a scan."* She moved the mono over the figure from head to toe, careful not to miss any sections of the prone robot. "Completed," Cyclops rasped, *"There are complex electronics inside which are inert, but also organic tissue, I have never seen such an organic-machine type device,"* Cyclops concluded.

She looked around, they were in a lowered section of the river where the rock shelf above had trapped the Android as it had presumably washed over the top. The water was cascading away from their position down a steeper rock slide, they were perched on a small pebble island which had formed, free from the majority of the wash. She sat on the dry section of river pebble watching the prone Android, lying like a sleeping traveller.

"Now we have to get that card in this" she said, rising and walking around the lying figure, while looking around as if there might be other foreign materials around.

"Well, we can't carry the thing, it's way too heavy and what use would it be I wonder?," she said, thinking. *"I could try and reactivate its power source, but then we have a new possibly dangerous scenario, the being looks stronger than you, and there are many unknown variables,"* Cyclops replied.

The effort required to drag the Android up the rock embankment she decided would be a days worth of energy, energy she didn't have and she gathered Cyclops and climbed back up the slope to the river bank edge and looked down at the lying figure on its pebble bed with wonder and a little concern. *"Will it suddenly wake up?,"* she thought.

Cyclops suddenly interrupted, *"I have some more information on the Android,"* he said. *"I have located its power source, but the interesting thing is that it has been disabled by what seems to be a chemical paralytic substance, its firmware is still active, therefore it could be activated, although I am certain it would be unable to exercise motor function"* "Ok, …will that try and kill me as well?," she said dryly. *"Unlikely, but we may be able to communicate with it, it may enlighten us on how to insert the card,"* the mono replied. "Let's do it," she replied.

She descended the river bank again. She examined the machine, the exoplated Android was segmented as if it had been made with armour plates like an armoured knight but she could see nowhere she could access to hardwire a terminal.

She rolled the machine to the side with considerable effort, behind was a different story. A small access panel was visible on the right shoulder blade. "Cyclops, can you scan this panel, let's see what this section is," she asked. "Copy, scanning…wait.

Complete. It is an auxiliary power inlet I would assess but what sort of connection it takes is not in my database," Cyclops replied.

"What about wireless power?, can you try?" "Affirmative, trying" *"Success, power request accepted, the machine has a*

224

firmware exocode protocol which is still functioning independent of its organic function., shall I use my fusion connection to transfer?" She looked back at the river wash thinking. "It may wake up, then we could be in for it," she thought.

"Any additional information about the machine that the firmware can give you?" "Not that I can translate, the machine language protocol is beyond my reasoning," Cyclops replied. "She tried her chemical transaction" "Machine, can you hear me?," she asked using the trace chemical that the rushes had accessed. The machine communicated some symbols, which appeared in her mind as symbols of the chemical seemingly visual as well.

She translated the symbols as a whole, "Please provide the Fusion power source" "What is your intent?," she asked. "To power-on," the machine replied."What is your intent after powering on?," she tried again. "Repair and assessment, my firmware reports I have been in the wash for seven hundred years" She laid the Android down again, the machine gave no indication of movement. The river wash sounded the same tempo as she scanned around thinking as the steam from the hot pools beyond the river plumed into the sky, a green background exosphere contrasting some high altitude cirrus cloud above. From time to time, the wafts of warm hot pool air came across the pebble, warming her legs like heating asphalt with a rising sun. She sent a chemical thought again, "Who are you, what is your purpose, why are you here?"

"I cannot remember, my memory has been erased, the firmware only is operating because of your input of wireless fusion power which has restored my limited firmware kernel function, I know the date and time, that is all, my vision cannot be restored without a full power input, nor my motor function," the Android replied. "Why can you understand *chemical communication?"* she asked. *"I do not know, but I can clearly understand the transmission after the firmware decodes the transmitter chemical into machine language,"* the Android piped, the chemicals instantaneous communication effect clear in the reply.

"I do know that I have been injured however, the firmware reports a pointed object within my lower abdomen," the metal man replied. She looked again at the Androids abdomen scanning the area but could not see anything obvious. "Cyclops, can you scan the Android, lets see what the layers contain.

"Affirmative, please pan for me. Slow movement, the length of the figure, then roll it over, and I can do the rear," the mono replied. *"Sending scans now to your tablet, there is a dart in the Androids chest, but not the same variety as from the tree that attempted to seed you. I would suggest this is the reason the machine succumbed,"* Cyclops reported.

She grabbed her tablet from the pack, the scans showed a clear insertion point, the dart still embedded in what looked like organic matter under the metal exo-skin, the darts passage a clear penetration through metal. "Cyclops, that would require considerable force, this dart is from something else, you are right" *"The machine has internal organs, you can see the arrayed organ types, the dart has penetrated the machines heart and stopped blood flow or whatever type of liquid keeps the machines blood pressure constant, although it seems the liquid has been retained and the machine has not bled out"*

She looked at the scan, the darts tip was protruding into the heart organ, a square shaped box of tissue, arrayed around were other strange features, what seemed to be lungs, and a other shapes like a children's toy box, not at all like a human or an animal's internal setup. She stood up, worried about the danger from the plain. "Cyclops, let's just get up on the bank for a moment so we can scan the horizon, so we don't get

226

eaten by surprise," she said dryly. "Affirmative," Cyclops piped.

She scanned the plain, which revealed a motionless white vista, the steam pools the only movement in the freeze, a billowing mist swirling into the sky. The day was calm and the far side of the river revealed a mass of the spike rushes growing close to the pools. The river beyond in the far distance glistened in the morning sun, the twin stars shining but weak in the elliptical sky. She could see the familiar basalt outcrops dotting the plains horizon out to the West. "Ok, all clear, you think Cyclops?," she asked the mono. *"There is no hostile movement that I can detect,"* the mono replied. They returned to the river pebble below the Android prone like a beach bather on the river island without a towel.

"Let's power up this puppy," she said to Cyclops, looking at the Android and wondering how the machine survived seven hundred years in a river bed, since the river would have changed multiple times since the war. *"It probably didn't even flow through here,"* she mused. *"Akseli, where are you when I need you,"* she thought, looking around. "So, you flowed here, that's certain, but from where I wonder, from what?," she mused to herself. *"Power initiated,"* Cyclops stated deadpan. The Android remained still, the only indication that the power was doing something were the green eyes of the machine which suddenly flickered she noticed then grew bright; two rings of green with a blue circle that looked like a pupil in the centre. The Android emitted an unintelligible command it seemed, the sound some sort of booting sound, then was silent. *"I have reactivated its power source, some sort of electric generator. It does not run on fusion power,"* Cyclops stated.

The Android suddenly shifted and rose to a sitting position like a wakening roadside accident victim, looking sideways and back again as if trying to remember what had happened. *"Activated, thank you Fusion power source, assessing, please*

227

wait" The machine flexed each arm outward from its body, now resembling a yoga exercise. *"Ah, yes, I can see, thank you Firmware my old friend"* The Android tilted its head to look directly at her, then around at the river bed where it sat, still seemingly testing itself; a seven hundred year sleep affecting its comeback.

"Cyclops, tell me the Android has no weapon systems," she asked the Mono. *"Negative, none detected, I am monitoring its boot process, there have been no weapon initiation commands,"* Cyclops replied. She wondered about the Androids' strength and retreated, gathering her pack and tablet and moving up to the top of the riverbank to watch the awakening. She looked at possible escape routes on the plain.

"Cyclops, prepare an escape plan just in case," she asked the AI. *"Affirmative, preparing,"* Cyclops replied. *"So what do you have?,"* she asked, getting a little nervous as the Android rose to a standing position flexing its legs like a surfer before entering the water. *"I have prepared an insertion virus, it will make the Android blind again if initiated and disable its motor leg function,"* the Mono stated. She looked down at the machine. The Android turned to them and raised a hand in greeting, then the chemical trace message overcame her:

"Thank You. My goodness, it has been a long hiatus, my firmware tells me that I have cold booted, so I cannot tell you anything about myself." She looked at the machine and used her mind to chemical back, sending Cyclops the text communication. *"That might be a good thing,"* she replied. *"I am a little afraid,"* the machine said, looking around urgently.

"Don't be,""*we will not harm you,"* she said, feeling sorry for the Android. The Android moved forward a little, taking its first step, looking around in a nervous manner, then up to her gaze again from the river bank position. *"How do you feel other than frightened,"* she sent. *"Fine, system-wise, my organic emotions are a little scattered through, hah, gee, I say,*

it's very weird, ..we?, there are more of you?" "Yes, I am accompanied by an AI, like you a bit" "Speak for yourself," Cyclops replied.

The Android again turned to her, "So what now?" the green circled eyes gazing at her like the world had been lost. They descended down to the Android, the figure standing seven feet tall, an imposing lost manikin upon the river pebble. "My name is Ye-Min and this is Cyclops," she said chemically, transferring the message to the Android pointing to the mono on her headset and craning her head to look up at the machine.

"What shall we address you as?," she inquired of the grey-purple exo-skinned robot before them, its eyes shining green, flexing its seven hundred year old hands, an appendage with seven fingers and an opposable thumb. "I am uncertain, what do you suggest?" the android asked, turning its head down towards them, then looking up to the sky as if in contemplation with the green exosphere. "Well, Lethe was the river of forgetfulness in Greek Mythology, be it in the underworld, that seems apt in many ways," she said, "what about Lethe?,"she asked the Droid. "Lethe," the machine messaged. "Greek Mythology?," the Android asked the chemical syntax in her mind clear and fast from its reply. "Yes, it's my species' fictional past, stories related to a past real civilization where I come from," she replied, wondering if it had been a good idea to bring up the suggestion, the Android understandably seemingly unable to make any meaningful connection to her words.

"I would prefer 45xTSNyhy77juim990-AXC, this is my manufacturer model," the Android syntaxed. "No," she said smiling, shaking her head. "By the time I say that we could all be dead in this environment, it's too hard to say. "What about Juim or 990?" "Very well, I select 990," the Android replied in her mind, looking at her, the green eyes, two twin ringed cylinders looking her way. "Alright, 990 it is," she said looking at the Android who was looking around as if searching for a lost key among the pebble.

"990, we need to get that card in your brain." She pointed to the arm aloft between the boulders." "It is a network card, things I am told will become clearer for you after we do that. Can you help us unlock the field? It is coded and wont let us take the card from the hand," she asked. 990 turned his head and looked at the arm. *"Yes it is a sentient lock my firmware tells me, I have the code, although I am not sure why,"* the droid replied."Where does the card go?," she asked. *"Here in this slot,"* 990 replied. The droid's head suddenly opened and a slice of the lobe opened like a piece of bread coming out of a toaster.

She walked back a step, the opening skull a surprise. She looked at the slot, the size of the card. The section was shimmering with a yellow light as though the droid's head contained light below. "Ok, 990 release the card and let's see if this works, you agree?," she asked the machine. "Very well," 990 replied. She walked over and grabbed the card from the hand which released from the seemingly impervious grasp. Before she could look to see where the enclosure opened the glass popped open revealing the card. The circuit board was an intricate mass of small fibres and glistening parts and she edged the piece from the glass and placed it in the slot. 990's head closed immediately and the droid looked around as if the card had initiated something.

"Come on, let's go up to the top of the river bank, there we can talk some more," she said walking towards the far bank where she had climbed down earlier. They stood on the river bank, and discussed what the alien had said and the hardware card, and the machine turned to her. *"I understand. You have initiated my conjoined network mode. I am now able to find others of my kind. I have detected many others of my type above the river's wash. I also have located another beacon*

source which is out on the distant Western plain. There are others of my kind there. My card instructions indicate we can travel there after this location where new information will become clear ""New information?," she asked the droid shining in a rare ray of light from the clouds above. *"Affirmative, but I cannot tell you the nature of the information, this is all I know,"* the droid replied.

990 let Cyclops mount on the Androids shoulder attached by magnetism, another of the mono's adaptations, the monocle perched now high and effective for the Mono's surveillance. She donned her pack and set off again, walking back to their camp, determined to make some headway in the clear day and fine weather, the sun reflecting off the Android, making the machine shine and contrast against the plumes of steam from the hot pools that surrounded the river.

During the day she talked in her human voice to the Android asking about its makeup to see if she could elicit a spoken response and was surprised when the machine answered directly at the first attempt. *"Yes, I seem capable of audible speech, although I am not certain how and when this occurred, ah it is quite the thing isn't it, to be able to project an audible sound and thus communicate?,* " the machine said after her initial inquiry. "I think you may be capable of a lot of which we are still unaware of 990," she replied smiling.

32

The next morning a blizzard blew and she remained under the terrain blanket which she probably would remain all day listening to the wind and the snow and watching as it piled on the tent from the windward side, through the basalt pillars providing a wind break. Cyclops and 990 stayed in the freeze,both seemingly impervious to such conditions. The AI was now connected to her tablet, as she reviewed the terrain maps, and comms from the others, cave bound on the coast.

The warmth of the tent was a constant nestled in among the lifesaving pillars of rock that were abundant at varying distances from the river across the plain. They had selected a large cluster of basalt that was raised slightly with a view over the river and beyond so Cyclops could traverse the plain with his excellent sight when the weather cleared and possible danger, her memory of the Terror Birds still fresh and not tempered by the latest plant encounter.

Her progress was slow and she wondered if Jessica and Iris had made headway. *"No point trying to contact them yet, if they survive the journey up the river we will see where we are at,"* she thought, she knew instinctively the terrain North of the plains were increasingly hostile, as she had already experienced, how she knew it would be the same for Jessica and Iris she couldn't say. *"Probably the same thing as the ability to talk to plants,"* she mused, lying like a wrapped pupa listening to the wind and snow outside.

During the afternoon the wind increased further, the energy tent was buffeted but the shield held sure and the warmth of the tent remained the same. She did some repairing of equipment, a dash into the driving snow to do her business and minor body maintenance then returned to the terrain blanket.

The next day dawned clear and cold the storm front abated and the still freezing snow laden lament as she emerged from the tent zipping her terrain coat against the well below freezing atmosphere, her breath a billow of steam and an effort to breath in the super-freezing air. She scraped some ice off Cyclops while 990 crouched in the snow, his great from still reaching her shoulders. "How is that, Cyclops?," she asked the AI. "Fine, your vision is my surveillance," Cyclops replied. "What are your temperature tolerances by the way," she asked the mono. "I can operate in a vacuum if necessary," Cyclops replied. "Good grief Cyclops, who made you again?," she asked. "Quantum Bound Industries, Military Research Division," Cyclops replied. "Yes, I remember," she said, looking out across the river to where 990 had indicated. "I guess we get a move on, but first I have to negotiate with a tree," she said looking at Cyclops.

"I am going to negotiate with a tree, let's see where this one goes," she thought standing a safe distance from the range of the darts. She assumed the darts were fired by an intelligent tree, there was no reason to assume it could not be now after her experiences and she tried chemically communicating with it as with the other creatures and plants.

"Tree bearing fruit ten metres away, can you hear me?"

"Yes, I can hear you," the tree intonated.

"Your darts missed me, what was your intention?," she chemically asked..

"To disable you and then absorb you after your death, your rotting corpse would be a good fertiliser for many months to come," the tree replied.

"Tree, bearing fruit, I would very much like to taste one of your fruits, what would I have to do to obtain one without you

attacking me?," she chemically asked again.. *"Provide some fertiliser,"* the tree chemically replied from a distance.

She spent the afternoon trying to find a flying fish pool as described by the fortunate amphibian searching among the rocks and wash. *"If I can get some rotting fish..that would do,"* she thought, looking around on the river bed, standing on a pebble mound section, the water surging around her. Much of the river's surface was now a flowing ice crust but the flow broke up where hot pools interacted with the flow from section to section.

Unsuccessfully searching, and made do with a wad of lichen that was milling near the warm shallow where a hot pool stream had penetrated the river bank and was seeping down into the freezing wash, and offered her catch to the tree.

"Yes, I accept the donation," the tree said. *"It's not a donation, it is a trade, meaning you let me take a fruit without harming me and I give you the fertiliser, agreed?,"* she replied with careful words.

"Very well, place the lichen around the trunk and partially bury it, you will have to release the fruit yourself, you may have the ripest one." She looked aloft, calculating how she would achieve the feat up the ten foot trunk. "Can I shake you?, I may be able to release a fruit that way," she asked. *"No, you may not,"* the tree replied. She looked out across the plain, Cyclops was on a boulder near the embankment keeping watch, 990 turned as he scanned the area. *"Far from ideal,"* she mused, thinking about her problem. She looked over the river bank down at the water which was surging strongly through the rocks. *"Ok, I shall return,"* she said looking at the tree.

"What about the Lichen?," the tree asked. *"All in good time,"* she replied thinking about the darts and her close call. She looked around the area where the tree had fired the darts, finding one and holding it up to the now fading light. The point was a three inch long needle, on a sturdy wood stem, behind the flight hairs, fanned like a shuttlecock. *"That's nasty,"* she thought, looking back at the tree. "Cyclops, analyse that dart and tell me what it's made of and what your theory is about this tree's behaviour," she said pointing the mono at the barb on the ground so it could scan the weapon. 990 placed Cyclops in several positions so he could get some analysis done using the scan ability and the AI computing power on theories of behaviour.

She skirted again down stream, 990 with Cyclops attached skirted forward. She was hoping to find some flotsam, a tree branch that she could use as a pole. She traversed down the embankment again and followed the ice and steaming pools of water keeping the river flow to her right. "Cyclops, keep an eye out for a long tree branch, one thin enough to handle as a pole to dislodge the fruit from the killer tree," she said. *"Affirmative,"* the mono replied. Glancing around a large boulder was her catch, a piled section of tree stumps and hanging stricken roots from uprooted trees that had become trapped against the stone. She selected a long branch, releasing her knife and using the multitool saw blade, sawing off the branch. *"A good looking tool for hitting the fruit off,"* she assessed. "Cyclops, how long is this, three metres?," she asked. *"Three point eight two metres,"* the mono replied.

She returned with the long branch, careful to keep her safe distance from the tree's dart range. Cyclops interrupted, *"I have finished my calculations on why the tree has lethal darts,"* he stated deadpan. "Go ahead, now would be the optimal time, Cyclops," she replied.

"It has nothing to do with fertiliser, the darts upon examination are designed to impale the victim but only injure

and designed to partially break off and fall to the ground after the victim is spiked. The spikes inject small seed pods into the victim. I found these pods within the dart after my scan of 990, but the droid was unaffected, therefore I suggest it was not the barb that disabled him. The needle is hollow like an intravenous needle. I suspect they have a delayed fertilisation time meaning they will open and disperse into the bloodstream at a later time. I suspect this mechanism is designed to allow the prey to think it is just a small injury, the victim moves away and therefore disperses the seed as far as possible by travel so the plant can proliferate at distance from the infecting tree to improve its chance of survival; not compete with the Mother plant for nutrients. The mechanism of seeding I suspect is one of internal growth, meaning the tree literally sprouts within the host and takes root, eventually killing the darted victim through slow haemorrhaging and trauma. I assume the victim dies a painful death, collapses and the tree takes root through the corpse and into the ground completing the seeding process."

She put her head in her hands and then looked up feeling very tired as if to say, *"Ok, that's it"* "Cyclops, let's veer away from any of these trees, I give up, no more negotiation with a devious tree for a piece of fruit" "I concur, the risk is too great," the Mono replied. She moved away from the tree, scanning the frozen plain. They spent the morning removing the dart from 990, the machine guided them as she cut the barb out, the droid prone on a flat piece of basalt like a surgeon's operating table.

"Do you feel pain," she asked the droid pulling the vicious piece of thorn from the androids midriff. "Yes, it hurts considerably but I have anaesthetised the site," 990 replied. She replaced the androids armour plate and 990 sat up and looked at her. "Thankyou Min," the droid said. She threw the barb into the grass and looked at the distant hostile tree again. *"Now I have met a terror tree, not just terror birds,"* she thought, feeling a chill from the cold and thinking about the

236

energy-tent's warmth as she grabbed her pack again following 990 and the mono as they instantly moved off as snow started to fall and descended upon the plain with black and grey cloud and a slight sleet falling on the river like a frosty murmur.

During the afternoon the plain was beset with a tempest, whirligig, a miniature Tornado that Cyclops alerted her of, the sand spinning vortex large enough to cause them issues, the plume tearing up the plain floor a desiccated mass of dead grass, sand dust and detritus skyward to the spinning plume above the pipe shaped funnel. They watched as the dust devil changed path at whim travelling fast Westward then turning towards them and dancing like a mad pirate a wavering step and rasping stride of sound as it turned again and headed across the river in the distance, plumbing water vapour with a marine fury as it crossed the wash, then desiccating the far bank and lifting from the terrain and whirling skyward before it disappeared and wisped up somewhere into the green sky.

The air grew warmer and she saw that instead of the temperature dropping as the afternoon encroached it was rising, the volcanic heat was apparent from the increasingly flat rock surface that the river ran through, their path rising a little as the terrain changed proper, a collection of steeper rock ravines the rivers water was running through. At the first noticeable rise a great rock pool had formed, the river was surging through an eroded gap and a small waterfall surged into the pool, she estimated at least one hundred metres in radial circumference. She tested the water and knew she had discovered her first opportunity to take a massive bath, the first time the water had been cool enough to attempt a soaking, the Terror birds and the moat experience utmost in her mind.

"The warehouses contained seven million unused electric vehicles, the components superseded by the discovery of fusion power drives which.." "990, can you stand here and keep watch, I mean look around for me while I test this water?," she said to the Android that was talking to itself,

testing its newly discovered speech using passages of literature Cyclops had provided from the satellite uplink hard drive that contained the crew's reading materials. She was surprised to find that the drive contained Science Fiction classics such as Stewart Cameron's best seller masterpiece *Horses of the Interstellar sky*, and other interestingly selected works, *Pig's Arse,* Elliot Packer's prediction of the disintegration of man, and her favourite, *"No. How to temper constant nonsense and wokeful thinking in a day."*

"Yes I can certainly do that Min, what are we looking for?" "Danger, Cyclops will brief you, he has excellent sight and other abilities," she said looking at the warm water swirling invitingly. She looked around by habit for prying eyes as she started to take off her clothes and placed them on the warm stone, the air wafting a freeze but greatly tempered by the landmass heat in the area.

Placed her white tortured feet on the stone and felt the warm lament rising up her legs, *"Oh, that's good, oh yes, that is good,"* she thought, standing and feeling the sensation. The rock pool edge had been worn smooth where the water surged through after reaching the end of the pool and flowing away down stream. The small waterfall bubbled and swirled crashing against the rocks below, making noises like a sea creature as it hit the pool. She didn't know if it contained toxins but her instinct said it didn't and she risked the water placing her leg in to test the heat factor. *"Hot but not burning,"* she thought. Naked she felt rushed and crouched into the pool's water. "Ahhhhh, oh my, aghhhh," she descended into the hot spring, the water seemingly making her exclaim.

The Android was scanning the area, turning as she had requested, still quoting passages from the novels, she tuned her ears to try and catch what the machine was quoting, and kept quiet in the delicious water like an Arctic monkey, already wondering what the change of temperature would be when she got out. *"And so in the fullness of time we see a dimensional shift, a crux of interrelated myriad of convection towards the source, a fungus-like lament and..*she picked the sentence 990 was reading, echoing across the flat rock and the rocky pool water.

"What novel is that, I wonder," she thought, a little bemused, smiling at the Androids' newly found ability. The water was alternating hot and colder and she shifted like a crab to assess the optimum spots, striding the rock below as she immersed in her first bath not involving a rag being rubbed over her body for the first time in three months. " Cyclops, is everything ok up there?," she asked, wanting to remain in the pool for an eternity if she could, the AI perched like a parrot on the Androids shoulder. *"Affirmative, assessment is clear, plain is still, no detected movement of significance,"* the mono replied deadpan.

"Min, is your bath to your liking? I see you are immersed in the pool, is this for washing or pleasure?," 990 asked. She smiled wryly, surprised at the Androids learning curve. Before she could reply the Android continued, *"Also, I see that you are a wholly organic species, covered in a layer of dermis to protect your inner vital mass containing organs and a neural pathway that leads to a control centre within your cranial space, I am guessing that you need to wash your outer layer fairly frequently to ward off infection and irritation,"* the Android added. She washed the pool's water over her head, not quite sure how to answer the machine which seemed to be learning at a rapid pace. "Very perceptive of you 990, yes, pleasure and washing," she replied, squinting her eyes, the warm water stinging the encrusted dirt from her cornea's, the blurred vision a caress. She scrubbed her hair, a matted mess and washed some of the water in her mouth cleaning her teeth with the mineralised water. As she waded, her head just above the pool's surface, she noticed a boobing shape about ten metres distant, a purple coloured item flashing green in the

sunlight, tossing to and fro like a small boat on a strong current.

"Cyclops, 990, can you come here and see this, please," she asked the pair. The Android turned and approached the pool, Cyclops's mono eye pointing towards her. The Android stopped at the pool's edge. "Over there about ten metres, that bobbing object," she said pointing across the water, the object slowly making its way to her like a floating pool toy attracted by the inlet current. *"Looks like an eye similar to 990's, it is still attached to the socket housing a broken off piece of the Android model" "I concur, that is an eye exactly like mine, still attached as you say Cyclops to the eye housing, this part can be popped out for repair and replacement on my model, how odd,"* the Android piped. She swam out and collected the piece, a twin green circled Android eye, she saw as she rotated it looking at the housing, a petal-shaped fitting plate, purple and seemingly in good condition.

"So, there are more of you around, it seems 990," she said, still looking at the eye, placing it again in the water, too light to sink, the piece rotating and bobbing again. Thinking about the pool eye, she swam to the edge and climbed out, looking at the waterfall as the likely transport route. She lay on the hot stone naked, comfortable in the surrounding heat from the stone and the pool vapour heated air and dried like a sea bird's wings, the heat a potent elixir, her muscles thanking her for the three month bath. After washing her clothes in the clear water, she waited until they dried, the hot stone steaming the fabric quickly and she dressed feeling renewed and a bit shaky, the warmth relaxing her muscles into a semi-rubber state.

They continued on, climbing the rocks past the waterfall, a flat long basalt plateau greeted them ahead before a high wall of piled massive boulders, she estimated two or three hundred metres long, much like a sea wall, looking like it was man-made and some giant dump trucks had deposited the stone in a heap. She could see out to the plain in this location,

240

the rock plateau veered up slowly above the wash, slightly below,
running down fast an eroded natural gutter of rock and over the waterfall behind her.

They reached the rock face, she estimated the wall about ten metres high, a climb with plenty of small shelves to rest on where flat faced boulders were arranged by chance for footholds. She noticed other Android parts, she could see 990 had stopped and was examining a piece, then picked it up, an entire leg, the Android showing her in a deliberate raise of the leg towards her. She started to climb, hauling her renewed clean body. She reached the top of the wall, and felt a little light headed. *"I need to eat,"* she thought. The Android was climbing up below with assured professional ascent like a free climber.

At first she thought it was the horizon, a light patch as she gazed over the top of the wall, but then realised it was a massive pile of bodies, Android carcasses, white, purple, green exo-skin parts and smashed plates of sections of machine anatomy, piled high, she estimated at a height of at least thirty metres, in three same sized piles side by side, reaching up into the sky.

She gasped and held her breath, the vision seemed an image of a Human on Human catastrophe, an end of world scene of viral death or scrapyard of discarded robots. The Android reached the top and looked at the scene, she looked at 990, mute from shock and wondering what the Android would make of it. "Cyclops, I...," she stopped and realised that the mono saw what she saw, there was no need to say anything. The Android stood silent and motionless viewing the scene as if turned off or one of the Android machines; a part of metal.

She suspected the Android was upset, she was herself, the fact that they were part machines seemed made no difference, the scene reflected mass murder or an end of a massive battle, all

241

that was missing was smoke,he crying of the slain and the victors searching through the mass for booty like a mediaeval killing ground or some far right pyre.

From patches in the three piles, she could see the green inert eyes of some Android heads peering from the wreckage like they were wounded and calling for help silently adding to the heaped carnage of ancient smouldering violence. Arms pointed out from the throng, legs akimbo and stand-alone torsos balanced on each other were mixed with the metallic thrum, shining with the light, the Android dead seemed impervious to weathering, their shells as if seemingly delivered by a factory floor on some conveyor belt industrial line beyond the piles they column't see, the smashed and discarded.

She saw some of the Androids had plants growing from their torso's and realised that the darts had played a role in their demise. "The terror trees," she softly said out loud. *"Oh, my word, my word,"* 990 said finally, still standing assessing the scene. She turned to the Android, not sure how to approach her new companion. Cyclops, in a familiar deadpan voice, broke the silence.

"These are the casualties of the war, it looks like I would estimate, a hundred thousand Androids, I cannot detect any transmissions from the piles, it appears they are inert," the mono stated.

990, suddenly expertly scrambled across to the piles, walking like an ancient priest across a sacrificial rock altar, stopping at the nearest Android carcass, then looking up to the top of the pile towering above, the machine in shadow from the mass.

"Cyclops, can an Android get upset?," she inquired of the mono, looking at the scene with increasingly disturbed feelings, the AI moving with the Android's shoulder as it surveyed the scene from below.

242

"It appears so, 990 is upset, I detect high thought levels, the Android has also compartmentalised its systems, a behaviour seen with AI combat machines during an anticipated assault"

"Anticipated assault?"she asked, alarmed. *"Do not be alarmed, I suspect this is an innate Android model adaptation build of this model, it is used for other reasons such as entering hazardous environments,"* Cyclops replied.

She made her way down to the base of the pile where 990 was standing, the Android had a severed Android hand in its hand, holding the body part by its side like it was a personal item, staring at its kind. "990, I am so sorry," she said, placing her outstretched hand on the Android's arm, the metal, a strange texture.

"You are mistaken, Cyclops, this is not from a war, this was a test-dummy factory, and these are the discarded models of my kind," 990 piped in perfect English. Side by side she and the Android looked above at the mass, she wasn't sure what 990 meant, Cyclops remained silent as if contemplating the Androids comment, the afternoon twin suns were weak behind the towering mass, the green sky above was dotted with patchy small cumulus and the floor of the killing field silent with a slight echo, she noticed as 990 threw the lone Android hand into the pile.

They moved on finding a valley through the metal bodies through a gap in the third pile. The eerie path led them to another seemingly hand crafted space, a dirt clearing, she could see a fence, a steel plated structure and posts holding the plates together and was taken aback at the sight. *"A fence? What the fuck is this place?,"* she thought.

Cyclops immediately suggested they find cover, the scene an unexpected discovery. They backtracked back down the path, the Android's tall presence leading the way, she assumed he and Cyclops had an understanding and they traversed the slope behind the piles flanking around to the left side out of sight of the area. Behind the piles and away out on the plain to the Western side they hid behind a large grassy hill, a place where there were mounds arrayed like a mole rat colony, the moderate size domes tempering the wind with their formation.

The day was closing fast and she wondered whether they should be here at all, the shadows from the pile she could see were lengthening, the twin suns halfway to the horizon. It was still relatively warm, she was sweating and the temperature had seemed to remain the same after the rock pool bath area. Her usual grassy plain freezing planet was changed, it seemed, her mind was swirling with quick theories, *"Another space colony?, an Android manufacturer factory?,"* she thought.

33

By the time they had fled the area, after Cyclops brought in the airstrike and she had hand to hand combat with an android, she was in a state of puzzlement. *"I can fight, like really fight, how can I fight like that?"* She could hear more assembled Android noises on the distant Easterly plain. 990, with Cyclops on his shoulder strode through the grass plain on a course back to the river and out of sight of the Android carcass mounds and the strange out of place fence-line.

An enormous cloud of smoke still billowed upwards from the air strike from the East and the darkness had descended, she noticing the first star appear in the green and black sky to the West. They didn't stop until late into the night, Cyclops navigated 990 to a position he had selected, a safe location where they could assess and rest for the night. They crossed the river again, having taken a wide arc track out to the Western table-top plain, an easier place to assess if they had been followed, but the horizon was clear and the stars put on a contrasting display of interstellar majesty.

She didn't feel tired and realised she had changed, she could fight, but had never been trained, her stamina was seemingly endless, she recovered from injury fast; her leg felt sore but otherwise fully functional. 990 had pulled a four inch piece of metal plate from her leg, if she was normal she would be in pain and limping, probably lame. *"No, I am not normal,"* she mused as they reached a high basalt outcrop, four hours after the Android attack, the stones arrayed in a tumbling mass, good position to hide the energy tent. She lay down and fell asleep, knowing 990 and Cyclops were outside and awoke at dawn as usual, feeling her leg under the terrain blanket, and not seeing, but knowing it had completely healed.

"The combat drone was packaged with the satellite, a classified drone; only Katie Arnold, Kylie Albott, Captain

Williamson and myself know about it among the crew. It was included for worst case scenarios and this is what saved us, I have full control over the machine if the satellite sees the need," Cyclops piped, on 990's shoulder, the Android scanning the surrounding plain for movement, through the low lying freezing mist that had settled on the plain, a windless cold white morning vista."The satellite?," what, is it an AI as well?"she asked, shocked.

"Yes, the satellite has multiple functioning, but segmented purposes, like a computer that has two separate hard drives that boot two separate operating systems. The 'AI in the sky' as it has been named, keeps overwatch on the crew and reacts if there is a need for the combat drone. I am a qualified combat ground controller, thus I brought in the strike. The drone has now entered the atmosphere and cannot return, but it has unlimited power with a fusion drive. It will eventually succumb to the elements and or through mechanical failure but until then it is at our disposal"

She shook her head in disbelief. *"There is still much to learn,"* she thought, looking at Cyclops atop 990's shoulder. "What else don't I know, Cyclops? Do we have any other AI's I don't know about? What about stashes of Tequila and beach umbrellas?," she asked dryly. *"No, ...beach umbrellas were deemed unnecessary, Tequila was seen as a threat to normal functioning,"* the AI replied deadpan.

She closed her eyes in annoyance, then smiled, trying not to laugh, looking out towards where they fought a small army, at times in hand to hand combat. *"The events still seem far-fetched, but I disabled, no, killed an Android with two meat cleavers and was calm about it,"* she thought. "And what about you?," she said, addressing 990, the Android turning to face her. "How all of a sudden do you go from a memory lost Android to a warrior that, I will say, with thanks, saved my life in concert with Cyclops?," she asked the machine.

246

"Cyclops has downloaded a Special Forces training module within my system, I am now a qualified Operator. I have to abide by the rules of robotics concerning harming a human, this does not apply to hostile machines. Cyclops has also downloaded language skills, and other pertinent knowledge to my store. I am at your service and have to obey your commands. There is a caveat, however, I have negotiated with Cyclops, that being, if I find my origin, then I can upload the programs and access my original system, in effect rebirth myself." "Ok, 990, that's fine with me, you have already saved my life," she said looking at the green eyes. The Android seemed to hesitate and stood looking at her not saying anything. "What, 990?, spit it out," she said in impatience.

"I ask you in reply, if I may, you dispatched that hostile Android with great strength and skill, in effect you initially saved your own life. Where did you learn how to fight like that?," 990 asked, its green eyes staring at her, while she looked with concentration at the machine. "I didn't, I just knew what to do, I am an Astronomer, not a soldier," she said, staring at the Android.

She nodded, still looking at the Droid. 990 turned and continued its surveillance of the plain, she had no comprehensive answer, the Android made a critical point. *"Am I still being controlled by the Alien?,"* she thought. *"Or, are these abilities I have had for some time they gave me, and only now do I realise that they exist?,"* she pondered. Cyclops piped again,

"The beacon signal is only two days walk away. Jessica Neuer is still 1667 km distant, 1035.8 miles, as the river flows. I anticipate making contact with Jessica Neuer within the next two to three weeks. I will continue the analysis of the Android army. None of them have followed us, they seem confined to the area we encountered them within; this is fortunate. I suggest a day's trek as usual if your injuries allow it "

"Well, Cyclops, that's the thing as well. I no longer have any injuries from about ten hours ago, they have completely healed. I am hungry however, so if you and 990 can help me find something to eat, I would be most grateful," she replied, standing and walking down to the river, hearing 990's steps behind her. She then thought about what Cyclops had just said; *"I will continue the analysis of the Android army"* and stopped, turning to 990 and the AI who halted looking at her.

"There is another Android mob on the plain, my estimate is that they number around five to six hundred machines, I cannot say where they are coming from though I have this drone photograph, an installation, a building one hundred metres square, that was East of where we were attacked, behind the mob that approached us," Cyclops reported.

She stared at the tablet aerial high resolution image, a white square building from above, the machines arrayed around the perimeter in great numbers, the small figures in the photo like a crowd at a football match, exiting the stadium. "Well, we are not going anywhere near the place, Cyclops," she replied, looking at their location, the camp on the open plain, the river turning West again. *"Agreed, however we must monitor them, they are still within range to threaten us,"* the mono stated.

They continued to follow the river Westward wash in the few days. The plain extended into the interior and the river became a green bordered highway through ever increasingly reddened sand and broken pebbles. The intelligent spiked rushes arrayed in scattered clumps, around the rivers marshy areas and the volcanic pools became larger, some lakes she could see in the far distance the steam rising in great clouds into the sky.

She noticed other changes in vegetation, small purple flowers, on high stalks with ten arrow shaped petals arrayed around a bright orange pistil, stumpy rough barked shrubs five feet tall with massive crowns of pandanus-like fronds splayed like a palm tree, always with bromeliad species growing from the trunks, red, blue, green and yellow epiphytes challenging for the trunks space, some with bending striking coloured flowers a coloured display under the grey rough bark of the trees. The hot pool plain heated the surrounds and raised the local temperature, heated the rock and air-conditioned the ambient air sections around the pools which contrasted the flow of the chilled river wash; itself, a meandering heated flow.

990, found a selection of edible plants and freshwater mussels, testing them with the OTAA, in the soft mud surrounding the rock pools. If the creatures and plants had entities, none spoke to her, she felt relieved as she made rudimentary salads and fried the morsels, content so she didn't have to bargain with the life she had to eat.

She sat with the rush species after making camp on the seventh day after the flight from the Android army. The plants told her about the differing path of the river over its Geological history, and about an ancient volcano to the South East, a Caldera and what they knew about the Androids.

"The machines came from the sky, they flew down in great bunches, there were flying craft that brought them, round hovering craft that emptied them onto the plain. They aligned the river one thousand years ago as if they were looking for something. The hoard moved away to the South West. Afterwards, they scattered and meandered individually mostly in small bunches as if they had been drugged and coursed through this location again, we assume they had been infected from the conflict. They were no longer organised and seemed to have forgotten their technical ability, their weapons laid scattered in heaps and they wandered aimlessly, most of them heading South East.

They have made a camp, the place where you were attacked, our kind have told us they are able to rebuild themselves quickly, they have a machine warehouse or some factory. They are all infected, the more of their kind they make, the same they behave. They have learned some things like crude weapon making but their abilities seem muted and tempered, they no longer seem to know how to use their original technology nor weapons."

"Can you survive that long? The rushes, one thousand years?" She chemically transferred, racking up the additional questions to come in her mind to ask the ancient plant., 990, she could see was out on a basalt outcrop she noticed scanning the area with Cyclops.

"We have evolutionary intelligence, knowledge is passed as a chemical marker over time from the protein synthesis during the first root of our seedlings, therefore all rushes have the same memories, even though our life-span is twenty to thirty years," the rush replied swaying in the warm wind now caressing the flat stone that dissected the rush marsh and the river boundary.

"They had advanced weapons?," she asked, concerned about the Android threat. *"Particle beam weapons, we saw energy shields being used and energy bombs,"* the rush replied. "But you have not seen them in any other place but the camp, for a long time?," she asked.

"No, they have contained themselves within the encampment and there they mill around it seems aimlessly in a primitive state, not like their advanced ancestors," the rush replied. "Thank you, Autotroph, I will disperse much seed for you," she replied. *"Your dispersal is welcomed"* , the rush replied.

She noticed some black beetles aligned on the stones beside her and she turned and looked, the ten beetles were evenly spaced on the flat stone, their glistening green and black exo-skins caught the light and the sheen filtered around reflecting.

"Ye-Min, you have secured the card, 990 will now show you the way forward. There is another beacon as 990 has described. Follow the source, the Archivist has his ways and will find you" She looked at the beetles then up at 990 who had walked to her watching the insects fly in formation into the sky.

Epilogue

Jessica Neuer looked at the scattered clouds that obscured the upper Troposphere descent, breaking to streaking light and breathtaking vista, a grass quilt-like mottled plain, Iris had computed well, "Three seconds...." The craft shuddered as the air-braking wings deployed and hit thicker air, the atmospheric air-speed indicator slowing from 800 km/h the counter in a frenzied countdown slowing, the beeping stopped as if the die had been cast and all bets were off. "One hundred and sixty to one hundred and eighty knots was the life-boats' lower landing speed limit," she thought. The terrain closed fast, sky dwindling, land rising like dropping into an earth sea.

In a sudden gasping moment the life-boat struck the sedge grass plain-runway at 200 knots with a terrific multi-shuddering slam, knocking the breath from her, the parachute deployed immediately then sending her squashing into the back of the chair like a highly vacuumed piece of meat in a plastic food preserver, accompanied by a ground-zero, bone-jarring, eye popping, jaw stressing, and ear watering tone that audibly sounded like a five hundred tonne bass drum full of rocks being thrown onto dry grass within a field of egg shells. Something broke, the beeping started again, blurred landscape, she instinctively braced with her arms around her head, relaxed her posture as in training for impact, but retaining grip, the slide to end all slides, "childrens dream, mud fantasy, Crap help!," she thought, her eyes felt like frozen marbles.

"Terrestrial surface contact" Iris stated in calm control. The life-boat emitted a high pitched whine like a wounded animal, the outside hiss contrasted by inside clamour and the incessant master-warning tone. The roar outside seemed to be the precursor to inevitable impact, terrestrial crush-depth, flayed metal, fire, compromised structure. It seemed inevitable something would be struck or blown away, unravel, ignite, but

the waiting continued as if torturing her with suspense, a surprise, then bad news. "Hang on Jessica, momentum slowing" Iris ejected the parachute, sending her forward with the momentum again, the craft speeding up then slowing dramatically in a burst, then becoming airborne again briefly as it hit a small rise, twisting and crunching again into the grass cover, jolting her like a puppet, shaking the breath out of her lungs and with mighty force, seemingly to tear the seat from under her, then swinging, jerking, buffeting, whirring, hissing, sighing then whispering, sliding at speed, sending lumps of mud into the air outside passing the portal in a heavy globular spray and grass detritus. The final slide spun it three-sixty, finally coming to a complete stop making her reflexively tighten her arms like she was on a Carnival spinning wheel ride. The Flexible-Atom-Acrylic-Glass was now a blur of brown sludge with streaking sand, smearing downwards in small rivulets, two warning signals blared at different tones as she reached above and silenced the master-caution.